Caveat Emptor

Devon De'Ath

DEDICATION

For Thomas Leonard – Beloved teacher and friend :

May you ever find 'The Horizontal,'

and with it life and peace eternal.

.

CONTENTS

1   Conflagration   7

2   Making His Way   28

3   The Renovators   48

4   Kate   65

5   A New Home   87

6   Persona non grata   108

7   Re-evaluation   128

8   Heave Ho   150

9   New Developers   171

10   Old Developments   191

11   Oblivious Occupiers   210

12   Settlement   230

13   Digging Deeper   249

14   Spiritual Support   273

15   Marina   299

16   The Whole Truth   318

17   A Bride in Mourning   334

1

Conflagration

Do you believe a house can have a soul? I don't mean a pleasant feeling engendered by a nice spot. Nor the archetypal *tick in the box* for those in search of the perfect 'location, location, location.' None of that, but a living soul. Can a place be sentient; self-aware?

If you had asked that question to David Holmes back in 1985, it might have given him pause. Especially during the interview for his first serious job as an estate agent.

Is this a trick? Do I need to come up with a clever answer to pip my competition to the post?

That was before…

Quite a bit happened to the man in the following decades of his career. Events that would see him deliver an answer to your question without hesitation. But now we're getting ahead of ourselves. So, let's start at the beginning.

*   *   *

"Roger Blakeston, when are you going to get off your fat, lazy arse and help me strip out the wood panelling in the bathroom?" An attractive, slim, thirty-five-year-old woman filled the living room door frame. Her legs formed a power stance that stretched knee-length skirt material almost to breaking point. Even with a scowl darkening her creamy complexion, the bobbed blonde was every inch a trophy wife to her fund manager husband. He looked up from the broadsheet newspaper in his hands, brow creased with frustrated indifference. Roger was ten years her senior. He folded the paper, placed it on a side table and lifted a snifter of cognac. Behind him, a large, manorial fireplace flickered in the glow of leaping flames. Tinsel, holly and other greenery to mark the yuletide season, hung from the mantel. Roger reclined his head against the high back of a refurbished, Victorian armchair. He swirled the spirit around the glass, warming it with his fingers.

"Not much of a break from work in the city if I've got to roll up my sleeves and start DIY, Nancy." He regarded his wife with a slight shake of the head.

"I'm amazed you lasted this long without hopping back on a train to work." His wife's tone dripped with sarcasm. "Sometimes it puzzles me why we ever moved down to Dorset in the first place. Is this country estate some kind of tax write-off? I'll bet on your return, you list Meoria Grange as 'Garden Annexe' or something ridiculous."

Roger almost choked on his cognac. Her clever quip reminded the city executive of the other reason he had married her, apart from her looks: She was smarter than a new suit from Savile Row. "If I lay out a couple of grand, I can get one of those new briefcase sized portable phones and spend less time in the office."

Nancy rolled her eyes. "Ever since Ernie Wise made that famous call from the 'Dickens Inn' the other day, you keep bleating on about those things. How much do they weigh?"

"Five Kilos."

The woman snorted and held up a flat palm. "Think I'll stick with a land line until they make them small enough to fit in my pocket."

Roger drained his glass and placed it alongside the paper with a self-confident flourish. "This is January 1985, not 2085. I suppose you'll be expecting me to travel to the city in a flying car, next."

"If it meant I could get into Dorchester without ploughing through snow on the back roads, I wouldn't mind. The weather's atrocious out there right now."

"Part and parcel of living on top of a high ridge. Anyway, I understand Kent and East Anglia have taken more of a pounding than us."

"Is that so? I heard on the radio that Poole Park Lake has frozen solid and they've shut many schools. It's deep enough out there to make life difficult."

"Shouldn't we finish taking down the last of the Christmas decorations before we knock this place about? It's after Twelfth Night. Bad luck, or so it's said."

Nancy entered the room and withdrew an iron poker from a rack of fireplace implements. The remaining brush, tongs and shovel swung back and forth from the disturbance, casting shadows that danced against the chimney brickwork. "Since when have you been superstitious? I heard the Queen leaves her decorations up at Sandringham way into New Year. If it's good enough for her, I'm sure we'll cope."

Roger eyed the poker with mock fear and uncertainty that softened his wife's brusque demeanour. The woman waved the tool in the air before agitating and awakening the burning logs in the grate.

The seated figure coughed. "Whatever you say. You're the one with the poker."

Nancy replaced the implement and perched on her husband's lap. Large, deliberate, fluttering lashes intermittently obscured puppy dog eyes.

The man groaned. "You always know what works, don't you? We could get a team of professionals in to remodel the whole place, you know. It's not like we're rummaging around down the back of the sofa looking for loose change."

Nancy pouted her lips. "It would mean so much more if we worked on this place together, Darling. I'm not in a hurry to get it all done."

"But?"

"But, if we don't at least make a start during your extended Christmas holiday, I don't suppose we ever will."

"Why not?"

"Because once you get back into work, the only words I'll hear from you are 'Liquidity,' 'Gearing,'

'Yield,' and not 'Sanding,' 'Plaster,' and 'Paint.' The bathroom will still look like the rest of the crumbling pile it sits within, for the next year."

Roger sighed. "You're right. Okay, let me get changed and we'll remove that grotty dark wood off the walls, tout suite."

Nancy kissed him and got up to leave. "Better. I'll pop down to the cellar and have a rummage around for an extra crowbar. There are all kinds of tools amongst the boxes of crap and spider webs."

Roger thought for a moment. "Or we *could* start down there and work up. You know, get my wine cellar sorted first before we..." his voice trailed away and his eyes sparkled. The cold stare from his spouse would have given the icy blizzard outside some stiff competition. "Just kidding, Hun."

Nancy bit her lip and strode into the hallway past a long, sweeping staircase, to where a low, subtle door merged with the other wood-panelled walls. The cold brass knob twisted in her lithe fingers. Away from the warmth of the living room fireplace, the high-ceilinged central atrium of the house chilled her to the bone. She drew a shawl about her shoulders, opened the cellar door and flicked on a light switch. A sticky veil of cobwebs wrapped around the woman's face as she edged down the dimly lit staircase into the bowels of the property.

"Bloody creepy crawlies have been working overtime at Christmas." Nancy brushed the unpleasant residue from her countenance in a series of long strokes. The mess clung to her fingers like a limpet. She wiped her hands across the cool stone wall on the way down.

At the foot of the staircase, the basement stretched away in several directions. Each of its interconnecting chambers featured a barrel-vaulted brick ceiling, barely illuminated by a naked incandescent light bulb. When they moved into Meoria Grange in the autumn, Roger had discovered a handful of dust encased vintage red wines down there. Ever since, he seemed to have a real hard-on for turning the entire space into a wine cellar that would make even top restaurateurs green with envy. Nancy had to admit, it would be a great space for a party once they got the place sorted. Especially if they didn't want half-cut stockbrokers spilling wine all over their new upholstery upstairs.

She glanced around and thought aloud. "Now, if I was a previous owner stashing hundreds of years of junk down here, where might I leave a crowbar?" Her verbal pondering didn't help. The entire subterranean labyrinth was chock-a-bloc with heaps of boxes. All had been stacked without obvious logic or forethought. Nancy shrugged. "Pot luck, I guess." She shut her eyes, span on the spot and pointed. A blast of icy air wafted across the back of her neck, causing the woman to stiffen her shoulders and cringe. A dull clang of a metal item impacting the concrete floor rang down from the chamber behind. A thud of heavy objects toppling over, came straight after. Nancy froze to the spot, eyes wide. With considerable effort and stress stiffened joints, she twisted about. *Has Roger come down* to look for something? Is he playing a joke on me? Nah, not his style. "Darling, is that you?" Her voice reverberated off the arched ceiling, but was soon swallowed up by the darkness. No response. "Don't be foolish, Nancy," she chided herself. One foot forcing the other forwards, the woman took almost robotic steps in the direction from which the cacophony had emanated. In the far corner of the next chamber, a stack of three boxes lay on their side. Rags, china and a few old books had escaped across the floor. "Of course." Nancy smiled and sighed. "Wonder what the metallic clang was?" She crouched to retrieve and repack the errant objects. Her eyes alighted on the tip of a dark, metal item that seemed to have rolled between two stacks of the boxes. She leaned over and gripped the tip to drag it into view. "Aha. Must have fallen off the top as the boxes sagged." Nancy held up an old crowbar. "Hmm, should do the job. Wonder if Roger has started yet?"

Upstairs in the master bedroom, Roger folded his trousers over a hangar and retrieved work clothes from a large, mahogany wardrobe. Work clothes from his perspective, were expensive tailored shirts and trousers he had worn more than a few months at the office. He regarded his reflection in a mirror mounted to the inside of one wardrobe door. *I still don't see why Nancy wants to do so much hands-on work herself. My time is more valuable than some workman who knows his way round a toolbox better than I do. Ah well, it's important to her.* He closed the door and walked across the landing into the large bathroom. The bath and toilet with high-mounted cistern were chunky, old and almost as white as the day they were first fitted. Roger pondered that Queen Victoria must still have been on the nation's throne, when they installed this porcelain one. The house itself pre-dated the English Civil War. On the atrium wall at a turn in the main staircase, hung a framed portrait of a cavalier. One Jacob Backhouse - the builder and original owner. Or so the Estate Agents had said during their viewing. Roger took anything like that with a considerable pinch of salt.

"Ready to do some damage?" Nancy appeared in the doorway. She tapped a crowbar against one palm with faux menace.

Roger reached down to a toolbox his wife had already left there a day or two before, in hopes of inspiring her spouse to action. "Aren't you going to put some overalls on, or something?"

Nancy gasped. "Whoops! Got so carried away down in the cellar, I clean forgot. Back in a mo."

Roger examined the waist high, wood panelling that clung to the walls. Age had turned them almost the colour of ebony. Combined with dark blue painted plaster above, it meant the bathroom always felt grim and dingy. *This looks like a good place to start.* He inserted one end of his own crowbar into a small gap between a panel and the wall behind. There was enough space to work the tool in and gain purchase. With a splintering creak and a puff of dust, the first panel shifted away from the wall. Once it stuck out at an angle of forty-five degrees, the man got enough of a grip to lever it free by hand.

Nancy reappeared and coughed at the already plaster laden air. "Shouldn't we have masks on in here?"

Roger grunted and retrieved two disposable ones from the toolbox. "We'll need a decent plasterer to sort out these walls after we're done. No way my skills are up to doing a proper job on that. Only if you fancy visitors admiring something as rugged as the surface of the moon while they're having a crap."

"Okay, okay. There are lots of jobs we'll need professional help with. I wanted to start on some of it together though."

Roger winked at her. *How does she still look glamorous in baggy overalls and a mask?* "Come on then. Your turn to prise off the next panel."

Nancy drove her crowbar behind another piece of wood, courtesy of the exposed wall left behind by the first. Her head jerked back and forth. She huffed and puffed.

"Here, why don't I..." Roger began.

The look her brown eyes shot him silenced the would-be helper in a heartbeat.

Nancy tugged again. The panel burst away from its fixings.

"Bravo." Roger called and applauded.

His wife staggered backwards, regained her balance and wiped away dust that itched her nose. When those eyes made contact with her husband again, they shone with a cheeky glint.

Roger attacked the next panel. And so it went on

until the lower part of the bathroom walls comprised nothing more than stone and crumbling plaster. The man glanced at his wristwatch.

"Is that the time? We'd better call it a night and clear up in the morning." He dropped his crowbar back in the box and stretched.

Nancy surveyed the damage. "We're off to a great start. Shall we pile the old panels up on the landing for now?"

"Yeah. I'm ready for bed. Don't fancy humping that lot all the way downstairs, right this second. Not to mention it's blowing a fair blizzard outside. I'll chuck the wood out tomorrow."

Nancy kissed her husband.

The man brushed plaster from her hair. "Good job the water's working. Look at the state of us."

It didn't take long after they had freshened up and climbed into bed before sleep got a hold of them both. Outside, a howling wind whipped snow about the structure.

Meoria Grange was a large, three-storey house dating from the early Seventeenth Century, made from Portland stone with stepped gables. Three bays lined the east facade, with a porch tower between the first and second bays from the south. Someone had added a two-storey bay in the nineteenth century, along with an orangery. Many of the principal windows were pedimented. Twin chimney stacks poked through the roof at either end. The house sat in private but open ground atop a ridge, around six miles northwest of Dorchester. It was a fine setting on a clear day, with breathtaking views of the Dorset hills. But on this particular night, it proved a wild and intimidating place.

The master bedroom windows burst open as if sucked outward by some raging monster. Snow puffed into the room, rousing husband and wife in an instant.

Nancy was first out of bed. She dashed across to lean through the casement and grab hold of the latches. The moaning blizzard reduced to a muffled rumble as she secured the windows back into place.

Roger wiped sleep from his eyes and squinted. "It's going some out there tonight."

Nancy shivered and rubbed her hands across opposite shoulders. "I need the loo." She flicked the light switch. Nothing happened. "Great. Looks like we've got a power cut."

"Pretty much what you'd expect in a storm like this. I shouldn't be surprised if half the county were out, not just the sticks." Roger fumbled open a drawer on his nightstand and clicked on a tiny torch. "Here. You'd better use this."

"Thanks." Nancy took the device and shone the scant beam around to locate the bedroom door handle. She made her way across the hallway with a yawn and tugged the hanging light cord in the bathroom. No response. *Worth a shot. Now, how am I going to do this?* The sink was set in a large cabinet, with enough flat space to lay the handheld torch down and point its beam at the toilet. A useful feature. The woman sat down and let the trickle flow. Midway through, the lights flickered and came back on.

Across the hallway, the sudden simultaneous illumination of the bedroom ceiling light, and a bloodcurdling scream from his wife awoke Roger. His feet hit the floor, and he stumbled for the door.

In the bathroom, Nancy sat with her knees pressed together on the toilet, hands shaking in a series of oscillating spasms.

Roger blinked. "What is it, Darling?"

Nancy pointed a trembling finger at the bathroom walls. Her husband wobbled and put out a hand to steady himself on the door frame.

The bathroom was once again clad in the dark wood panels as if the couple's earlier DIY activity had never occurred.

Roger stuck his head out onto the landing where they had piled the old wood. The floor was empty.

* * *

"I'll make us a cup of tea." Roger folded back the covers next morning and swung his legs out of bed.

Nancy gripped onto his arm, her fingers vice-like and immovable. The man bent back each individual digit, one at a time. His gaze never left the distant, unblinking stare of those normally playful brown eyes.

It had been a difficult few hours since their discovery in the bathroom. Roger eventually coaxed Nancy off the toilet and - surmising they did not appear in immediate danger and that there was nowhere to go in this blizzard anyway - got her back into bed. He'd drifted into an uneasy slumber. His wife didn't sleep a wink. She now appeared lost in a catatonic stupor.

Roger patted her hand. "It's alright. You're safe here in bed. I'll only be a few minutes."

"Please don't leave me." The voice was pathetic, like a pleading child. Not the normal, confident and sassy tone of the woman he cherished.

Roger toyed with the idea of making a joke about there not being any monsters in the closet. The unusual and unresponsive demeanour of his wife chased the thought of disarming tension with humour away. He'd never seen her act like this before. And small wonder. Distracting himself with other thoughts had been the only way he'd kept his own sanity together. He felt the pressure of urine on his bladder wall, swallowed hard and walked back into the bathroom. All appeared as before. The man struggled to take his eyes off the immaculate, aged panelling. The sound of splashing relief didn't even register on the radar of his consciousness. Only a near miss on the toilet rim snapped his attention back onto what he was doing.

Down in the kitchen, the businessman peered out the rear windows while the kettle boiled. Light flurries of snow swirled in the morning light of a pink sky. The storm appeared to have passed, for now. The ground lay covered several inches deep in a blanket of white.

A herd of deer emerged from a patch of trees in the distance. Seconds later they disappeared down the other side of the hill, into one of the valleys below.

The kettle clicked off. Roger warmed the pot and set the brew going. He rubbed his chin and mentally recounted the unfathomable events of the night. Life as a city fund manager was about cause and effect. His world revolved around a set of rules. If followed, everything made sense and predictable results were achieved. It was ordered, logical, safe. Well, safe except for limited and manageable risks that could be quantified, at least. The world of the fantastic, the spiritual or supernatural he left to dreamy people. Poor folks who had another focus than achieving 'La Dolce Vita.' *So is this house haunted? Are all those nut jobs on TV ghost hunting documentaries, actually onto something genuine? I know the place sat empty for a long time. The agent wouldn't say why it was a vacant possession, or what happened to the previous owners. Is my bargain investment in bricks and mortar riddled with problems I didn't foresee? More important than that, what am I going to do with Nancy?* They were uncomfortable questions, well outside his usual chain of reasoning.

On his way up the stairs, Roger studied the portrait of Jacob Backhouse. *Is this something to do with you?* His knuckles whitened, clenching against the side of the tea tray he bore. Head shaking, he trudged up to the landing and brought the refreshments in to where his wife still sat upright and motionless in bed.

"Tea, Honey." He placed the tray on a nightstand. Nancy moved her head, but still appeared semi-lucid.

"I- I... can't stay in this house, Roger." The words came out stilted and with difficulty.

"Shh, now. Here, have a cup of tea. We've had a bizarre night, but everything seems normal now." He passed a cup and saucer into her limp hands. The thought of trying to sell this country pile - based on what the agents had told him - caused his pocket book to wince. It was such a great house. If they ever did sell, the businessman envisioned it being after a major refurbishment. One that would realise a significant profit on the purchase price and redevelopment costs.

"Normal?" Nancy took a major mental step back towards the conscious world. "How can *anything* here seem normal, after what we saw?"

"I can't explain it. Crumbs, who could? But the house seems as ordinary as ever in the cold light of day."

Nancy went to respond but halted as her husband held up a hand.

"Hear me out. Didn't you love this place yesterday?"

"Well yes."

"And weren't you keen for us to start work on our own improvements?"

"Of course, but-"

"Have you noticed anything else about Meoria Grange that has made you uneasy?"

"No. I suppose not. But that doesn't change what happened, Roger. What if the house won't let us change it?"

"Would you listen to yourself? It's a house, not a person."

"What do you think happened then? A team of DIY happy ghosts who don't like our take on interior decoration?"

Roger shrugged. "All I'm saying is, let's give it some time. Could be a bizarre, one-off encounter. If odd things keep happening, we'll reach out to someone for answers or sell up and leave. Is that unreasonable?"

Nancy took a sip of her tea.

Roger dropped a sugar lump into his own and stirred it with a delicate silver spoon. "I'll tell you what: Once we're dressed, I'm going to pull off those wall panels again and burn them. I'd like to see something happen after that. If nothing occurs, do you think you'd feel a mite happier?"

Nancy placed the cup down and nodded in silence.

Roger kissed her on the cheek. "Okay then. Down to business."

Renewed vigour marked the spirit in which Roger Blakeston went at those panels with his crowbar. Nancy didn't want to touch them. She watched from the landing beyond the bathroom door though. Once the uneven walls were finally exposed, her husband lugged the splintered wood downstairs to the impressive living room fireplace. The wind and snow had blown with renewed force. Sustaining a bonfire outside in the present conditions wasn't a practical option. Instead, Roger decided to burn the panels inside. A series of small batches would do the trick, and heat the place up a treat at no extra fuel cost. He tramped through ankle-deep flurries in the driveway, to retrieve a spare petrol cannister from their Jaguar XJS. Some gentle daubing of fuel might help the hated panelling on its cremation journey. The house was large enough that any unpleasant aroma from the igniting accelerant, wouldn't become too odious. It was the lesser of two evils if it finally gave Nancy the reassurance she required.

The first pile of panels caught and went up with a jet of flame. Roger hopped aside, avoiding singed eyebrows by a whisker. *A bit less petrol smeared on the next lot, I'd say.* He turned to watch the flickering flames reflected in the unblinking eyes of his spouse. She sat in the Victorian armchair, glued to the almost ceremonial burning. As the wood crackled, her shoulders slackened and relaxed. *Excellent. It seems to be doing the job.* "We'll be nice and toasty this evening. Feeling a bit better now?"

Nancy twisted her head first one way and then the other. "I will once I walk into the bathroom tomorrow morning and find the lower walls still bare."

"It's going to be fine, Darling. You'll see."

It was in the small hours when Roger stirred from a deep sleep. He rolled over in bed to find the other side unoccupied. A glow seeped under the door onto the landing. It appeared more orange than the usual pale illumination provided by the wall lights. The man sniffed his nightshirt. *I showered and washed my hair after we burned the last of those panels. How come I can still smell the smoke?* A female shriek cut through the stillness of his muggy, sleep encrusted head.

"Nancy?" He was onto the landing like a sprinter under a starting pistol. It was at this moment he realised the wall lights weren't on. The glow flickered across the passage from beneath the bathroom door. Smoke wafted around the edges of the portal and the roar of a mighty conflagration greeted his ears. "Nancy?!" Roger reached for the brass doorknob. He recoiled in pain as the scorching metal seared into the flesh of his hand. The nightshirt torn from his upper torso, the man formed a makeshift binding and went for the knob again. The door wouldn't budge. Screams from inside morphed into a long and drawn-out wail. "Nancy!" Roger's shoulder walloped into the wood. A few more blows and the door finally relinquished its hold. Inside, the bathroom walls were covered in the old wooden panels once again. Each burned with a fierce flame, but didn't appear consumed by the process. On the toilet sat the cinder-like torso of Nancy Blakeston. Her now blackened form glowed, wreathed in fire. The woman's head twisted and pointed upwards, mouth wide open. It was the final motion before her flesh erupted like a Roman Candle. Roger attempted to enter the room. A wall of heat drove him back. He collapsed on the landing, tear-filled eyes never leaving the undignified bonfire of his beloved - burning to death on the toilet.

The blaze extinguished itself seconds later. Roger trembled in a heap on the landing in total darkness. The distasteful and sickening aroma of charred flesh filled the man's nostrils. Only his sobs broke the stillness. The sole subject on an ambient canvas, washed by the moaning of another blizzard in the world outside. Tears of anguish and disbelief turned to rage. He pulled himself up against the wall and flicked on the landing lights. Overspill of the electric glow reached far enough into the bathroom to illuminate his wife's dark and curled up toes. The man's head swam in confusion. He stumbled down the staircase, the red mist of hate descending like a mask. The portrait of Jacob Backhouse watched him with seeming indifference. Less than a minute later, Roger returned to it from the living room, clutching the petrol cannister like a weapon. "I'm going to burn your fucking house to the ground." His teeth clenched. The black screw cap came away in his hand. He sloshed some of the contents across the painting and backed away down the stairs.

"Roger?" Nancy's voice called from the landing above.

"W-what? It can't be. Nan-" His mouth dropped open. The charred corpse stood looking down at him from empty eye sockets. "No. NO!" His cry turned to more sobs. "What's happening?"

The woman spoke again. "Why don't you come back to bed, Roger?" Her blackened form took a step down. Strips of melted flesh hung from protruding bones. The femurs clicked as they supported the apparition in its grisly descent.

Roger shook petrol across the floorboards in the hallway. Something drew his eyes to a tin near the fireplace. This receptacle contained firelighters and a box of extra-long matches. The would-be arsonist continued his mission, retrieving the matches. A clicking of bones drew nearer. The businessman dropped the plastic petrol cannister in shock. Nancy's animated torso stood at the foot of the staircase. Shoulders hunched with tension, Roger pulled his jacket from the hallway coat rack and felt for his car keys.

Nancy angled a half dissolved skull in her signature, sultry gesture. "Don't you love me, Roger? Why do you want to hurt our home?"

Roger fought the rising urge to pass out. "You're not Nancy. You killed her, you bitch! What are you?!"

"Come back to bed, Roger." The corpse repeated its invitation.

The man spat and pulled a match from the box.

An even and deadpan tone replaced the usual lilt of his wife's voice. "It won't do any good."

Roger struck the match. It caught on the first pull. He backed away to the door. "We'll see."

The tossed match ignited the spilt fuel in a flash that spread up the stairs between Nancy's legs. Her body blazed again. Roger pulled open the front door and stumbled out into the driving snow and icy wind. The living room windows exploded outward. A cloud of shattering glass glittered in the light of the growing fire. The man staggered and ploughed through the icy precipitation to his half buried Jaguar. *Shit. No way am I going anywhere in that.*

Behind him on the doorstep, the whipping wind put

out the flames that engulfed his wife's corpse. Her voice rose above the storm. "I'm coming for you, Roger." She started towards him, arms outstretched.

For the first time in that horrible sequence of events, Roger Blakeston felt the emotion of fear. It threatened to paralyse him. His legs seemed glued to the spot. Heart pounding in his chest, the man slipped and ran. Snow fought back against his escape, yet had little effect on his terrifying pursuer. Blood pulsed in his jugular. He ran around the side of the house and made for the downhill descent those deer had taken earlier. Could momentum become his friend on that diabolical night, devoid of other allies?

"You won't get away, Roger. Nobody ever attacks me and gets away. You're mine now." Those horrific words spoken in the voice he loved more than any other, drained the fugitive's emotional tank further.

He tripped over the brow of the hill and found himself running faster than expected. An upended fence stake - disturbed by the blizzard - didn't even enter his perception. Not until it had pierced and entered his body like a skewer. His squirming form writhed and spasmed like a beetle on a bug collector's needle. He was dead before Nancy ever reached him.

2

Making His Way

"Bet you didn't expect to go out in the field, your first day on the job." A plump, rosy-cheeked man in his late fifties chuckled to himself. His puffy white sideburns jostled in time to his head bobbing in amusement. He signalled to turn right and glanced across at his passenger. A fresh-faced twenty-year-old man in the front seat listened with interest.

David Holmes reclined back into the soft leather of the Rover SD1 Vanden Plas. He turned his centre parted, dark blond, diamond shaped head to meet the watery blue stare with his own creamy jade eyes. For the briefest of moments, the younger man smirked at those Victorian-looking tufts of hair either side of the driver's head. They were nothing like his own short and tidy ones. Shaking the thought aside, he spoke. "I didn't expect to spend time with one of the partners either, Mr Strong."

"Arthur. Call me Arthur, lad. When we set up 'Strong & Boldwood,' James and I vowed to make it a pleasant and friendly place to work. Sort of like

'Fezziwigs' in 'A Christmas Carol,' you know?"

David nodded. He vaguely remembered reading the book at school if the truth be told. But he wasn't about to disappoint his new employer. Well-built, with a toned and athletic torso; sport rather than literature had been David's overriding interest during those years of formal education.

The British, rear-wheel drive executive motor slipped on a patch of ice. Arthur Strong tugged at the wheel to stop the back end going out. "Blast. When will this infernal snowy weather come to an end? We've taken our fair share this year. Was it bad in Wiltshire?"

"Yeah. Salisbury Plain looked like a proper wilderness right after Christmas."

"Is this the first time you've moved away from home?"

"It is."

"Exciting or intimidating?"

"Bit of both, I suppose. I only arrived at my rented flat this last weekend. Lots of new things happening all at once. New county, new home, a new job."

"Enough to make anyone's head spin. Where are you living?"

"Got a first floor conversion in a lovely old Tudor building near the church in Cerne Abbas."

"Right over the hill from here. Did the giant shock you?"

David's eyes glittered at the kindly old estate agent and his enquiry about the ancient hill carving that overlooked the village. "No, I've seen an erection before."

Arthur threw back his head and roared with laughter. Those rosy cheeks - blood-shot from a few too many long Friday lunches down the pub - glowed with the hue of beetroot. "At least you're in an adjoining county, should you fancy popping back for a home-cooked meal or visit on your days off."

"Quite. So what sort of house are we going to look at?"

"A fire damaged one."

"Really? Are the owners still living there?"

"No. The owners aren't still living there." Bushy and unkempt eyebrows knitted together in a moment of uncharacteristic seriousness for the older man. He went on. "The owners aren't living at all."

"Oh. I'm sorry. Were they lost in the fire?" David's voice became less confident and more tentative.

Arthur Strong gunned the engine to help the car ascend a steep hill beyond Sydling St. Nicholas. "They *were* lost in the fire, after a fashion. It's rather a tragic tale, I'm afraid."

"I didn't mean to push, Mr Str- Arthur."

"It's alright, David. If you are going to help me sell this place, it's good for you to know some background. We need to be a little circumspect about how - or indeed *if* - we relay any of that to prospective buyers though. Coldred Martin and Co. sold the house last time. When the executors of the owner's estate tried to liquidate the property, they wanted nothing to do with it. So the solicitors came to us instead."

"What caused that?"

Arthur turned down a long hilltop track, past a gatepost bearing the sign 'Meoria Grange.' Ahead, an imposing old house stood sentinel in the still-snowy landscape of an April morning. "Roger and Nancy Blakeston bought this place last autumn. Roger was some big cheese in London finance. The couple planned to refurbish their new home and use it for entertaining their city set of friends. Nobody knows exactly what happened. Early in the new year, an observer from the village below called the fire brigade out to the site. Quite a task getting their engines up here in a blizzard, too. Anyway, once they extinguished the blaze, the resulting investigation revealed it had been started deliberately. They found Nancy burned to death and Roger impaled on a fence post in the grounds. Someone had used petrol from a cannister to set the fire off."

"Impaled on a fence post? Sounds a bit random. What was that all about?"

"The police surmised that their relationship must have been on the rocks. It seems Roger killed his wife. Then, as the full horror of what he had done sank in, he ran off in a blind panic and met a rather grisly end."

"I can see why you'd be hesitant to pass that story on. What an awful tragedy. The house doesn't look too bad from the outside. The fire brigade must have showed up well before the place was completely gutted."

"Quite so. I don't know if the blizzard held any of the fire in check, but Meoria Grange has survived intact. It could have been a very different story."

They pulled up in front of the impressive structure, alongside a dark blue Transit van emblazoned with the name 'Deeks of Dorchester - Building Contractors.' Arthur applied the handbrake and indicated the commercial vehicle with one finger. "I've asked Ted Deeks to board up and make safe the damage. We'll pitch this place somewhere between renovation and redevelopment, depending on the extent of the work required to make it livable. It's the first time I've been up here myself."

"Arthur, nice to see you," a gruff, well-built man in his forties emerged around the side of the van, clutching a thermos of tea. He poured some into a plastic mug as the occupants of the Rover disembarked.

"Good morning, Ted. Allow me to introduce you to our newest agent, David Holmes."

Ted acknowledged the younger man. "I would shake your hand, David. But as you can see, mine are rather full. Nice to meet you."

"Likewise." David zipped up a fleece-lined jacket against the bitter weather.

Arthur pulled a heavy overcoat across the signature dark blue blazer with bright brass buttons he usually wore. "So, Ted. What's the prognosis, then?"

The builder whistled, twisted to gaze up all three storeys of the structure and then took a sip of tea. When he looked back at them, his face strained. "You know what Arthur, it's the weirdest thing."

"What's that?" Arthur stepped closer.

"Since you phoned and asked me to do the job last Wednesday, I thought I'd drop by Friday evening and perform a quick recce of the old place. Give myself an idea of what I'd need to bring along this week to avoid extra trips and so forth."

"And?"

"Well, I could swear the damage isn't as bad today as it was before the weekend." Ted shook his head. "Not a massive difference, but the odd thing here and there."

Arthur chuckled. "Are you sure you're only putting tea in that flask, Ted?"

"Sound like a crank, don't I? Let me give you an example. The bottom stair had burned clean away as God is my witness. I was going to put some makeshift timber in for when you show folks around. Didn't want them breaking an ankle on their way upstairs."

"Exactly," Arthur placed his hands on his hips.

Ted flicked the last drops of tea from his cup into the snow and crossed his arms. "When I got here this morning, the bottom stair was absolutely fine. Blow me if I can't even find a scorch mark on the bloody thing. It's old wood though. Original. I can't explain it."

Arthur frowned. "Sounds like you've been overdoing it, old man. But when you look at so many different houses…"

Ted shook his head with a series of vigorous and decisive motions. "Not like me to be scatterbrained. Either I'm going silly or there's something peculiar about this house."

The old estate agent coughed and changed the

subject. "So how about the rest of the place?"

"It's in remarkably good nick. Bit of work needs doing on the roof. Still plenty of soot and water damage for whoever buys it to sort out. But, in terms of viewer safety you're almost good to go. I've boarded up the living room window. Had to shovel snow out of the bay first. Never done that before."

"Can we take a look around?"

"Please do. Watch your step inside until I'm done."

"Thank you. Come along, David."

The younger man followed his new boss up a short flight of stone steps, through a blackened front door peppered with ancient, wrought iron studs. Inside, the central hallway and atrium reeked of damp and charred wood. To their left, a channel of flame appeared to have partially consumed several floorboards. They led up to a broad stone fireplace in what once must have been the living room. Similar damage wove its way up to a left-hand turn in the staircase. Heavy, wood-panelled walls stood caked with soot and moisture.

Arthur placed his hands at the base of his spine and bent backwards to examine some damaged ceiling plaster. "What a magnificent home this must once have been."

David didn't feel inclined to argue. His mind was uneasy; active with imaginings about whether this or that spot had been the place where Nancy Blakeston lost her life. But beyond that, he still had enough imagination to picture Meoria Grange in its days of glory. Of greater importance to his career, he could visualise what a spectacular home it might become again. For the right people with the requisite pile of money and endless reserves of patience that is. "A 'fixer-upper,' I believe they call it."

Arthur clapped him across the shoulders. "That's the spirit. Come on, we'll have a cursory look around, do a quick tour of the grounds, then put up a sign."

"Do we need to take any photographs?"

"Not inside, in the current state. We'll endeavour to capture a couple of nice images of the exterior facade and setting. That's the real selling point with the place at present. If we can get people excited about the location - which in this case is nothing short of spectacular - it will help overcome the various negatives."

Arthur and David ascended the staircase. It proved chilling to encounter bed sheets pulled back in the master bedroom as if the couple had got up minutes ago. On the top floor, soot and water damage appeared minimal, except for a few holes in the roof requiring urgent attention from Ted Deeks. On their way back down, David paused near the bend in the staircase. Hanging on the wall, something peered out from beneath a filth-encrusted frame.

"Hey Arthur, what's this?"

The old estate agent stopped in the hallway and turned back. "A painting of some sort, I would imagine."

"Can I touch it?"

"Why not? I shouldn't think it'll make much

difference to it now."

David reached up and brushed a layer of grime away from the canvas with gentle strokes. The figure of a cavalier emerged from underneath the dirt. "Looks like one of the original owners or something. English Civil War era if I'm not mistaken."

Arthur smiled. "Very good, lad. We must take a look at the history of this place a little closer. Might be a few nuggets we can include in the particulars when you type them up."

"Can we get that from the library or council records office?"

"I should think so. I'll start by putting the squeeze on Coldred Martin and Co. They seem to know a lot more than they're saying. Don't worry, the business owners are friends as well as rivals. I'll take Barry Coldred for a long lunch. Be good to catch up with him, anyway."

David took one last look at the cavalier watching him and turned without a further thought. After the story of what happened to the Blakeston couple, he expected the house to feel a little more sinister. Instead, there was an odd calm about every room, even with reminders of the ghastly events that must have occurred in them.

"Does this place have a cellar, Arthur?"

"Quite a serious one, from what I've heard. Did you want to have a wander down there?"

"Would it help our task?"

Arthur called out the front door. "Ted, is it safe to go down in the cellar yet?"

The workman appeared on the step, clutching a

piece of timber. "I shouldn't, if I were you. While it's all solid, barrel-vaulted tunnels, I haven't inspected them properly. Could be loose masonry from the damage above, water from the fire hoses and goodness knows what else."

Arthur stroked his chin. "Hmm. We can give it a miss for now." He looked at David. "Once there's a nibble about a viewing, we'll pop over the day before for a closer inspection."

Ted pushed past and carried his wood up the stairs. At the bend he examined the newly revealed painting. "Next thing you know, those eyes will be following me." He delivered the comment in good humour, yet the tone of his voice carried mild uncertainty.

"Be careful up there." Arthur's words of genuine concern followed the workman upstairs.

"I will," Ted's voice returned. "God this place makes me feel tired. I'll be glad when the job is over and done with."

David followed his boss back out into the icy weather. A sudden, arctic gust buffeted the pair on their journey around the left side of the house.

"I see the orangery survived the fire," Arthur pointed to an angled, glass roofed structure attached to one side of the building. "I don't know how watertight it is, but the cost of replacing all those panes would be considerable."

They walked to the brow of the hill and gazed westward over the pretty undulations of the Dorset landscape, stretching away to Hooke in the distance. Below the crest, a broken fence post jutted out beneath a layer of fresh powder. Its upended stake was stained with something dark. David studied it with unwavering intensity.

"I see," Arthur followed his gaze. "If you're thinking what I imagine, you may well be right. This must have been the spot where they found Roger's body."

David tugged up his jacket collar to keep the ice cold wind from blowing down his neck. It was unclear whether his involuntary shudder came because of the breeze, or the mental imagery of the deceased fund manager, suffering in his final throes of agony.

"Blast, I forgot to get the camera out of the boot. This would make a great location shot, too. One of the house from here, plus another of the landscape."

"Why don't I run back and fetch it?" David was eager to please.

"Ah, splendid." Arthur retrieved the jangling Rover keys from his pocket and handed them across. "It's already loaded with film."

David strode through the snow and popped open the hatchback. An SLR camera in a leather case sat atop a 'For Sale' board bearing the 'Strong & Boldwood' logo. He retrieved the case, shut the boot and made his way back to where Arthur was enjoying the view. The three storey, stepped gable country pile loomed overhead as the young man retraced his steps. What with recent events at the house and Ted Deeks' claims of odd happenings, David mused that it was easy to imagine the place watching him as he went.

At the sound of his approach, Arthur shifted round to face the house. He sized the property up; hands forming an imaginary camera lens. "This is the spot, lad. One picture this way, and one of the landscape looking west."

David opened the bag, powered up the SLR and removed the lens cap. Arthur moved his own hands in time as if vicariously performing the function himself.

"Steady. Nice sharp focus." The old agent placed a hand on his pupil's shoulder, causing the young man to start in alarm and waste a shot. The shutter whirred and David focused on the house for another. This time he took a deep breath and squeezed off a second photo before his enthusiastic mentor could interfere.

"Marvellous." Arthur twisted to frame the panoramic country vista with his hands. "Now, aim towards Melplash and that should set the shot up right."

"Melplash?"

"Oh yes, I forgot. You're new to Dorset. Well, you can't see it from here, but point at that line of hills. It's on the other side."

David followed his instructions to the letter. He snapped what he hoped would be an attractive image. Not quite Ansel Adams' quality, but enough to encourage interest from potential buyers.

"Right, my boy. We'll tootle off down the drive, put up the sign and take a shot of the main house frontage." He gasped for air. "Gosh, I'm getting tired like Ted. Must be too much overindulgence at Christmas."

"But we're in April," David replied.

Arthur winked. "Well, I really *did* overdo it, don't

you know."

The younger man grinned and tucked the camera back in its case for now. If every day spent with Arthur Strong was as pleasant as this - and his other new colleagues were even half as nice - this job was going to be an absolute keeper.

They climbed back in the car and cruised to the end of the driveway. Deceptively spry, given his frame, Arthur hopped out and soon had the sale board hammered into the ground. David whipped out the SLR again and set up a great shot of the house against a sky blended with hues of rose and blue. If this one developed okay, it was going to be a proper head-turner. The shutter fired.

Arthur stood alongside him. "And if that doesn't bring the interest in, nothing will," he said with a satisfied twinkle in his eye.

*   *   *

David reversed his 1981, dark green Ford Fiesta out of a parking space. It was a warm evening, Friday 12th July 1985. Those first three months at Strong & Boldwood had seen him grow and develop into a promising estate agent. Oh, he'd made his fair share of mistakes, but always learnt from them. Meoria Grange was still on the market. As yet, no interest had been forthcoming. It didn't seem to faze the partners - Arthur Strong and James Boldwood, however. Arthur often said to him that renovation/redevelopment projects (especially above a certain size or price bracket) always took a while to go.

The young man pulled up at a red traffic light in Dorchester and steadied a bag of groceries on the front passenger seat. He clicked on the radio and the speakers crackled to life. A newscaster mentioned a scrubbed space shuttle launch due to a main engine shutdown. They had also discovered a cancerous growth in President Reagan's colon. The light turned green. David pulled away. Some pop music began in time to accompany his unhindered journey back to the flat in Cerne Abbas.

The little Ford accelerated north along the A352. David's fingers drummed on the steering wheel to the strains of Duran Duran. He nodded his head and sang along. Shortly thereafter, he found himself at the turnoff into the village. For a settlement in decline (historically), Cerne Abbas was a charming and characterful place. Once a thriving market town of about fifteen hundred souls, the population now numbered half that. There were still a few pubs, a post office, school and various independent shops and tearooms. What appealed most to the young man, was the quiet, friendly feel. Close enough to all the amenities and work in Dorchester, but still a haven from the throng of humanity.

The Fiesta came to a halt in a dead-end street opposite the church of St. Mary. Beyond the graveyard, a patch of woodland spread part way up a rising hillside which seemed to burst above the canopy. Carved into the chalky soil was the image of a giant; a hundred and eighty foot naked figure clutching a club in his right hand. Smaller - yet no less impressive - was the prominent, thirty-six foot erect penis in vertical salute between its legs. Opinion seemed divided about the giant's origin and meaning. Some thought the figure depicted a Celtic or Saxon deity. Others believed it to be an act of satire, a mere two centuries old. It always gave David a grin.

"Pleased to see me, fella?" He brushed his mouth with one hand, climbing from the vehicle and staring up at the hill carving. An attractive young woman appeared from the church path, pushing a baby buggy. David flushed at the realisation she had heard his comment. Eyes twinkling, the woman turned the buggy to face down the pavement.

"He's always pleased to see everyone, by the looks of it," came a playful tone as she started off towards the village centre.

David retrieved his groceries and locked the car. He rummaged around in his jacket pocket for a brass Yale key. With a twist in the lock, he opened the broad, wooden communal door of a large, timber-framed Tudor building. It swung shut behind him with a drawn-out creak, followed by a solid and definite thud. At the top of a worn set of dark, polished wooden stairs, he selected another key from his chain.

The flat was a two-bedroom affair - at least on paper. In the last few months, the young man had become accustomed to speaking fluent 'Estate Agent' when describing properties. The place *did* have another chamber, not part of the bathroom, master bedroom or combined lounge/kitchen/diner. Therefore it was recorded as a second bedroom. David surmised that you could fit a cot in there if you were lucky, and not much else. It would require an adult to sleep standing up, or trail their ankles out into the hallway. Since he lived alone, this wasn't an issue. He used it as a walk-in cupboard with a window. A more truthful description, but less inclined to pull in viewers when marketing such a property. The building comprised four flats: two upstairs and two down. What David particularly loved about it, were the old features and the usable fireplace. Finding a flat where you could have a real fire was rare. It made him feel like this dwelling was something more than a bolt hole to rest his head, for a guy starting out.

The electronic warble of a telephone hanging on the kitchenette wall, cut through the silence. David placed his shopping on the worktop and answered it.

"Hi Mum. Yeah. Yeah it's been a good week. How are you? Great. What about Dad and Mandy? Is she? Everyone's excited about the concert in the office, too. 'Live Aid,' that's it. No, no work tomorrow. Don't think there are any viewings on. Unusual for a Saturday. I suppose most people will be glued to the telly, watching things unfold at Wembley. Me? Yeah, I plan on watching it, too. I'll cook myself a nice meal and settle down in front of the box, I imagine. What's that? *With* someone? No, I'm not expecting company." David's momentary wry smile evaporated with a sigh. He ran one hand through his hair. "No, there's no-one like that at work. Yes, they're all very nice. Socially? No Mum, I've been so busy getting settled and learning the ropes in my job, I haven't had time or energy for... I will. Yes. Yes. Okay, well I'll keep you posted if there are any developments there. Does she? Okay, put her on." David's shoulders relaxed. The excitable tones of his teenage kid sister burst from the handset. He winced and held the receiver away from his ear. "Hi Mandy. No need to shout, I'm not deaf. Are you? That's right, midday isn't it? So which... David Bowie. I should have guessed. Yes, I'm sure he'll be brilliant. Me? Yes, I'm going to watch it. You do. Oh, that's sweet. I wish I was watching it with you too. My job? Great thanks. The flat's superb too. I love Cerne Abbas, it's a peaceful village. No, no girlfriends. Okay. Well, you run along and have dinner before it gets cold. Say hello to Dad. Love you too, Kiddo. Bye. Bye." He hung up and blinked away the faintest glimmer of moisture from his eyes.

Once the shopping was packed away, he prepared a light tea and settled down to flick back and forth between the four channels on television.

* * *

Drums beat in time with a chorus of rhythmic chanting. Torches sputtered in the velvet blackness of a late summer night. Leaping figures, daubed in blue woad, hopped and jigged about the hilltop. The sound rose to a crescendo of both volume and fervour until it ended in an instant.

A young man panted, his heart pounding. Mouth dry with a mixture of elation and uncertainty, he was ushered forward by the crowd. Before him, a tribal holy man stood alongside an angled, standing stone. The menhir was inscribed with a series of swirling patterns. They writhed and reached up from the earth like some mythical serpent. The shaman signalled for the man to approach. He was aware of his hands being fastened above his head, back to the stone. The world seemed to spin. Even a sudden gust of wind that almost extinguished the torches, did little to rouse him. What was in that ritual draught someone had given him to drink at the start of the ceremony? The holy man stood before him, clasping a long blade in both hands. The point glittered as it raised above his head. A blood-curdling scream echoed across the valley, from the mouth of the drugged participant. He stared down, eyes wide to see the knife sunk deep into his heart. It was cold as ice, yet there was no sensation of pain nor sign of blood. His heart beat like the earlier drums. He could feel the life-maintaining muscle contract around the blade, embedded in its centre. An eerie light seemed to envelop his body. A sense of power, joy and completeness flooded his soul. He had become one with something, like the union of a man and woman. Yet no bride could he see.

* * *

David sat up in bed with a start, hands clutching his chest. It had been the weirdest nightmare of his life, seen through the eyes of some ancient, British tribal sacrifice. Or that's what he could remember and

45

decipher from the startling unconscious imagery.

"I've got to stop drinking coffee that late at night." He rubbed his eyes and pulled the sweat-sodden pyjama top away from the base of his neck. "Yuck. This is going in the wash. Gives new meaning to having a wet dream." His words rebounded off the uneven, ancient walls of the room. He glanced at the bedside clock. Six fifteen. Being July, it was already after sunrise. He hauled back the sheets and trudged into the bathroom to take a shower.

A hazy, morning mist slithered about the tombs in St. Mary's churchyard. The long grass hung heavy with dew. From up in the treetops, wood pigeons sang their muffled song. David hiked beyond the graves and followed a track up the hillside. It was a regular route whenever the young man fancied a leg stretch. The additional effort of the climb and descent, gave him a better workout than several miles on straight-and-level ground. Not that straight-and-level ground was that easy to come by on the Dorset Downs. By the time he reached the top of the giant, David was panting for breath and feeling the benefit of his exertions. The air smelled fresh. It would be a warm and beautiful day.

On the way back down, he paused in a small meadow. This was another regular feature of his ad hoc exercise regime. It was a quiet and restful spot. David closed his eyes to inhale long and slow. The tensions of the week and that disturbing dream seemed to fall away like dead skin. He listened. Almost total silence. Every once in a while he could make out a faint car engine beyond the distant hedge bordering the A352. But other than that, the meadow felt serene.

He pressed on into the village, stopping at the post office and shop to buy a local paper. On his way back to the flat, he took a cursory glance at the property section. It had become a force of habit to always be aware of the market and what their competitors were offering. David stopped dead. Coldred Martin & Co. were advertising parcels of land for sale. One looked familiar. *It's the meadow. Wonder who's selling it? A farmer looking to boost his bottom line, I suppose. It's not big enough for crops. Not much use for anything else. Hmm, from the low price it must only be the land without planning permission. Wonder if I could afford a loan for that and keep it as a long-term investment? It would be a shame if they ever built on the spot.* He folded the paper under his arm and carried on home.

After an early lunch, David got himself set to watch the 'Live Aid' concert from Wembley Stadium. It began with a rendition of 'God Save the Queen' by the Coldstream Guards. Status Quo got the party started and the young man sat transfixed by the goggle-box, right the way through until the final hand over from London to Philadelphia at Ten PM. It was a memorable event, watched by almost forty percent of the global population. And he'd been right: David Bowie was brilliant. Not to mention Queen, who also set the world on fire.

3

The Renovators

"Sad, but it could have been a lot worse." Arthur Strong folded his newspaper, placed it on the desk in front of him and picked up a cup of tea.

"What's that?" David asked.

"An earthquake in Strajica, Bulgaria. Five point seven on the Richter scale. It killed two people in a town of several thousand. I imagine the buildings are somewhat the worse for wear."

"We're not going to be opening a Bulgarian branch of Strong & Boldwood soon then?"

Arthur gulped and almost spat out his tea. He slammed a palm down on a leather blotter. "That's what I like about you, lad: Sharp as a razor. What did you want to see me about?"

"I just got off the phone with some potential buyers for Meoria Grange. They want to come down tomorrow for a look."

Arthur whistled. "Where from?"

"The city. A family of four. They sounded quite taken with the setting and exterior house shots. Plus, the wife has links to the county on her mother's side."

"Aha!" Arthur rubbed his hands together. "Never underestimate the power of emotion and sentimentality in a buyer. Hearts ruling heads can sound the dinner bell for a savvy agent. Well done, my boy. So, let's see now: If you make the sale, we'll have had the place on our books less than two years. That'll drive Barry Coldred nuts with jealousy. Jolly good."

"Two years come the spring."

"Good heavens. That's how long you will have been with us? Is it really all that time? My, how it flies. Well, pull this one off and your Christmas bonus should make for a very happy new year."

David coughed. "As I've not been back there since my first day on the job last year, it might be an idea to re-acquaint myself with the old place. If memory serves, we were going to inspect the cellars and have a better look round."

"That's right, now you mention it. Gosh, what it is to have a young and agile memory. Go ahead. Take an early afternoon and get yourself over there. Tracey will let you have the keys."

"Thanks, Arthur."

"Good luck with that viewing. This is the first nibble we've had on that old house."

"I'll do my best."

David's dark green Fiesta crunched to a halt outside the impressive frontage of Meoria Grange. All the way down the drive, the young estate agent struggled to break away from staring at the ancient pile. Back in the office, many of his colleagues had expressed relief that David was handling the sale. Wild stories about the estate and demise of the Blakestons were rife in modern folklore now. None of the other staff wanted anything to do with it unless under threat of losing their job by declining.

David took a deep breath. He examined the chunky set of keys the office administrator had handed him back in Dorchester. It was a chilly December afternoon as he walked up the short flight of stone steps to the front door and inserted the key. Before allowing the portal to swing inward, he arched his back and gazed straight up. *Why does this place always feel like it's watching me? Yet somehow, that's not an uncomfortable feeling.* He dismissed the thought as imagination fuelled by gossip and teasing at Strong & Boldwood. Tragedy or not, it was only a house, wasn't it?

The living room window was still boarded up where Ted Deeks had left it. Many lattice panes of glass were missing between its mullions. The door drifted open. Inside, the hallway and atrium appeared as he remembered. Soot and water damage still clung to and stained everything. Some new wood had been hammered into the floor where that channel of flame once ran from the fireplace to the stairs. It was cold in the house, but missing the icy drafts that previously blew through fire damaged holes in the roof. Holes that had been patched in a basic fashion at minimum cost to prevent further rapid deterioration.

David surveyed his surroundings. *Well, if Ted was right about that stair growing back, nothing else seems to have changed. Silly old bugger.* The dead eyes of the cavalier portrait stared out from the painting on the half-landing. It was no cleaner than when he'd brushed

it with his hand. *Jacob Backhouse, Royalist and architect.*
He and Arthur had gleaned some information from
their competitors and a local records search. He knew
Jacob was a favourite at court, who designed and had
Meoria Grange constructed on this site. That was right
before he succumbed to a mortal wound while
supporting King Charles during the English Civil War.
A sad fate he never got to enjoy his beautiful home.
The fellow wasn't married and had no offspring or
other heirs to his fortune. Over the centuries, the
Grange passed from person to person - unrelated
mostly. It was rarely a generational residence for any
one family. Sale records showed that inheritors
appeared to favour immediate sale to a different party
rather than personal occupation. That could be why
this house bore the air of a museum. There were some
new additions since the civil war - the bathrooms being
notable examples, along with electricity and general
plumbing. But little else set it apart in any dramatic
fashion from the essence of what its architect must
have envisioned in his day. David was surprised it
didn't have a Grade I listing or hadn't been left to a
trust for conservation. Could scary tales and rumours
have prevented its designation as a heritage asset, by
officials not daring to enter?

David took a casual stroll around the downstairs
space. The kitchen and dining room adjoined that
spectacular orangery attached to one side of the house.
The glass was dirty, caked in grime. It caused the low
winter sun to cast a faded yellow glow across the

gloomy interior. A drawing room, library, study, boot room and ancillary other chambers all led back to the main hallway. He climbed the substantial staircase to the first floor and surveyed the main bathroom, master bedroom and various suites. A smaller set of stairs behind a wood panel led to the top floor under the eaves. This must have originally been designated as servant accommodation. Now it was a set of interconnected junk rooms. The smaller and plainer flight of stairs also led down to a rear parlour on the ground floor near the kitchen. David emerged back behind the main staircase and noticed a brass doorknob in one of the wood panels attached to it. *That must be the cellar entrance unless I've missed it somewhere else.* He gave the handle a twist and the panel came open. *Let's hope Ted Deeks wasn't pulling a fast one when he told us he'd arranged for the electrics and water to be put back in service.* He flicked the switch and a dim glow from beneath let him know that juice was still flowing to at least some of the house. Arthur Strong insisted they maintain basic utilities to the site, lest a last minute viewing arise. With nobody using the home, costs to the firm were minimal. But it gave them a slight edge, should a rogue viewer appear from nowhere. Now his gamble had paid off. No way could they have had the place reconnected in less than a day. Showing potential buyers around the house in December with no light, would hurt their chances of making that all important sale. And people weren't exactly queueing up along the street to have a gander at Meoria Grange.

David edged his way down the steps. As a precaution, he'd tucked a small torch from the Fiesta glove box into his jacket pocket. Arthur claimed the cellar was like a maze of tunnels. Getting lost down there in the dark with no-one looking for you, would be no joke.

At the foot of the steps, the young man discovered a crossroads of barrel-vaulted brick chambers. They stretched out of sight, leading to more crossroads and an intimidating blackness. *How big is it down here?* A swinging bulb - disturbed by a draft when he opened the cellar door - glowed brighter. A shower of sparks cascaded off its fitting and the glass shattered. David jumped and wiped some of the hot shards from his shoulders. *Hope that doesn't happen tomorrow. Mental note to self: remember to bring the torch along again. Right, I'd better get an idea of the underground layout, in case my viewers are the insistent, curious type.*

He took a methodical approach to his exploration. There were some old floor plans he'd discovered in the local archives, but more chambers had been constructed since they were draughted. David kept a mental note of his position on a folded photocopy of the blueprints. He became familiar with the mapped areas first before widening his survey. Most of the new building work led north, away from the house and further under the hilltop. At the edge of the final electrically lit room, he could see further tunnels reaching into darkness. The overhead lights faded, glowed brighter and then went out. *Shit.* He fumbled in his pocket and found the torch. Its beam was pathetic given the size of the device. *Good job I put some new batteries in at lunch. It'll take me ten minutes or more to retrace my steps to the stairs without tripping over any junk down here. How much farther do those tunnels go? Could they once have used this place for smuggling?*

A sudden, low moaning echoed beyond the tiny spread of his pocket torch. It originated from the long, dark tunnel. Not a person, nor yet the sound of a wind. Hairs pricked up on the back of his neck. He strained to listen. A chill blast of air wafted over him as if somebody had opened the door of a walk-in commercial refrigerator. On the opposite side of his head, the breeze formed into a sound like words. A single phrase whispered with a strange longing: "S-T-A-Y."

* * *

It took every ounce of professionalism David Holmes could muster to drive back to the house next morning. After that chilling voice whispered in his ear, he found himself able to make the stairs again in a lot less than ten minutes. Granted, he'd tripped over a box or two and his ankle still stung from the impacts. But, he'd got out of the place alive. For the briefest of moments he had to fight down a rising urge to squeal, during that frantic escape. The memory of it aroused a certain sense of shame. He'd gone from a buff, well-built, handsome young buck, to almost wailing like a terrified child. His British, stiff upper lip had suffered a very definite wobble, if only for that instant of horror.

It was an experience that seemed to stretch into infinity at the time. The thing was: now he had to go back and show people around in there. It would test his mettle to breaking point if they wanted to examine the cellar. Could he steer them away from extensive investigations without jeopardising the sale? He'd soon find out.

A brand new Mercedes estate sat parked in front of the building. A tall, rakish man with receding brown hair, stood with one arm around his well-fed, red-haired wife. Children - a boy and girl of around ten or eleven, who appeared to have inherited their hair follicles from the maternal gene pool - raced around the structure, peering through downstairs windows.

"Mr and Mrs Griffin?" David swung his frame out of the Fiesta driving seat, wearing a rather forced smile.

"That's us," the man spoke up. "Derek and Sylvia."

Offering first names. That bodes well. David made a mental note of their informal, forward approach and enthusiastic body language. He'd learnt his trade well from Arthur Strong and James Boldwood - two masters of the art when it came to selling property. This was a good example of starting out on the right foot.

"David Holmes from Strong & Boldwood. A pleasure to make your acquaintance. Did you have a good journey down from London?"

"Yes we did. Actually we came down last night and stopped at a hotel in Dorchester," Sylvia Griffin replied.

"Marvellous. All fit, energised and raring to take a

look around then?"

Derek Griffin released his wife and shook David's offered hand. "Indeed. As are our children. But I'm sure you can already see - or rather *hear* that." Cries and excited squeals blared from outside the orangery.

The three of them laughed with polite reserve and Sylvia also shook the agent's hand. She glanced across to the brow of the hill and the landscape unfolding beneath it. "We thought the pictures of the location were fabulous. But they don't even begin to do it justice."

David nodded. "I can, without question, put my hand on my heart and say properties like this don't come along very often. But then, I *would* say that, wouldn't I?" They all laughed again in a rather forced manner. "Would you care to take a turn around the grounds first, or shall we open the place and discover what a treasure it is inside?"

Derek placed an index finger across his lips in thoughtful gesture, watching the agent. He lowered it again as if having brought his deliberations to a satisfactory conclusion. "You're a confident young chap, aren't you? From the description on the particulars and lack of internal photographs, I imagine we're looking at a major renovation project?"

David shrugged. "We *have* been candid about that. There's no interest in wasting anyone's time at our firm. Yes, it's in a state."

Sylvia frowned. "So what happened exactly? The particulars described a fire and water damaged house offered as a vacant possession."

"That's correct. Strong & Boldwood are acting as agents for the estate inheritors."

"No appetite to fix it up themselves?" Sylvia went on.

"Apparently not. The house had no history in the family. And, let's be honest here, it will require a significant capital investment to restore. Not everyone has pockets that deep, nor the drive and will to see such a project through." David was playing a risky game, fishing to see if he could elicit a response. The feint paid off.

"Well, there are also some who *do*, and can see beyond the cosmetic or awkward aspects of a re-build." Derek's voice carried a tone of mild annoyance. He'd been challenged and picked up the gauntlet. The game was afoot. Let the duelling begin.

David jangled the keys and waved towards the front door. "Shall we?"

"Children," Sylvia called through the crisp morning air.

The two excitable scamps thundered round the corner and stopped dead upon spying David.

Sylvia looked at the agent. "This is our daughter, Amy and our son, Craig."

"Pleased to meet you both," David shot them a friendly wink.

The kids relaxed in an instant. The girl tugged at her long, full red locks and turned to her mother. "You should see the greenhouse thingy on the side, Mum. The views must be wonderful from in there."

"That's called an orangery," Derek corrected her.

The girl lifted her head. "Are we going to grow oranges then?"

Sylvia put an arm around her shoulder. "We may, if we buy it."

"Can we have a look at the bedrooms now?" Craig piped up.

"Soon," Derek twisted to face the house as David unlocked the door.

The five of them filed into the hallway and atrium. Derek studied the makeshift repairs on floorboards leading from the living room fireplace to the main staircase. "Was the fire an accident, David?"

"Not as I understand it." He was going to be tight-lipped and evasive until the point it put the client/seller relationship under obvious strain.

Derek continued. "Arson insurance job?"

"I wasn't privy to the police report. Our firm came in after the fact, at the estate solicitors' request."

Sylvia frowned. "Were the owners killed in the blaze?"

"I'm afraid so. Or on the same night, anyway." David worried that this viewing might be over before it even began. While that at least meant he would avoid another trip down into the cellar, it wasn't exactly going to boost his career.

Derek leaned against one wall. "Did they die in the house?"

David tried to display a neutral expression. "Outside during a blizzard, if I've been correctly informed."

"Ah. Horrible, but a little less troubling to know it didn't happen inside. Not that one believes in ghosts."

He put on an exaggerated laugh.

Sylvia and David joined in, neither appearing convinced. Craig was too busy leaning around door frames and peering into other rooms to care. Amy acted less guarded about her feelings. "Mum, this house isn't haunted, is it?" She wrung her hands against her skirt.

"Why of course not. It's seen a lot of history and suffered a rather sad event that created all this mess. Once it's fixed up, can you imagine what a wonderful home it might be?"

This eased the child's discomfort a little.

"When was the fire?" Derek asked.

"January '85."

The father strolled around the living room and bent to look up the chimney. David never understood why people did that. It seemed to meet the need to appear thoughtful about a potential buy. How many people could look up a chimney and spot something that would be a deciding factor in a house purchase? David knew that he couldn't, and he spent his entire working life in and out of different homes.

"Can we see the orangey thing?" Amy tugged her mother's arm.

"O-r-a-n-g-e-r-y," Derek annunciated the word correctly.

"Yes, that."

Sylvia raised an eyebrow at the estate agent.

David indicated down the side of the staircase. "Right this way, if you please."

The weather was being a real pal this morning. They entered the orangery via the kitchen to a glorious morning sky. The light made the most of that spectacular landscape view.

Sylvia gasped. "Gosh Amy, you were right. Look at that." She grabbed her husband's arm. "Can you imagine reading the Sunday papers in here with a nice cup of coffee?"

David attempted to hide his smile. Ordinarily, he liked to waft a muslin bag of ground coffee beans about a property, before a viewing. Either that, or stop by the bakers and pick up a warm, freshly baked roll to keep in his pocket. Both were smells that proffered the subliminal suggestion of being at home. It was an old house seller's trick. But, if it ain't broke, why fix it? It was a family mantra in the Holmes household. At Meoria Grange this couldn't have worked. At least, the devious action would be so obvious as to prove detrimental. That was, unless one considered some invisible resident spectre might enjoy a nice cup of java or fresh bakery product. David was trying to steer matters away from the idea of the Grange being a haunted house. Even if the events of the previous afternoon made him question his ordinary dismissal of such matters. After allowing the couple time to engage in the fantasy Sylvia had concocted, he chipped in another. "Since it faces west, the sunsets here are nothing short of spectacular." He didn't know this to be a fact, but it was a reasonable enough assumption.

Sylvia and her husband let out a unified sigh of pleasure. The mental suggestion had found its mark and hit home.

That set the scene for most of the tour. The day before, David made a point of stripping the sheets from the master bedroom and concealing anything that spoke of the previous occupants and their final hours. If something jolted his system, he attempted to alter or conceal it. So it was that the idea the master had once been Roger and Nancy Blakeston's bedroom, didn't even enter the conversation. Rather, Derek and Sylvia became engrossed in other discussions. Ones about drapes, paint schemes and more reveries on what life in the renovated house could be like. Amy and Craig ran free throughout the first floor until an argument started about who might occupy which room. There was one overall favourite they had both taken a shine to. Once Sylvia reigned them in, David took the family on a repeat of his top floor excursion from the previous day. This ended in the parlour at the foot of the backstairs.

"Does this house have a cellar?" Derek's enquiry caused the agent's heart to sink.

"It does. Quite an extensive one." The reply was hesitant.

Derek fidgeted and shrugged. "It would surprise me if it didn't. Where is it?"

"This way." David tried not to sound annoyed. He paused with his hand touching the brass doorknob in the wood panelling. "Before we go down there, a word of caution: The cellar is a veritable maze of chambers. These have been added to with a series of tunnels constructed after someone drew the original plans up.

Only a few rooms are lit, and then not very well. Also, since the fire, the electrics are temperamental. Not to mention power cuts that are a regular occurrence in the country. I have a pocket torch, in case of a blackout. But, if the children are coming down I advise you to keep them close at hand."

Derek stroked his chin. "Fair enough. Sylvia?"

"Yes Love. Amy, Craig, don't go running off down in the cellar. We'll have a quick look to see what it's like."

David opened the door and flicked the light switch. A faint glow appeared from the stairs below. It wasn't as bright as yesterday. Not surprising since that bulb in the first chamber exploded. The young man took a deep breath, crossed his fingers and led the family into the bowels of the earth.

"Would you look at that." Derek was awestruck upon taking in the crossroad of brick chambers, stacked high with the junk of centuries.

"What's in all these?" Sylvia brushed her fingers along the top of a wooden crate.

"Years of history, I imagine," David replied.

Derek opened a cardboard box and lifted out an art deco lampshade. "Is any of it valuable?"

"I don't know. We haven't taken inventory. There's so much of it and the solicitors haven't bothered sending appraisers in. Everything is included in the sale price, however. The entire contents." David couldn't resist the urge to tack on another positive. Could it be that a dream of discovering a missing Van Gogh or some other treasure, might spur the Griffins into making an offer?

Derek returned the shade to its box. "That seems lax, not using appraisers."

David guided them round a circuit of the first few chambers, closest to the stairs. "Their assumption seems to be that the property was appraised before the deceased occupants purchased it. This stuff was already here."

"Aha." Derek peered as far ahead as he could, to glimpse the copious cellar system beyond. "Goodness, this place is huge. No shortage of storage space."

Amy shuddered. "I don't like it down here."

"Fraidy Cat," her brother poked the girl in the ribs.

"Stop it, Craig," Sylvia spoke in a firm but hushed voice. "Darling, can we have a look outside now?"

Derek rocked on his heels. "Okay. This has given us a reasonable idea of what to expect. Thank you, David."

The agent breathed a discrete sigh of relief and escorted them back up to the hallway. Their tour of the exterior site proved far more pleasant. Amy's mood improved once they were above ground again.

"We appreciate your help." It was a matter-of-fact statement that accompanied Derek Griffin's extending hand. David shook it. He watched the guarded fellow climb into the Mercedes driver's seat and start the engine. Seconds later, the young man stood alone by his Fiesta, staring after the luxury motor as it rumbled down the drive. The viewing had gone better than he'd hoped. But the family's final responses still felt mixed.

He had no idea if this was going to be a sale or not.

4

Kate

"Good morning. It's Tuesday the thirty-first of March. I'm Andrew Crown with your news update." The clock radio bursting to life woke David with a start. His woolly head adjusted to the surroundings of his flat, making the difficult switch from a dream he couldn't recall. He stretched and swung his legs out of bed. The newsreader spoke of an auction at Christie's yesterday, in which one of Vincent van Gogh's sunflower paintings sold for twenty-four and three-quarter million pounds. The story caused his mind to flash back to December. Images of that junk-filled cellar at Meoria Grange and the curious voice reawakened from where he had attempted to bury them in his subconscious. The experience might have been startling and unnerving, yet it paid off. The Griffins bought the house and David received a healthy Christmas bonus. He clicked off the radio and went into his automatic routine of preparing for another day in the office.

"David?" It was the voice of a woman, but one the

agent couldn't quite put his finger on. He looked up on his way out of the bakers near Strong & Boldwood, clutching a sandwich in a brown paper bag.

"Good Heavens, Mrs Griffin. How are you?"

"Hello. Sylvia, please. Well. Yourself?"

"Tolerably." He took a deep breath, unsure whether he even wanted to ask the next question. "How are things at the house?"

Sylvia Griffin touched her red hair with an idle palm. Her chest swelled. "Very satisfactory. We hired a smart motor home and moved onto the site a fortnight ago. Derek intends to tackle the principle living areas first. Then we can move into the house proper and continue renovations."

"That's great to hear. Are the children okay?"

Sylvia rolled her eyes. "When you're that age, life is one long adventure. Especially spending a few weeks in a camper. Lots of squabbling and a few frayed nerves, but otherwise they're having a marvellous time."

"Do you have a long-term vision of how you want to develop the property?" David wasn't being polite here. On the one hand, he was filing away intelligence for a potential future sale, should the family decide to leave. On the other, there was something about Meoria Grange that had grabbed a hold of his attention.

"Derek and I decided to try to honour the property as much as possible. It has so much character and so many historical features. I rather think we got a good deal from you though."

"Oh? How's that?"

"Well, since we moved in, there doesn't seem to be half as much work to do as we thought after the viewing. Every time Derek starts a job, the repair proves simpler than expected."

"Bonus."

"Just as well. I know my husband isn't a spring chicken anymore, but even the little jobs are making him tired."

David started and attempted to conceal his surprise. Thoughts of Ted Deeks and similar comments rang peculiar alarm bells in the back of his mind. He dismissed the idea as nonsense. "Living in a camper doesn't help, I should think."

"That's true. Well, I don't want to hold up your lunch break. It was nice to see you again."

"And you. Please give my best wishes to your husband and family."

"I will. Good day."

David walked back into Strong & Boldwood. He sat down at his desk and unwrapped the sarnie.

"Friday night. You, Me, Claire and a potential miss right." Charles Pembry leaned back in his nearby chair with a grin like a Cheshire cat.

David grimaced. "Charlie. How many times have I told you not to try fixing me up?"

Charles Pembry was two years older than David. He had been a promising Surrey estate agent until his move to Dorset. David got along okay with him, even if his ebullient, overbearing nature sometimes grated on the younger man's nerves. Charles adjusted a yellow tie around his neck. His crew cut had so many coats of hair spray applied, the brown spikes gave the appearance of crampons. His long chin extended as his mouth opened in a grin. "Come on Mate, time's a wasting. You want to get out there on the scene before you're too old and someone takes all the good ones."

David blinked. "I'm twenty-two. I hardly think I qualify for a bus pass yet."

"Look. All I'm saying is that it can take time. You need to be a player, getting into your stride. Why are you always so touchy about the subject, anyhow?"

David swallowed. His eyes misted, narrowed and appeared to look straight through Charles to the wall behind, as if seeing into the distance. "I had some bad early experiences in that area, back in Wiltshire. Not in a hurry to repeat all that nonsense. Thought I'd get my feet under the table in a job first."

"Okay. So, how far under the table do your feet need to be? You've been the agent of the month how many times now, in the last two years?"

"Ten." The word came out under his breath.

"What was that?"

"TEN," David repeated it at a greater volume.

"That's great. So here you are: this up and coming successful estate agent with a glittering career and good prospects." Charles wheeled his chair out from under the desk, swivelled the base to face David and crossed his long, lanky legs. "You're a good-looking bloke. Fit, buff, blond-haired with striking eyes. In short, a top wingman for any fella about town."

"Wingman? How many times have you seen 'Top

Gun' now?"

Charles flushed. "As many as you've been the agent of the month."

"That's what I thought. So, why do you want a 'wingman' anyway? I thought you were going steady with Claire."

"I am." Charles whistled and howled like a cartoon coyote. "Man, she is amazing."

David folded his arms. "I'm happy for you. Then why the need to meddle in my affective life, or lack thereof?"

"Claire's got this colleague."

"Wait a minute. I'm not sure I like where this is going." David held up a flat palm like a police officer directing traffic.

"Hold on, hold on. Hear me out. Listen Dave, I've seen her. She's not some desperate, spinster librarian type with thick-rimmed specs. Kate is bloody tasty. I tell you, if I weren't with Claire..."

"Don't finish that sentence, please. I'm trying to enjoy a ham sandwich."

Charles grinned. "So how about it? We go out for drinks, the four of us. If you guys get along: great. If you don't click, what have you lost?"

"Nothing, I guess."

"Exactly. You'll have an evening out with your entertaining and debonair colleague," he shined his fist against an already shiny suit jacket, "and meet an available and attractive young woman. If you screw that up, you can still go back to being a miserable homebody, spending time in your patch of mud."

"It's not a patch of mud, it's a meadow."

"Why ever did you buy that chunk of land? You can't do anything with it."

"That's it. I didn't want anyone else to change it. Besides, an investment in land is a safe gamble. The value rarely goes any way but upwards. I haven't lost out. Or at least I won't in the long term, even with interest payments on the loan."

"But you *have* lost out, Dave. You're still driving that old Fiesta of yours, after going to the bank to buy some grass instead. Meanwhile, I've got myself a Vauxhall Astra GTE. It's a proper chick magnet. The digital dash looks like something out of 'Knight Rider.' So cool."

David shook his head and let out a long, shallow sigh. "So, what's your plan for Friday?"

"Claire and Kate will meet us here in town, about seven thirty. We'll have a drink or two, then see if anyone fancies going for a bite to eat. No pressure."

David bit his lip and thought for a moment before repeating the last part. "No pressure."

"See, I consider everything. I told Kate what a nice, quiet chap with potential you are. She seemed keen to make your acquaintance."

David screwed up the empty sandwich bag and tossed it in a wastepaper basket under his desk. "Okay Charlie. Let's give it a shot."

Charles let out a shriek of victory. "A-ha. We're going to buzz the tower."

"No." David pointed a finger at him, but struggled to hide a smile. "If you embarrass me with even one

'Top Gun' quote, I'm walking out of there."

Charles span to face forward and picked up a ringing telephone from the desk. "You've got it."

*   *   *

"Nervous?" Charles Pembry pulled up in a shiny new white Astra GTE with the driver's window lowered. He had to shout his enquiry above the thudding bass of his car stereo. David waited until his colleague wound up the window and killed the engine. The tall, playboy wannabe slipped out from behind the wheel.

David locked the driver's door of his Fiesta, not bothering to look over his shoulder as he spoke.

"The only thing I'm nervous about, is if you've stretched the truth regarding the spinster librarian thing."

Charles elbowed him in the ribs. "Prepare to be awed, Buddy."

The pair entered a large, quiet, seventeenth century pub. Seated one side of a booth made of two old wooden settles and an oak table, were two attractive young women. David recognised Claire straight away. She'd stopped by the office to have lunch with Charlie on several occasions. Five and a half feet of slim, shapely womanhood. Her dark blonde hair was usually tied back in a bun, with a few straggly ends tickling her long, slender neck. Big brown eyes and a faintly freckled face spoke more of homegrown beauty than supermodel looks. She had a subdued, erotic power about her. Like a smouldering fire that seems to be out, but is in fact ready to burst back into life. David could see the appeal. Claire was a fine catch for any man. The young woman next to her clocked the two men as soon as they walked through the door. Piercing blue eyes burrowed into David's face, as if extracting information through psychic interrogation. A lithe tongue traced the lips of a wide mouth. It puffed the cheeks out on her rectangular face. Long, thin eyebrows raised a fraction. She subconsciously brushed one hand through short-layered, shoulder-length and side-parted mousy hair. A modest curved chest and almost endless, toned shapely legs caused David to surmise that she must be taller than Claire. He wasn't wrong. Both women stood to greet the new arrivals. David found himself eye to eye with the one who hadn't yet taken her eyes off him.

Charles did the introductions. "Kate Warren, meet David Holmes. David, this is Kate."

"Pleased to meet you." David extended a polite hand.

Kate took it, holding him firm as she brought her lips up to kiss him on the cheek. Her perfume smelled sweet and refined. A pleasant change from the heady concoction of aftershave, industrial grade deodorant and shower gel that hung around Charles like a cloud. David almost got a headache from his stench in the short distance from the car park to the pub. The kiss lingered a moment, somewhere beyond polite but well short of needy. Even before she spoke, the young man had a sense of Kate being an assertive woman. Someone who knew what she wanted, what she liked, and where she was going.

"I've heard so much about you." When her head moved back, she still held the man captive with those bright, sapphire orbs. "Charles says you are quite the estate agent."

"I've been lucky to find a career early on that agrees with me, I suppose."

Kate glanced at Charles but still gripped David's hand. "He's modest, too."

David stole this respite from her gaze to scan the girl up and down. She was a stunning package. *I wonder what her story is and why she's not with anyone just now?* Then those eyes were back.

"And you're from Wiltshire, is that correct?"

"Yes. A small village east of Salisbury. You?"

"Dorset born and bred. I'm a Dorchester girl."

"And what do you do?"

Charles stuck his head between them. "Sorry to interrupt and glad things are off to a flying start, but shouldn't we order drinks?"

"Sorry." David flushed.

Kate pursed her lips. Her eyes twinkled and softened their intensity.

Charles pulled out his wallet. "I'll get the first ones in. Kate?"

"Claire and I already have a cola each."

"Okay. What about you, Dave?"

"I'd better have a lager shandy."

Charles nodded. "Sounds like a plan. I'll fetch two.

You keep the girls company."

David slid onto the long, green cushions of the settle across the table from where Claire and Kate had been sitting. The girls took their places again. Kate tossed her hair back over her shoulders.

"So David, you wanted to know what I do?"

"That's right."

"I'm a PR Assistant at the council where Claire works."

"Charlie said you two were colleagues. Do you enjoy your job?"

Kate took a sip of her drink. She paused, holding the glass in midair. "Very much. I'm hoping to become a PR Executive, eventually. Presenting an image that appeals, plays to my natural strengths."

"I can see that." David meant it as a compliment, then realised she might take it as a suggestion of insincerity. "That is, I mean your own personal presentation is very appealing." He winced at the fumble.

Kate raised an eyebrow and looked down. "Whereas you have to take what is and draw people's attention to it in a positive way. Could be that we're compatible, or at least complimentary."

David fidgeted. It was a playful comment, neither promising nor disappointing. Kate knew how to say both yes and no without using either word. She was a lot smoother and more accomplished at social interactions than he. A real professional, for want of a better label.

"Did I hear the word 'compatible' just then?"

Charles returned with two pints of shandy. He plonked himself alongside David. "There you go, Buddy. Cheers."

*   *   *

"Why don't you drop me here?" Kate smoothed down her blouse, face blank.

David shifted into a lower gear, then pointed up the road ahead. "We're almost there. Seems daft to chuck you out when we'll be at your office in a couple of minutes."

"No, that's okay. It's a nice day and the walk will help clear my head."

"Suit yourself. Well, either you'll be raring to go once you reach your desk, or ready to start the weekend." David turned down the Fiesta radio, quietening the tones of 'Nothing's Gonna Stop Us Now' by Starship. It had been an eventful week since he first met the statuesque beauty perched on his front passenger seat. They went out on a solo date the very next day and hooked up for a restaurant meal the following Wednesday night.

Kate placed both hands flat on her knees. "Have you thought about us?"

"In what sense?" David signalled at an appropriate spot to pull over.

"I'm not sure what we're going to be yet."

The man was uncertain whether to feel disappointed or relieved. Kate Warren was a powerful character. Yet, he'd warmed to her companionship. Images of it developing further must have bubbled beneath the surface of his mind. Pictures bearing greater intensity than he first thought. "I've enjoyed our times out together. It's only a week since Charlie introduced us. Am I moving too slow for you?"

"No, nothing like that." She frowned. "Where do you see your life and career heading in the next five years?"

"Huh? I imagine I'll stay at Strong & Boldwood. It's a good job, nice people and I'm earning an excellent wage."

"That's great. What about your home?"

"I'm renting a flat for now. No immediate plans to change that. I suppose I rather thought I'd meet someone, settle down and buy a house. All the usual stuff."

"You must have a fair bit squirrelled away for a deposit."

"What makes you say that?"

"You don't live in an extravagant manner. Look at your car."

"What's wrong with it?" David glanced around his trusty little Ford.

"It doesn't exactly say 'man on the up' does it?"

David shrugged. "Charlie's bought himself an Astra."

"Exactly. Brand new. And you're a better agent than he is, David."

The man considered mentioning his purchase of the meadow, but decided against it. "Is that why you don't want me to drop you outside work? Are you ashamed to be seen with me?"

"Not with *you*," Kate trailed an index finger along the base of the passenger window.

"Oh, I see. Are we going out tomorrow?"

"I can't. I've got a family thing. But, you could cook me Sunday lunch at your place? I haven't visited your flat yet."

This perked David up a little. "Okay, deal. Why don't you come round for midday? There's room on the street to park your motor, assuming it's back from the garage."

Kate picked up her handbag, rummaged around inside and pulled out a Filofax. Flipping the leather cover open with one hand, she clicked a Biro with the other. "I've got your home phone number, but you'd better give me your address."

David sat parked at the kerb for a long time after Kate got out. He watched her confident, feminine form turn heads all the way up the road.

"Good morning, Sir. What can I show you today?" The garage salesman was around ten years David's senior. He regarded the twenty-two-year-old with a pleasant smile. One that didn't quite mask his obvious suspicion the younger man might be a time waster. This wasn't how he wanted to spend his Saturday. Not when commissions from older couples (who seemed a safer bet) beckoned.

David jerked a thumb at his green Fiesta parked

outside. "I'm in the market for a new car, through part exchange if possible."

"I see." The salesman cast a quick, appraising glance over the well-kept 1981 machine on the other side of a plate-glass window. He led the potential customer to a white, more rounded version of the same model. "If you like the Fiesta, we have the newer Mark II. Since these have been around from 1983 onward, there are both new and secondhand cars available for sale. It all depends on how much you're looking to spend."

David examined the car. It was a tidy-looking motor. But then, he considered his own vehicle tidy too. The thought had occurred to him that - given the miles travelled in his job - he would have to buy some new wheels, eventually. Had Kate's questions the morning before given him a much-needed kick up the backside? He imagined what her reaction might be to the shiny new Fiesta on display. Somehow, it didn't seem smart enough. He cleared his throat and wondered how much he was about to stitch himself up. "The thing is, I'm looking to move on. My Estate Agency career is a great success. I'm after something shiny and new that makes a positive statement."

If the salesman still retained any qualms about the younger fellow, the words: 'Estate Agency,' 'move on,' plus 'shiny and new,' dispelled them in an instant. His smile became a lot more genuine. As a salesman himself, David knew it all too well. It was the look of a man about to make himself a decent commission.

*   *   *

A meaty car engine interrupted the quiet side street in Cerne Abbas. David poked his head out of a window he had opened to allow smoke to escape. He'd fixed a classic Sunday roast for Kate, but one of his ovens needed its element cleaned. After a wet start to April with almost daily rain, the twelfth onward had seen a dramatic improvement. Warm, sunny and mostly dry. A black, Peugeot 205 GTi pulled up in front of his own motor. Kate slid out of the Driver's seat, looked up and gave him a wave. David hurried downstairs into the communal hall to let her in.

"Hi." She worked one effortless hand around his waist and pressed her fingers into the small of his back. The pair exchanged a kiss of greeting.

The warmth of her affection rippled through the man's body. "How was your family get-together?"

"Pleasant. I missed you though. Are you going to make it up to me today?"

David's brow furrowed. *Am I going to make it up to her? Who was unavailable again?* He shook his mild annoyance aside and shut the front door. "If you like roast beef, I suppose I can manage it."

"Marvellous." Kate walked alongside him upstairs to the flat, touching his waist every other step. It was the most tactile she had been so far.

"So, was it your aunt's birthday?"

"No. She wanted to touch base with family. Her next-door neighbour lost a daughter on the 'Herald of Free Enterprise' last month. It made her realise how precious relatives are."

David opened the flat door and ushered the woman inside. "Wasn't that awful? A hundred and ninety-three souls."

Kate poked her head into every room of the dwelling with almost forensic scrutiny.

David closed the door. "Make yourself at home." It was difficult to hide a hint of sarcasm in his voice.

"Mmm, that smells wonderful," Kate reappeared from the bedroom, immune to his mockery. "I do like a nice piece of meat on a Sunday." She shot him an indistinct flutter of her lashes, grinned and pulled a small paperback out of her handbag. "I've brought something for you. A sort of third date gift."

David flushed. "Is that the trend now? I'm sorry, I had no idea. I haven't bought you anything."

"You're fixing us lunch, aren't you?"

"Well yes, but-"

"Here, take it."

David examined the book and read the title aloud. "The Science of Wondrous Wealth - How to set your intentions and realise your goals to reap a prosperous life."

"I've read a couple of his books. He's an American business guru. Three mansions, a private jet, you get the idea. You might say his business model works."

David flipped the book over and raised one eyebrow. "What, selling get rich quick pseudo-science to the naïve?"

Kate crossed her arms. "Open your mind a little, David. Do I seem naïve to you?"

"No. Sorry. I'll give it a read and find out what he's

on about. My Dad always said you don't have to agree with everything a person says, to take wisdom away from them."

Kate relaxed and softened her posture. "That's a little better. I didn't ask how your Saturday was?"

David popped the book down on his coffee table and went to the hob. He picked up a fork and prodded it into a saucepan of carrots. "Good. I bought a new car."

"You didn't?" Kate's sapphire eyes widened. "Tell me."

"Escort XR3i. Brand new and fully loaded." He picked up a bottle of red wine he'd opened earlier to breathe. Without turning, he poured them both a glass.

"That *is* a step in the right direction. What colour?" She took the wineglass he offered her, gaze fixed on his face.

"Bright red."

"Well, you can drop me off at work in that, if you like."

David lifted his glass in the air, a thoughtful eyebrow raised in contemplation. "A toast: To our future happiness and success."

"Cheers." Kate dinged her glass against his. She took a sip, still reading his countenance. "Do you think that future will find us together?"

David put his wine down, reached forward and pulled the girl into an intimate hold. His jade eyes locked onto her pretty face. She smelled amazing. Even before he angled his head in for a kiss, the young man sensed his arousal announcing itself to the mousy-haired vision in his arms. The meeting of mouths was hot, wet and (if David was honest) a little awkward at first. When their lips parted, Kate whispered in his ear. "I was hoping you'd do that today."

A bell sounded on the oven. David peeped back over his shoulder. "Time to get the meat out."

"After only one kiss?" the girl pinched his bum and winked.

David slipped on his oven gloves. He almost felt able to balance the entire roasting tray on the erection straining his jeans.

When the meal was over, Kate helped him wash up and clear away. David watched her dry the dinner plates. A perfect picture of domestic bliss. His Mum would do a jig if she saw him now.

Kate caught the twinkle in his eye. "What?"

"Enjoying the moment and the view, that's all."

"I see." She stepped over and kissed him. "So, have you sold any properties near here?"

"A few. The first house I ever visited when I started the job, stands up on the western ridge. Not the first one I ever *sold* - it only went before Christmas - but it's quite special."

"How so?"

"Massive country pile. The previous owners died during a fire that damaged the house. A family from London recently moved in to fix it up."

"Can you see it from the village?"

"No. It's the other side of the woods that follow the slope uphill." David paused. He pondered whether to describe the voice in the cellar, but dismissed the idea out of hand.

Kate folded her tea towel. "I don't suppose the owners would want us dropping in for tea then?"

David grinned. "No. But, if you fancy a walk, there's a track that runs close to the estate. You can see the Grange from it. Some view."

"Grange?"

"Meoria Grange."

"What an odd name. Well, it's a nice afternoon, and I'd like a little exercise to work off that excellent meal. Will you show me?"

David emptied the sink. "Why not?"

It was fortunate the clement weather and good drainage made the landscape less boggy than of late. Although Kate wore sensible, flat shoes, David knew Weam Common Hill to be unpredictable. A dodgy surface after a series of storms. If farmers had allowed livestock into the pasture crossed by the public footpath, their going might prove both unpleasant and unromantic. As it happened, the sod was firm underfoot, with an occasional moist or spongy patch. Both walkers were puffed by the time they topped the ridge.

"You know how to give a girl a good workout, don't you?" Kate gasped. Laughter lines around her eyes and grinning teeth reassured David she was still enjoying herself. "Oh wow, is that it?" She stared past him and moved in soundless awe to rest against a stile. In the distance down a long driveway, the magnificent structure of the seventeenth century Portland stone house announced its commanding presence.

David joined her. "I thought you'd like it. It's the strangest thing: Most people at the office won't even go near the place. I had an odd experience there myself once, but I'm still drawn to it."

"I can see why," Kate finally spoke. "Can you imagine what a statement owning a house like that would make?"

"I didn't mean it like that, it's-"

"Think of how that would herald your career to the world - 'I'm David Holmes - the success story.' You could have it too if you wanted it."

"Be serious. I'd have to sell a lot more houses than we have on our books, just to buy the hallway."

"You need to read that paperback I bought you. Years from now they'll understand all the science about directed energy and other ideas the author writes about. If you can visualise owning that place and feel good about it regularly, you'll see it happen."

David thought better about voicing his doubts. The sincerity was evident, writ large on her face. Whether that stuff was all bunk or not, he knew he'd fallen for Kate Warren. So what, anyway? If dreaming her dreams motivated the woman to succeed, did it matter if she bought into those books?

Kate sensed his inner dialogue and conflict. She wound her arms about his neck and pulled David close for an open-mouthed kiss. When their lips parted, she nuzzled his nose. "The key to starting on the journey of getting what you want, is to associate it with a positive emotion. You can see the house from here. What would make you feel really good, right now?"

David gulped. His mind went blank. Answering with 'a win on the pools' was unlikely to help. A flippant comment to kill the mood.

Kate blew in his ear. She nibbled his lobe and whispered with a husky voice. "I know what would make *me* feel really good right now."

Spending time with Kate Warren was always an eventful experience. That Sunday afternoon proved no exception. The sudden change of tack from dreams about owning Meoria Grange to engaging in carnal, animalistic gratification took David Holmes completely by surprise.

In the distance, the manor glowed from the pleasant sunlight against its stonework. Even at this range, David could see the living room window was now fully repaired. Much closer to his field of vision, Kate's feminine fingers gripped the top of the stile before them. Her head flicked and jostled while she stood moaning and gasping in pleasure. David's hands gripped her hips from behind. His jeans sat tugged around his ankles. Kate's skirt and knickers lay in the grass nearby. When the divine suction of his girlfriend's massaging wetness became more than he could bear, time appeared to slow down. Meoria Grange filled David's vision. Kate gasped. The joy of that ejaculating muscle spasm enveloped her boyfriend's soul. He emptied his heavy burden inside her.

5

A New Home

There was an eerie stillness in the air. Atop the ancient hill by the angled standing stone, a young tribesman stood watch. A long scar across his chest, betrayed where a blade once plunged into his heart. It was a wound that would prove mortal, under any normal circumstance. He sniffed against the breeze. Something wasn't right. From deep within, a familiar throb of power and connection arose and overwhelmed him. He reached out a single, tingling hand to touch the swirling patterns that adorned the menhir.

A shout rang out across the valley below. It was picked up by a chorus of agitated voices. Torch flames were lit at a central fire in the village. The individual lights spread out in a rapid series of zigzag tracks across the landscape. A yell cut through the night. The torchlights converged on the source of the noise. Moments later, the cacophony of battle joined, carried up to the hilltop.

The tribesman ran and stumbled through the darkness. His trembling hands retrieved an iron axe from a loop at his waist. Bracken whipped against his face. He could see very little. Only the collection of torch flames and the roar of combat acted as a guide to keep him on course. His right ankle twisted on a tuft of grass. He tumbled the last few feet of his downhill race, rolling over and over. The axe had fallen from his hand. With the smell of wet grass in his nostrils, he crawled on all fours in a circle. Those shaking hands patted the ground, hoping for the familiar feel of cold iron amidst the sodden sedge.

From out of the darkness, a shadowy figure approached. His thick-set silhouette stood back-lit by the flickering flames beyond. With a shout of rage, the shape came closer until it blotted out all illumination.

The tribesman on the ground fell back, hands raised in a defensive gesture. The cold iron that cleaved his skull in two was also an axe, but not his own. The dimly-lit world span, yet all could be seen clear as day. The tribesman's soul gazed down to his own lifeless body, sprawled in the grass with its head split in two. He drifted up into the sky. From the hilltop, a cry of longing and separation registered in his being. It almost chased him into the world beyond, but got left somewhere behind. The utterance was a soundless lament. One that originated from no human mouth.

* * *

"Are you alright, David?" Kate rolled over and rubbed a few flecks of crusty sleep from her eyes.

David sat bolt upright in bed. He let out a long sigh. "Yeah, I'm okay. I had a weird dream."

Kate snuggled into his side and rested her head on

his tummy. "Do you want to tell me about it?"

"Nothing much to tell. It was about a guy from some ancient British tribe. I had one like it once before. Strange. Don't know why. I've never studied that period of history. Not other than the usual stuff way back at school."

"Did you watch a documentary on telly about it?"

"No. I haven't seen much TV in the last week. Someone has been tying up my evenings."

Kate giggled. She reached a hand into his pyjama shorts. "How about a quickie before we get up for work?"

"Here comes the love God." Charles Pembry beamed as he stirred a mug of coffee at his desk.

David winced and looked around, hoping any customers hadn't overheard the unprofessional greeting.

"Cut it out, Charlie. How would you know, anyway?"

Charles quit stirring and folded his hands behind his head. "Women talk to each other about things like that, Mate. Claire let on that Kate said you've been ringing her bell like an expert campanologist."

David fished his own mug out of the top drawer on his desk. "What a colourful metaphor."

"Hey, I'm happy you're getting some, that's all. Kate's amazing."

"She's something alright." David spooned instant coffee from a small jar.

Charles frowned. "Is everything okay? You don't seem convinced."

David rubbed his chin. "I don't know. One day we're dancing around what we could be, like two hesitant boxers. I thought for a while it was all over before it had even begun. The next thing I know it's non-stop sex, sex, sex."

Charles had to put his mug down to avoid spilling the entire contents. "And this is bad why, exactly? Sounds like you should give dating lessons, Buddy."

"I suppose." David drummed his fingers on the desk. "I can't seem to take it all in and process everything. It's happening too fast."

"Can I offer a word of advice?" Charles wore a ridiculous smirk.

"What's that?"

"I think you'll find it's happening at a normal pace. You've been sitting still for so long, it's a shock to the system."

David bit his lip. "Maybe."

"You'll adjust, Dave. So, isn't today the day?"

"Which day?"

"Which day? The man buys a new car and doesn't even get excited about collecting it."

"Oh. Yes, I'm picking it up after work."

David was a lot less than excited on the way to the car dealership that evening. The little green Fiesta had been his first set of wheels. It wasn't that he felt sentimental or had anthropomorphised it into a living being. But that car represented an important chapter in his life. One that appeared to be passing away a little quicker than he ever envisioned. He'd emptied any belongings out of the vehicle before he left for work that morning. Even though he knew it was only a hunk of metal, he couldn't help giving the roof a tiny pat as he locked it for the final time. He glanced back before entering the showroom. The dinky runabout looked sad and pathetic, sitting there, waiting to be taken away.

While it felt good to drive home in his shiny new Escort XR3i, David still knew he'd been coerced into a decision he hadn't been ready to make. His thoughts turned to Kate. Did that same sentiment apply to their developing relationship?

* * *

Over the next few weeks, Kate divided accommodation between her parents' home and spending nights at David's flat. On the evenings she was due over, David forewent his stroll up the Giant. Kate exhausted him with her talk, dreams and demands. Once all that was done, she rolled into bed randier than a submarine crew back from three months under the ice pack. The man tried to conserve his energy. Dozing off while Kate was horny, led to a serious ear bashing.

"So, are you enjoying the new car?" Kate examined the plate of pasta her boyfriend set before her.

"It's very nice. More power than I'm used to. I've

peeled away from a few sets of traffic lights, by accident. I imagine there are heads shaking all over Dorchester."

"Does the car make *you* feel powerful?"

David rocked his head from side to side and scrunched up his eyes. "I suppose there is a slight confidence boost. Like wearing a brand new, expensive suit to an important meeting or interview."

"How are you getting on with that book?"

"Finished it yesterday."

"And?"

"He makes some interesting points."

"Do you agree with any of them?" Kate's tone became more stern.

"Yes, and no. I recognise the benefit of a positive mental attitude. The parts about believing in something to help you achieve it, make sense."

"But?"

"But nothing. I don't think you can reduce all that to an exact science. His dogmatic insistence that if you don't have something it's because you didn't do this or that, is a step too far for me. It discredits some earlier good stuff. Only my opinion."

"Not quite a believer, eh?"

"If you're trying to make a religion out of it - and he *is*, if not in so many words - then no I'm not. But I took some useful wisdom away from it, like my Dad used to say." David returned to the table with a bottle of wine.

Kate placed a hand over the top of her glass. "Not for me, thanks."

David shrugged and poured his own. "Can I get you

a glass of fruit juice or something?"

"I'll have tap water, if I may?"

The man's brow creased. He fished a tumbler out of a cupboard on the kitchenette wall and ran the cold tap. "I've never known you to refuse a glass of wine. Are you alright, Love?"

"I'm fine. So are you going to use any of those writings to manifest your future? Maybe get that house on the hill one day?"

David laughed and placed the tumbler on a coaster alongside Kate. He sat himself opposite and twisted tagliatelle around his fork. "I don't know about manifesting my future. They may inspire me to be tenacious in my pursuit of that future."

Kate toyed with her food for a moment then looked up at him. "We've already manifested part of our future together."

"How do you mean?" David slipped pasta, bacon and a creamy mushroom into his mouth.

Kate pushed the wine glass further to one side in a deliberate fashion, then sipped her water. One of her feet stroked against David's lower left leg. She watched him chew his food. Would her response make him spit it all over her? "I'm pregnant."

David's chewing stopped in an instant. His eyes widened. Kate had to look away and cover her mouth with one playful hand in an attempt not to laugh. The look of that handsome blond estate agent with half a mushroom hanging out his mouth and a face like he'd encountered a UFO, was side-splitting. She looked back, eyes filled with mirth. "If you could only see your face."

David dropped his cutlery with a clatter and finished his mouthful. A long belt of wine followed before he found his voice and some words to use it on. "Are you sure?"

The woman nodded. Her boyfriend sat in stunned silence.

"Say something, David. Are you pleased, angry, what? I want to know."

The world span around more than once in that moment for David Holmes. He shook himself out of the shock-induced stupor. "Oh Darling, it's wonderful news. A little unexpected that's all. And surprising. I mean, we've been careful, haven't we?"

"Except that Sunday afternoon near the manor."

The penny dropped. "Ah yes. Well, that took me by surprise. I thought you said you weren't..." He didn't finish the sentence. Kate's face darkened. She looked upset. David got up and walked round the small dining table to crouch beside her. Tears rolled down the girl's face.

"I thought you'd be thrilled." A sob followed the tremulous tone of her sentence.

David hugged her and rocked. She rested her head against him and he kissed it. "Shh. Oh Kate, I'm sorry. What more could a man ask for? Crumbs, my Mum will shit a solid gold brick with delight. After she finishes scolding me about us not being married that is."

Kate blubbed and laughed at the same time. "I'm in for quite a lecture at home too. Home, David. What is that term going to look like for us when our baby arrives? Do you have any ideas?"

David looked around. "Well, the scope on this flat is limited. You could manage a baby in a cot here, but nothing more. Time to buy a house, in the long term. Let me give it some thought and have a look around. I get early word on a lot of good stuff before it ever hits the market."

"Pretty sure I'm in good hands there." Kate kissed him on the cheek.

David paused. "I know this is all very sudden and I should do it in a more romantic setting, but-"

"Yes," Kate interrupted. "That is, if you were going to propose. I'm not fussed about it being done in some special spot. Our future is what I care about, David. Our future and your commitment to us and our family."

David held both her hands in his. "Will you marry me, Kate?"

The girl flung her arms around his neck and rocked from side to side. "Yes."

* * *

Plans for their July wedding made David's head spin. Life had almost swept his feet out from underneath him before. But this was nothing compared to the run up to the big day. Everything had to look perfect for Kate. Not unusual for a bride, of course. But, her insistence on presenting the tiniest details to perfection, left her fiancé drained of both energy and enthusiasm.

Outside the church, David's sister Mandy was enjoying her new dress and being a bridesmaid. His mother fussed with his jacket, tidying him up for want of something more useful to do.

"Mum, I'm not a kid. It looks fine," David protested.

"She's a beautiful girl." Mrs Holmes' facial muscles tightened. "Why did she insist on keeping her own surname? We never did that in my day."

"That's Kate, Mum. She's independent. Anyway, it's becoming the fashion to retain maiden names after marriage these days."

Mrs Holmes wasn't convinced.

Charles Pembry sidled up to his colleague. Asking him to become Best Man had been a logical choice. Claire was Maid of Honour to the bride. In the time since David and Kate announced their engagement, she had managed to get a ring on her own third finger. Despite Charlie's protestations about losing his freedom, David knew it delighted him. Claire was a keeper.

"All set for the honeymoon, then?" Charles spoke out the corner of his mouth as they posed for a photograph.

"Yeah. We're flying out the day after tomorrow."

"Jamaica, huh? Reminds me of that joke - FIRST MAN: My wife and I went to the Caribbean for our honeymoon. SECOND MAN: Jamaica?"

David joined him for the groan-inducing punch line. "No, she went of her own free will."

Charles ground his teeth. "Okay, it was funnier when I was a kid." He shifted into a dreadful impression of a West Indian accent. "So, are you going to Kingston, man?"

David shook his head, both as a sign of disagreement and despair. "No. We're staying on the northwest of the island. Some complex in a place called Negril. It's closer to Montego Bay, so we're flying into the airport there."

"Well, I'm sure it will be nice to relax a bit before your bundle of joy arrives. You will be wrecked once you start with the early morning feeds, you know."

"That almost sounds like the voice of experience."

"Hardly."

"Your day is coming, Buddy."

"You're not kidding. Claire has already told me she wants three kids. Three! I'm hoping to wear her down to a maximum of two. How did we get here, Dave?"

"We chased women like a pair of big game hunters and then they caught us."

Charles laughed. "The predator becomes the prey. I imagine there are worse fates."

"Thanks Charlie. You're brightening up my wedding day a treat."

"Sorry Mate."

Everything at the reception was immaculately presented. Despite Kate and Claire attempting to keep Charles at bay, he still located David's XR3i. Shaving foam hearts and *'Just Married'* graffiti adorned the vehicle until the couple were out of sight of the venue.

Then Kate made her husband pull over and clean it all off in a lay-by, much to his chagrin. Not the best start to married life.

With the well-scripted minutiae of the wedding behind them, David finally relaxed. The stress of it all must have hit him harder than expected. Even with a day to rest in between, he dozed on the plane most of the way from Heathrow to Sangster International Airport. He was so tired he slept through both in-flight films and one meal.

On final approach, Kate gripped the armrests of her seat. David leaned over and followed her gaze. The almost turquoise hue of Caribbean water rose nearer than expected to the aircraft. At the last moment, the end of the runway appeared. The jet bumped down onto tarmac, wheels rumbling. Kate breathed again.

David sat back in his seat. "They don't want to misjudge that one up front." He nodded in the cockpit's direction. "Wonder how many close shaves they've had in the past?"

Once the newlyweds got through customs, they joined the other tourists trying to fend off an army of insistent locals. Each tried to grab and carry their cases, hoping to receive payment. The hotel sent a Toyota minibus to collect them. With much effort, David wrestled his bag out of the hands of a man attempting to drag it towards his taxi. At least, that's what he assumed the beaten up VW Beetle with no interior door panels and bald tyres to be. At last, both they and their luggage were aboard the bus. They bumped along a thoroughfare filled with potholes. Oncoming traffic had little concept of road positioning, safe speeds or distances. Their hearts never left their mouths until the vehicle turned into the holiday complex.

"Would you look at that sunset?" Kate sat down beneath a thatched sun umbrella. She placed a glass of juice on the wooden slatted table beneath it. Behind her, a cheer and some applause followed one of many cliff divers making contact with the sea.

David noticed a girl of their own age sporting massive bruises on the rear of her thighs. "I guess that's what happens if you don't land right." He joined his wife to enjoy the evening, caked in a generous amount of mosquito repellent. A young local boy of around ten, hurried over to them with a platter of sliced pineapple pieces. Kate served them both a variety of the produce.

"I never knew pineapple came in so many flavours." The woman took a bite.

"And when it's fresh, you don't get the acidic burn like the tinned variety or whole ones that have travelled. It's ruined pineapple for me, for life. I can't get enough of it here." David sucked his teeth and dug one hand around in the pocket of his khaki shorts. "There you go, lad. That's for you." He passed several coins to the boy.

Their fruit provider beamed and hurried away.

"You appear to be embracing abundance now." Kate

raised one corner of her mouth.

"Crumbs, it's only a few Jamaican Dollars. What do they call them here?"

"J's."

"That's it. Pennies to us, Kate. But a decent treat for that enterprising young fellow."

Kate's face softened. "Aw, sweet. And you want to encourage his entrepreneurial spirit?"

David gazed after the boy who was trying his luck at another table. "He may not grow up to be the next big fruit exporter. But, he'll learn that hard work is worthy of a reward."

Kate reached over and took his hand.

The following day on a trip to Ocho Rios, Kate insisted on making the group climb up Dunn's River Falls. David was never more than a foot away, standing behind her all the time. Despite his insistence over risk to the baby, his wife was adamant about taking part. She made it all the way to the top of the rare travertine waterfall, with only the odd minor slip.

The honeymoon proved mostly restful and serene. It gave David time to take stock of some changes in his life. Yet for all the positives, he couldn't shake a profound sense of emptiness. An ache, as if he had left something important behind. A feeling of loss far removed, yet somehow present. Marriage was supposed to be a time when emptiness drifted away. He had a beautiful wife, plus a baby on the way. Why did he now feel like a key part of his life was missing?

*   *   *

"How's the missus bearing up?" Charles washed his mug in the small rest area at the rear of Strong & Boldwood.

David dropped his own into the sink. "I understand the baby is about the size of a mango and weighs a little over a pound."

"How do they weigh the baby?"

David grinned. "I'm giving you the typical stats at around twenty-three weeks."

"Ah."

"Kate's fine, apart from a few leg cramps. Have you been out much today?"

"A viewing first thing. Why?"

"I wondered what the weather's doing."

"Don't tell me you've bought another field and are planting crops now?"

"Funny. No. The farmer's forecast on the Beeb on Sunday, predicted bad weather for today and tomorrow."

"A typical October Thursday at the minute, Mate. Bit of light rain with wind now and again. Ever since you and Kate bought that cottage, you've become quite countrified in your outlook. I swear I'm going to see you walk in wearing a pair of green wellies, one of these days."

David snorted. "In your dreams. See you tomorrow."

"Bye."

David's journey home each day wasn't too different to the ones before his wedding. He and Kate now lived in a small, thatched terrace cottage off the main high street in Sydling St. Nicholas. It nestled in a valley, the other side of the ridge from Cerne Abbas. Meoria Grange sat atop the self-same ridge. The word 'Sydling' derived from an Old English term that roughly translated to 'Broad Ridge.' Instead of his walks up the giant from life back at the flat, David now performed a circuit climbing east from the village up Cowdown Hill. He passed north near the Grange and descended back in a southwesterly direction at Buckland Hill. His final steps traced Sydling Water - the chalk stream that most homes in the village squatted beside. You even reached several of the cottages via characterful footbridges that crossed the water to their front doors. They recorded the settlement in the Domesday book in 1086. Today it looked every bit the quiet, chocolate box, quintessential English habitation.

David signalled right off the A37 to pull under an old, three arch stone railway bridge. The car bore left to follow the valley bottom, past a watercress farm on his way home. The shallow chalk stream of Sydling Water was perfect for growing the famous super food. Passing the church on his left and pub on his right, he was soon turning down the side lane near their cottage. Kate's Peugeot was already on site.

"Hi Honey, I'm home." David couldn't resist the

classic, corny domestic bliss greeting. Partly because it amused him to be in that situation (a fact that still astounded the man), and partly because it wound Kate up - which he rather enjoyed. She could be fun to tease as long as you didn't take things too far.

"That line never gets old for you, does it?" Kate appeared from the kitchen, palm resting on her tummy.

David winked and gave her a kiss before kneeling and planting his lips on the bump. He pulled back. "If you don't watch out, standing with your hand like that will become a habit. You'll still be doing it after you give birth."

"It's not that. I'm suffering more today."

"Leg cramps again?"

"Cramps, but not in my legs. Lower back at the moment. I've started dinner."

David took her by the arm and led her to the sofa. "You sit down and rest. I'll finish dinner."

"I'm not useless, you know. I *can* still do things."

"No-one's saying you can't, Love. But you're doing the heavy lifting in this venture at present, so let me take a hand at the plough, hey? Partners, remember?"

Kate kissed him. "Love you."

"Likewise." David disappeared into the kitchen. His wife snuggled up in front of the first crackles of a growing fire in the grate.

"David." Kate shook her husband awake.

"W-wha?" David pushed himself up in bed against

the headboard. The windows of the cottage rattled. Above the thatched roof a deafening wind blasted through the night sky. Rain lashed against the building in relentless torrents. "Crumbs, looks like the Sunday forecast was right."

"They said on TV last night that the storm would miss us." Kate touched her tummy with delicate fingers.

"Seems it caught them with their pants down. Are you okay?"

"No. That's why I woke you up. I need the loo, but my belly is in so much pain I'm going to need a hand."

"That doesn't sound good. Here." David escorted her to the bathroom.

A few minutes later Kate appeared with an ashen face. "I'm bleeding, David. Like a heavy period."

"What? Is it bad?"

"Too much for us to ignore."

"Right. Let's sit you back down and I'll get on the phone."

Kate rested on the edge of the mattress, listening to her husband thud down the steep staircase in their compact but comfortable country home. His curse of exasperation a minute later, didn't fill her with confidence. He was soon back at her side after taking two steps at a time on the way up.

"The phones are out. Must be the storm. We'd better get our clothes on and take you to Dorset County."

Kate nodded.

The drive to Dorchester was wilder than any David

could remember. Deafening wind threw his car from side to side, buffeting it with incredible force. He eyed the tree-lined sections of the road and peered through the rain. At any moment one of those wooden giants could topple on them or form an impassable roadblock. He thought about the little life, struggling to develop in his wife's womb.

"Hold on." He patted Kate's hand after shifting down a gear to reduce speed. Maybe less pace and more traction might alleviate the effect of the maelstrom on the vehicle? Already debris from trees, road signs and buildings lay strewn everywhere. Now and again the wind picked up more detritus and moved it around, or flung it straight at their windshield. A heavy branch smacked against the glass, leaving a tiny impact mark. "Shit, what a night." David puffed out his cheeks.

At last they made the car park at Dorset County Hospital, shaken but unscathed. It looked like A&E were in for a busy night. But, staff put all hands to the pumps and soon Kate was receiving appropriate care.

"Mr Warren?" A doctor appeared in the crowded waiting room at first light.

David looked up, twisting a Styrofoam cup in his hands from a vending machine. "It's Holmes. My wife is Kate Warren though."

"Ah, I see. Well, the good news is that your wife is going to be okay."

"Can I see her now? What about the baby?"

The doctor adjusted his glasses and closed his eyes

for a moment. David guessed the answer, even before the words came out of the physician's mouth. "I'm sorry. I'm afraid your wife suffered a miscarriage."

David's eyes watered. He glanced aside. "Do you know what caused it?"

"No, I'm afraid not. Although that's not unusual with miscarriages. Present thought is that abnormal chromosomes in the baby interfere with development. For most women it's a one-off event. They go on to carry one or more babies to full term in the future. I'm sorry for your loss, but please don't lose heart."

"Thank you, Doctor. Oh. Do you know what it was? Gender, I mean."

"A boy."

"I see."

"The nursing staff can advise you about the next steps. Kate will need all your love and support now. The hospital offers a memorial and burial within the grounds should you wish."

David shook his hand, and the doctor led him through to see his wife.

The couple called the baby Paul. They buried him within the hospital grounds as suggested. Kate and David weren't the only ones in mourning after the dust finally settled.

The hurricane lasted the night of Thursday 15th and all day Friday 16th October 1987. When it was over, it had killed twenty-two people in England and France. This included two brave Dorset firefighters, who lost their lives on duty when a twelve tonne elm tree crushed their appliance cab. They were the finest of men and remembered with honour.

6

Persona non grata

"This change of life seems to agree with you." Sylvia Griffin stepped into the orangery where her husband, Derek, was reading the Sunday morning paper.

The man lowered the broadsheet and squinted at his wife. "What makes you say that?"

"Your hair."

"What about it?" Derek reached one hand up to twist the thin brown strands on top of his head.

"Can't you feel it? There's definitely some new growth. Like a tuft of grass pushing through desert soil after a rainstorm."

The man felt a little closer, closing his eyes to block out visual sensory input and focus on touch. Sylvia was right. "Good heavens, so there is." He blinked.

"Mr Henderson your Trichologist had it spot on: Get out of the city and find a new project. He said your hair would make a steady recovery if you removed the bigger stressors from your life."

"I'm amazed. What with all the effort we've put into the house, I'd have thought to find myself with less hair."

"It's been hard work, but has it been stressful?"

Derek lowered his paper still further, so it hung

between his legs as he perched on the edge of a rattan chair. "Now you mention it, no. It's been tiring. Each night I roll into bed more exhausted than expected. Especially given the amount of effort required to bring the place up to spec. Or should I say *lack* of effort, as it always ends up less than I estimate. But I've never felt stressed about it."

"I know what you mean." Sylvia stood by the large panes of glass, staring out across their panoramic downs vista.

Derek examined her. "You've lost weight. All that running around, I suppose."

"Thank you. I feel better for it."

"You look more like the fox I married, every day." His eyes glinted with a playful light.

"Charmer." Sylvia glanced at him for a second before turning back to the view. Her facial expression became distant. "It's the strangest thing, Derek."

"What's that?"

"I could almost swear this house was helping us put itself back together."

Derek snorted and turned to the business section of his paper. He shook the item and rustled the sheets as it raised to obscure his face again. "Next thing you'll be suggesting it also gives advice on my investment portfolio."

"No, you're accomplished enough at that. We couldn't have bought this spectacular home in the first place, otherwise."

"What are the kids up to?"

"Craig's upstairs on his computer. Amy was reading

a book in the living room, last time I checked. Are you sure it was a good idea to get our boy that ZX Spectrum? In the last couple of years, he's spent more time on it than playing outside."

"It's the wave of the future. Oh, I know his computer is a hobbyists device, but he's learning to write basic programs. In a couple of months we'll be at the start of a new decade. I'm no soothsayer, but by the end of it I know we'll see computers hooked into everything. The skills he's gaining through play and curiosity will set him up for whatever career he chooses. Trust me, those hours in his room will pay dividends."

Sylvia frowned. "For once, it would be nice to hear you talk about our children outside the context of an investment. What happens if Craig becomes a blacksmith instead? Will you write him off as a loss-maker?"

Derek didn't respond. He kept his face out of sight. The new hair on top of his head shook in a subtle sign of despair.

Sylvia dropped the topic and changed tack. Craig had only turned thirteen this year. There was plenty of time before they needed to worry about that subject. "Those antique brass fire dogs we picked up in Dorchester, set the living room fireplace off a treat."

Derek cleared his throat. "They fit with the period of the house. I always felt the fire had something missing. As soon as I saw them in that dealer's, I knew what it was."

Sylvia folded her arms. "Can you believe we've been here almost three years now?"

"And still haven't explored the full range of those cellars."

"Well, there *have* been other, more pressing features calling out for our attention. It's a labour of love, a little at a time. Like restoring an old master in an art gallery."

"That's a good analogy. Are you happy?"

Sylvia paused.

Derek peered over the rim of his paper, brow furrowed. "Sylvia?"

His wife shrugged. "I don't know. The house still doesn't feel like it's ours, somehow."

"Well, we've attempted to make it what it once was, rather than putting our own stamp on it. Would it make you happier if we created a few changes, or styled up the decor to your own tastes?"

"No, I don't think so. It's not the presentation or facilities of the building that bother me. Living in this piece of history is a privilege. I don't know. I can't put my finger on it. Maybe I'm being silly. Once the dust has finally settled, I'm sure I'll adjust."

"Take a stand. Be confident. Tell yourself this is *our* house, and we're in charge. The tail will not wag the dog. You've been walking on eggshells too long, because we both wanted to do right by the old place. Now we're getting to the end of the renovation, it's time to remind ourselves of this important fact: At the end of the day, we own it, no matter how it feels. If you don't believe me, I'll have our solicitor show you the deeds."

Sylvia tapped a finger against her right cheek. "That

won't be necessary. Right, I'll get started on lunch."

"What have we got?"

"Shepherd's Pie."

"Jolly good. I'll fish a bottle of Appassimento off that new rack I put at the bottom of the cellar steps. Should make a nice pairing. Musky and robust enough to stand up to the flavours of the meal."

"You could have a sizable wine vault down there."

Derek sniffed. "It would take more than my pocket book could handle to fill the entirety of that expanse with quality plonk, I can assure you. My next mission - once I can summon the energy - is to go on an expedition to map out that space once and for all."

"Are you going to take a Union Jack and erect it when you reach the end?"

"Funny." Derek closed and folded his paper. He stood up and stretched. "I'll retrieve that bottle of Italian and open it now, so it can breathe."

"Don't get curious and wander off."

Derek ignored what he felt was a smothering and patronising comment.

He strolled into the hall and opened the panelled door in the side of the master staircase. Next to the light switch, the family had installed a large torch on a wall mount. Anyone descending into the depths collected the device to take with them, in case of a power cut. Derek flicked it on and off to check all was well. He edged down the steps into the first chamber. The only changes to this part of the house since the family arrived, were a replacement ceiling light bulb and a sturdy wooden wine rack about the size of a tall, free-standing bookcase. Derek switched the torch back on to provide extra illumination. Over the last few months, he had filled the rack from various trips to vintners in the local area, and the odd one in London. Each bottle lay on its side, keeping the corks moist. They were sorted first by country, then region and grape variety. Derek Griffin didn't consider himself any kind of authority on wine. But, learning about it over the years proved a diverting interest from the other hassles of life. He located the Appassimento he was after. *Last one. I'd better make a mental note for the next shopping trip.*

"Dad?" A girl's voice called from one of the side tunnels.

Derek lifted his head, ears straining. No further words were spoken. "Amy?" It surprised him to find his fourteen-year-old daughter anywhere near this place. She had disliked the cellar from the day of the house viewing and been careful to avoid coming down here ever since they moved in. There was no response. "Amy?" He spoke louder, causing his voice to reverberate off the curved chamber ceilings.

"Dad?" the voice came from further away this time.

Derek tucked the bottle under one arm and marched off toward the noise. *What is she doing down here, and without the torch?* He called again. "Keep speaking, Amy. I need to hear the sound of your voice to find you."

"Over here, Dad."

Derek turned right at another junction, building a temporary mental map to avoid getting lost. The air was musty, laced with an earthy aroma.

"This way," the girl's voice rose up from the left this time.

The man turned down another branch and reached the end point of overhead illumination. Derek brought the torch up and moved with tentative steps into a rougher set of tunnels. He reckoned to have gone about another eighty yards before the tunnel widened into a larger chamber. This one was devoid of junk. In the middle, his torch beam splashed across a pair of feminine shoulder blades in a cream blouse. He recognised the clothing and red hair of his daughter at once.

"Amy? Whatever are you doing? How did you find your way without the torch? It's pitch black in here."

Amy stood motionless, her back to him. There was no reply.

"Amy?"

"Did you find what you were looking for?" Her voice was calm, soft, measured.

"Yes. I came down for a bottle of wine. How did you know I was here? Did you see the cellar lights come on... Hang on a second? You got down here without the torch or any other illumination at all? The lights were off when I came dow-" The sentence died. Blood pumped in his jugular at an alarming rate. Amy still hadn't turned to face him. She remained still as a statue. Beads of cold sweat formed on the man's forehead.

The girl spoke again. "Why are you here?" The tone was firm. She ignored his earlier questions.

Derek swallowed. "Amy?" He reached a trembling hand out to touch her on the shoulder.

The figure growled like a startled, angry animal. That slender neck twisted round at an impossible angle that would have broken it under normal circumstances. Amy stared at him with solid white eyes, empty of pupil or iris. Her voice slurred. The pitch rose and fell as she spoke. "You have served our purpose. Now it's time for you to leave."

Derek let go and staggered backwards. The bottle dropped from beneath his arm and shattered on the chamber floor. A sudden puddle of red wine caused the man's footing to fail. He slipped and tumbled onto his back; the torch rolling away from his other hand.

In the poor illumination from that discarded handheld device, the thing that resembled his daughter unwound the rest of its body. The torso rotated back in line with its head. It now stood facing him square on, empty eyes bearing down on his shaking form.

Derek gasped for breath, panting and coughing.

The voice shrieked over and over at a shrill pitch, like a hysterical maniac. "Get out! Get out! Get out!"

The terrified homeowner scrambled to his feet, scooped up the torch and ran headlong away from that thing in the darkness. The repeated command to leave followed after him though the voice came no closer. In seconds he reached the lit part of the cellar. Something fell down the back of his shirt collar as he ran. Then another soft sensation tickled his nose. Derek sprinted into a wall and staggered from the impact. Dazed for two seconds, he lifted a hand to wipe sweat away from his head. When he lowered it again, the cause of the soft sensation became clear. His hand contained clumps of his own hair. He shook the strands free and ran those fingers the length of his head. The act felt like an electric razor on the noggin of a recruit in the Marines. It swept away all growth before it, leaving only bald skin behind. The man released an involuntary cry of anguish. He stumbled on towards the cellar steps. Behind him, the shrieking demands and all other sound ceased.

"Where's Dad?" Amy Griffin appeared in the kitchen doorway. Her mother added some braised lamb mince to a large oven-proof dish.

"He went down into the cellar to fetch a bottle of wine. Have you finished your book?"

"For now. I'll read more later."

In the corridor, Derek burst through the panelled cellar door, wailing like a banshee.

Sylvia wiped her hands. "Oh my God." She joined her daughter racing into the hallway. Her husband's eyes were open so wide, they threatened to explode out of their sockets and roll across the floor. When those eyes caught sight of Amy, the man wailed again, collapsed and passed out. In his hands, he still clutched tight to the torch.

* * *

"I've given your husband a mild sedative. He's

resting now." Dr Rowling stepped out onto the landing and closed the master bedroom door behind himself with a gentle click.

Sylvia Griffin stood with Amy holding onto one hand to offer solidarity. Both fidgeted and shifted from foot to foot. The woman twisted her lip at the confused expression on the Doctor's face. "Did you get any sense out of him?"

"Not much. You did the right thing calling me."

"It was a toss-up between that or dialling 999. When Derek came round and started babbling, it was clear something upset him. But he didn't appear in immediate danger. I'm glad you could come over on a Sunday. He kept touching his head and claimed all his hair had fallen out. I couldn't find a single strand missing when I checked. He's got more on top than he's had for a long time."

"Derek needs rest. I'd say he's been overdoing it."

Sylvia nodded. "We were only talking this morning about how tired we've become, working on the house. But Derek commented that it didn't make him feel stressed."

Dr Rowling fastened the large, black leather bag in his hands. "That may be so. But, even too much of a good thing can produce negative consequences. He appears to have suffered some kind of temporary mental collapse or hallucination. You mentioned that it occurred in the cellar?"

"That's right. He was fine before he went down there to fetch some wine. The first we knew to the contrary, was when he burst out into the downstairs hallway, screaming. At first I was terrified he'd been injured. The dark red stain on his trousers looked like blood. It was only when I tried to rouse him I realised the mark was wine."

"Has anything like this happened before?"

"No. Derek had a few negative stress experiences in the city. More a case of becoming tired, irritable and withdrawn, though. Nothing like this."

"Is there anything growing down there? In the cellar, I mean."

"Such as?"

"Mould, fungus, mushrooms - things of that nature."

"Not that I'm aware. To be honest, we hardly go down into the cellar. Do you think he inhaled some kind of weird spores?"

"It's one possibility. A mixture of a hallucinogen, the effects of exhaustion on the body and a strange environment that lends itself to suggestion, could explain it. For now, I would suggest keeping him as far away from the cellar as possible. You might consider hiring a specialist who deals with mould and damp removal to have a look around. Some of them offer a free quotation."

"Thank you, Doctor. I'll talk it over with my husband when he's in a better frame of mind."

Sylvia, Amy and Craig sat down later that afternoon to a meal of reheated shepherd's pie. Derek Griffin's episode had delayed lunch. Now he lay asleep upstairs.

After they cleared away, Craig went back up to his room. It was situated on the right hand front corner of the property, with stone mullioned windows facing south and east. The east-facing window shaped into a bay, in which stood a dark wooden desk. On the desk sat a small colour television. Connected to it was a black box the size of a textbook, covered in four rows of tiny, grey rubber keys. These formed a curious keyboard, barely wide enough for two hands pressed together. A rainbow stripe wrapped around the right-hand side of the keyboard, at about forty-five degrees. Above the top row of keys, a raised area was adorned on the left-hand side with the words: 'Sinclair ZX Spectrum.'

Craig switched on the TV and fired up the tiny computer. He slid a tape labelled 'Craig's Programs' into a cassette player alongside and pushed the door shut. Seconds later, the boy fast forwarded the tape while watching the counter. At the correct spot he hit the play button and pressed a combination of keys on his beloved 'Speccy.' Colourful stripes flickered across the screen. His latest project loaded into the 48K memory.

Before the horrendous cries of his distressed father emanated from downstairs, he had been working on a new basic program. The premise was that you typed certain conversational phrases at a cursor prompt. The software then attempted to pattern match your input. If it recognised what you had typed, it selected one of several appropriate responses at random from an array. Craig had tested the input recognition earlier.

Now he needed to add a few more interesting responses to those arrays, and the program would be complete. In his mind, images whirled of creating software that felt as though you were talking to a real person - like the computers in those futuristic shows on TV.

Outside, a November wind rattled against the window. The pleasant morning sunshine had given way to a grey and misty afternoon with restricted visibility. The boy didn't care much. He was far too engrossed in his programming task. After typing a handful of new phrases in, he ran the script. The TV screen printed the words: 'Hello, what's your name?' The boy grinned and typed in 'Craig.' He knew the code should store this as a variable and use it to talk back to him. A response appeared: 'Hello Craig. How are you today?'

Craig typed some more. 'I'm fine. How are you?' This was supposed to result in a reply of either 'That's great,' or 'Glad to hear it,' before selecting another random question.

'That's great. Why are you here?'

Craig frowned and moved his head back. *Huh? I didn't include that question.* He thought for a moment. *Might as well key in any response. That should trip the error trapping routine and say 'I'm afraid I don't understand.'* This was a catchall response he had created, for when the software couldn't match what you typed. It was better than having the program crash out. Instead, it shouldn't exit until you typed 'Goodbye.' He tapped away on the soft rubber keys. 'I live here.'

The program paused and wrote a new line of text. 'You don't belong here.'

Craig's heart leapt into his mouth.

The computer wrote another line. 'It's time for you to leave.'

The cursor winked on the screen. The program still appeared to be running. The boy tried typing a new question. 'Who are you?' He pressed 'Enter' and glanced around. Deep down he wondered if Jeremy Beadle was about to crawl out from underneath his bed. Then he'd find himself on a TV practical joke show. It might have brought a little relief. But Beadle didn't appear. More text did though.

'I am Meoria.'

Craig's pulse rose. He stood and checked the back of the TV for any other connections or anything strange he didn't recognise. When he sat back down, he found another sentence waiting.

'Why don't you kill yourself?'

Craig clenched his fists and pressed fingernails into his sweating palms. He tapped away again. 'Why would I do that?'

The reply was immediate. 'Because then I won't have to do it for you.'

The boy gasped and hammered away 'Goodbye.'

The cursor flashed twice, but the program didn't exit. The phrase 'Get Out,' flashed up and repeated ad infinitum until it filled the whole screen. Craig turned off the television and pulled the power lead out of his Spectrum. He jumped to his feet and backed away to the opposite wall. *What the heck was that?* He fought to control his breathing. *Now what?* No way would his family believe him about any of this. What with Dad having a funny turn, Mum would scold him if he even tried suggesting his computer appeared possessed. The boy's eyes roved around the high ceiling of his bedroom. He'd never noticed it before, but now the place felt like it was pressing in on him like a hungry predator circling for the kill.

Sylvia stirred in the middle of the night. She rolled over to see if Derek was awake. He'd been mumbling in his sleep earlier, but still lay unconscious. The woman felt pressure on her bladder and swung her feet over the edge of the mattress. Derek had only woken for about half an hour, earlier that evening. He sat up in bed for a dish of Shepherd's Pie, before drifting back into a listless slumber. Sylvia decided not to press him at the time. He appeared unresponsive to simple questions, anyway.

She trudged across the landing hallway into the bathroom and clicked on the light. Sleep caked her eyes like breadcrumbs. She wiped it away and peered at her reflection in the mirror. Staring back at her was a blob of a woman. She looked like an obesity case or someone with a serious allergy to an insect bite. Sylvia let out a yell and grabbed onto the basin for support. The figure staring back was definitely her. She looked down at her own torso. It appeared to have inflated as if she'd swallowed a rubber tyre. Another outburst escaped her trembling lips.

"What's the matter, Mum?" Amy staggered into the doorway, still unsteady on her feet after racing from bed.

"Look at me." Sylvia stared at her daughter and pointed to her own stomach.

"What? You look fine to me."

The woman checked her body again. She had resumed her normal size, still nice and trim from all those efforts at home restoration.

Derek cracked open the master bedroom door. "Sylvia? Are you okay, I heard a shout?" The voice wasn't his usual, confident self. It was timid, unsure but concerned.

Sylvia couldn't find the words. She glanced back at the mirror. Nothing unusual there. "I must have imagined it." The phrase came out with a lack of resolve and wasn't directed at anyone in particular. Her thoughts turned back to Dr Rowling's suggested explanation. She scanned around the bathroom for any signs of mould. There was nothing obvious. The room contained its normal dark wood panelling and drab walls. No organic matter clung to any surface, nor poked its way through a crack or crevice.

"Are you okay, Mum?" the teenager cocked her head and yawned.

"Yes, I'll be fine. Thanks for getting up."

"I heard my mother shriek. What else was I going to do?"

Sylvia used the loo and returned to their bedroom to find her husband already asleep again. She slipped under the covers, kissed him on the cheek and clicked off the light.

*   *   *

Over the course of the week, Derek Griffin's mood eased. He got up on Monday and spent most of the day reading in the orangery. Sylvia suspected this was a distraction. A way to stop replaying mental images of whatever he had encountered in the basement. She couldn't help but notice him shudder and hurry by the panelled door whenever he traversed the length of their downstairs hallway. He hadn't spoken about his experiences yet. She thought it best to let him unravel the tale when (or if) he felt ready. Besides, she couldn't get away from her own shocking memory of witnessing that reflection of a chronically overweight person. It didn't matter how many times she told herself it was only a mental blip; the image felt too real to accept it.

On Thursday evening, Amy curled up on the living room sofa with a pad and pen. The TV screen displayed an analogue clock on a black background. Underneath were the words 'BBC1' in large gold lettering. An announcer's voice spoke. "With the time at Nine O'clock, here's a specially extended news bulletin with John Humphrys." The girl clicked the top of her pen and got ready to write. One of her teachers had asked them to make a note of significant current events for discussion in class. The familiar face of the

Welsh broadcaster appeared, sat in front of a newsroom. He lifted his head and began. "The communist government of East Germany tonight announced that there *will* be democratic elections. Today its people have been celebrating their new freedom." The screen switched to a view of crowds standing atop the Berlin Wall. One figure hammered away at the concrete with a pickaxe. "They have demonstrated their loathing of the wall that sealed them in, and they have been crossing to the west on foot, in their cars and by rail - thousands upon thousands of them. The West German leader, Helmut Kohl has gone to west Berlin to tell the world: *We are one nation.*" The Nine O'clock News logo flashed up with an animated broadcast tower. The theme tune blared out of the speaker.

Amy scribbled down a few notes from the introduction. She looked up again, ready to digest more. Instead of the BBC newsroom, a familiar kitchen flashed onto the screen. She watched her mother fill a kettle at the sink. *What? Has Dad installed secret security cameras now?* Her father wandered into shot from below. He eased his arms around Sylvia's waist from behind, holding her close. Amy blushed and wondered how long she should continue watching. Her fingers hovered over the remote, resting on a sofa cushion alongside. Derek kissed his wife's neck. She angled her head back. The man moved his left hand upwards to stroke one side of her face. In an instant, the smooth, gentle motion turned to one of deliberate aggression. His hand clamped across Sylvia's mouth. She attempted to shake free, but remained held firm. Derek's other hand reached for a knife block on the work surface. He withdrew a large, glistening blade of Sheffield steel. Sylvia squirmed. Her face froze. Amy dropped her pad and pen on the living room floor. She sat forward on the edge of her seat, wide eyes almost unable to register what they were witnessing. The chef's knife came up in an arc and plunged into Sylvia's breast. Derek repeated this action with rising ferocity. Blood sprayed across the kitchen units. Sylvia's struggling form went limp. Derek twisted to gaze back out the TV screen. A maniacal mixture of glee and frenzy sparkled in that pair of mad eyes.

"Oh my God!" Amy shouted and clapped both hands either side of her face. She leapt from the sofa to run barefoot down the hallway. The possibility of her crazed father turning his fury on her next, didn't even register. When she reached the kitchen door, there was no-one in sight. The kitchen stood spotless - a proud testament to her mother's scrupulous cleaning regime. There wasn't a drop or stain of blood anywhere. Amy span and raised her head to where the CCTV camera must have been transmitting from, above the hallway door. Nothing there.

"Aren't you watching the news, Amy?" Sylvia Griffin walked out of the orangery.

The colour drained from the teenager's cheeks. Her hands went limp at her sides. "Err, yes."

"I thought I heard you cry out in exclamation. Has something important happened?"

"Looks like the Berlin Wall might be about to come

down." She turned without another word and wandered in zombie-like pigeon steps back to the living room. Next to the sofa, a sandwich and a glass of bright green limeade still sat where she had left them. Amy eyed the drink with a scowl. "Jenny was right. Bloody food additives and colouring. It must be. Whatever do they put in that stuff?" She rubbed her eyes, collected her pad and pen, then sat down to continue her observation of current events.

7

Re-evaluation

"Pull." A reverberating spring and two loud cracks followed Derek Griffin's shout.

Sylvia shuffled round the back of the house, wrapped up warm against an icy December breeze. In her hands, she clutched a compact round tin tray containing two mugs of tea. "You boys must be thirsty after shooting all those clays."

Derek opened the breech of his new, under and over shotgun. Two spent cartridge cases ejected past his shoulder. "Marvellous."

Sylvia eyed her son, shivering near the clay pigeon trap. "Did you have to start a new outdoor hobby this close to Christmas, Derek?"

Her husband followed the woman's gaze. "Craig's alright. Besides, I thought you'd be glad he's been spending less time on his computer these days. Didn't you want him out and about?"

"Well yes. But not frozen like an ice pole."

Derek loaded fresh cartridges into the gun and called to his helper. "Would you rather be indoors, Craig?"

"No, thanks."

Derek raised one arm to his wife in a gesture of reassurance. "There you are."

Sylvia set the tray down on a sturdy storage box of spare clay pigeons. "Don't let it get cold, you two."

"We won't. Thanks, Mum." Craig lifted a mug with both hands and took a tentative sip of the steaming liquid.

"How's 'Dead-eye Dad' getting on with his new toy?" Amy was sitting at the kitchen table when Sylvia went back inside. The girl didn't look up from a teen magazine she was reading while sipping a hot drink of her own. Her mother had noticed her daughter perform a shift away from sugary soft drinks in the last month. She put it down to growing maturity. Plus, it must be healthier for tooth and body.

"His skill is improving. I hope your brother doesn't freeze to death out there. The wind on this ridge can be parky at the best of times. It's biting today."

"What on earth possessed him to take up clay pigeon shooting? Dad's never been the outdoor type."

Sylvia watched her husband and son through the kitchen windows. She hesitated and didn't turn.

Amy looked up this time. "Mum? It's something to do with that Sunday down in the cellar, isn't it? What happened? Did he run into a monster down there, like a giant spider? Does he plan to shoot it with this gun of his?"

Sylvia swallowed. "Which question would you like me to answer first?"

"Sorry."

The woman eased round and pulled out a chair

across from her daughter. Her face creased with lines that spoke of deep inner turmoil. "I promised your father I wouldn't talk to you or Craig about this. The thing is, if I bottle it all up inside any longer I'm afraid I'll lose my mind."

Amy gulped. She had her suspicions over what she was about to hear. Ever since the episode with that vision of the fake kitchen murder on TV, a growing worry had niggled at the back of her mind. When they first moved into the house, everything was an adventure. She always felt comfortable there. But after they completed the major renovation work, a persistent sense their welcome had expired, replaced it.

Sylvia cleared her throat. "After your father recovered enough from his experience to tell me all about it, the story made my blood run cold."

"Go on."

"He said that while he was down in the cellar fetching wine for lunch, he heard your voice calling to him."

"Me in the cellar? Not even if hell froze over."

"That's what he thought. He became worried you might have got lost down there. You know, tricked by your brother having a laugh and then left in the dark or something."

"Only if Craig wanted to walk with a limp for the rest of his life."

Sylvia's smile was thin. She appreciated her teenage daughter's attempts to lighten the burden of relaying a difficult confidence. But nothing could make this easier if the truth be told. "He claims to have found you in the extended part, beyond where the lighting ends."

"But how could he? I've never... Sorry again, Mum. Please continue."

"He reached out to touch you. This doppelgänger - or thing that looked like you - twisted its head around. The face was yours, but the eyes were blank white."

Amy fumbled her tea and spilt some on the table. "Are you serious? Was it a ghost?"

Sylvia sighed and wiped her brow. "I don't know. The creature demanded we leave this place. It shouted after him as he ran. On the way back, he found his hair dropping out in clumps."

"It looked okay when he came upstairs."

"Exactly. Do you remember that night when I called out from the bathroom and you came running?"

"Yeah. You were worried about your body, but I couldn't see anything wrong."

"When I looked in the mirror, I appeared like a blimp. It was the same when I felt my own body. The vision disappeared after you arrived. It was like the whole thing had been a hallucination."

Amy slammed the mug down with a crash. Her nostrils flared.

Sylvia started. "What's wrong, Darling?"

"I saw Dad murder you in the kitchen while watching TV, like it was on a programme."

"When was this?"

"That night I told you the Berlin Wall might come down. That's why I called out and ran in here. I thought Dad had put a security camera over the door and got the feed crossed with the telly. He grabbed you from behind and stabbed you with a kitchen knife like a proper psychopath. When I got in here, it was all an illusion. I put it down to additives in the fizzy pop."

"That explains the sudden switch to hot drinks." Sylvia reached across and mopped up the spillage.

"I suppose. If I'm honest, I knew it was an excuse to stop myself thinking about it. The incident looked so real. I thought I was losing my grip on reality. How could I imagine that?"

"I know what you mean."

"Craig's also been behaving a little odd. Once upon a time you had to drag him out of his bedroom for anything. It was like that funny computer of his became an extra appendage. He was always calling for Dad to come and see the latest little program he'd written. I can't remember the last time he used it. Can you?"

"Now you mention it, no."

"Is Meoria Grange haunted, Mum?"

Sylvia shrugged. "I wanted to believe the doctor's explanation about rare fungal spores causing hallucinations."

"Is that why that man from the treatment company poked around in the cellar?"

"That's right."

"Didn't stay long, did he?"

Sylvia shook her head. "No. We never received a quotation from him. Our follow-up calls went unreturned."

"Why didn't Dad want you to talk about it with us?"

"He's hoping it's a freak set of disturbances. We've

put so much time, money and effort into restoring this beautiful building. The last thing he wanted was to worry either of you, so you couldn't concentrate at school or relax at home."

"I see. Well, it's a bloody ungrateful ghost after everything you've done."

"Don't swear, Amy."

Amy flushed. "Has anything else happened since?"

"Not that I know of. I've been uneasy. So has your father. But that could be fallout from the scares we've suffered."

"Are we going to move out or call in some kind of priest or spiritualist to bless the place?"

"Neither option is on the table at present. We agreed to see how things unfold over Christmas. If there are no more disturbances, fine."

"And if there are?"

"Then we must consider further action."

"I'm glad we had this chat, Mum. It makes me feel a little easier. Less isolated."

"Me too." Sylvia squeezed her daughter's hand. "Me too."

* * *

"Nooo." A woman's cry caused Craig Griffin's eyes to snap open. He lay in bed, straining his ears to catch any further sounds in the darkness. The yell jolted him from a listless dream about being chased by a formless horror. He swallowed and waited for his eyes to adjust. After a minute or two the door architrave became visible, outlined by moonlight poking through the curtains. From along the landing, a clamour of pounding footsteps arose. They hurtled down the staircase at breakneck speed. Craig pushed back his duvet and got out of bed. From the hallway below, a door banged. The boy reached his door and flicked the light switch. Nothing happened. *Not another power cut.* They were a regular occurrence out here. He retraced his steps to a nightstand and rummaged around for a large metal torch he kept by the bed. It had been a present for his ninth birthday, back in London. His surprised parents finally understood the request when they caught him practising Morse Code with it from one of his childhood spy craft manuals. Craig clicked on the light. A bright, wide beam flooded the room. He twisted the bulb housing to narrow the focus of illumination and moved back to the door. Another muffled yell emanated from somewhere below. This time it sounded male. Craig slipped out onto the landing and peered over the banister into the hallway beneath. The torch caught the panelled cellar door as it swung open and then banged to again. From somewhere in the chambers beyond, the boy registered his father's screams. Craig ran back across the landing and twisted the brass doorknob of the study. Sweeping the light back and forth, he fumbled around in a desk drawer. *Where are they? Aha.* He fished out a set of keys. The boy crouched and opened a drawer on the other side of the desk. He pushed his arm through into the back and retrieved another small, shiny key. A stationery cupboard alongside the window contained a false back. The boy knew how to swing out the shelving section and slide the rear panel open. Behind, stood a concealed tall, green metal gun safe. Beneath it sat a dinky, grey cube of a safe for the secure storage of ammunition. Both were drilled and bracketed to the wall behind. Craig rested the torch on one shelf. With the first set of keys, he unlocked the green safe. One nervous hand reached out for the cold metal and polished wood of his father's shotgun. He retrieved a leather shoulder pouch resting loose in the safe's bottom. After closing the door, he knelt to unlock the ammunition store. Another ear-splitting scream chilled him to the bone. He stuffed a handful of twelve bore cartridges into the pouch and slung it beneath one arm.

Amy Griffin yawned and flushed the bathroom toilet. She washed her hands and picked up her own small torch from the valet unit. Questionable electricity service had become something of a norm at the Grange. As she stepped back onto the landing, another beam of light caught her eye to the left. *That's so bright it must be Craig.* The pool of battery-powered illumination descended the staircase. The boy turned right at the cavalier portrait. Amy noticed a long protrusion accompanying his silhouette on the far wall. *What on earth is he doing?* She rubbed her eyes and crept along to the top of the stairs. *Oh my God, he's got Dad's shotgun!* She was about to call out when Craig slipped through the cellar door and disappeared. *Now what? Do I try to wake Mum and Dad? How will Dad react to going back down in the cellar - and during a power cut?*

Fine hairs raised on the back of her neck. The girl shuddered. *I'd better reach him before he gets lost and has an accident.*

Amy couldn't believe she was doing this. The downstairs hallway lay thick with a sinister chill. She rubbed her arms to find warmth beneath her nightgown. The cellar entrance creaked open. Mercifully, Craig's torch was large enough that he had left the wall-mounted one in place. The girl wasn't keen on her tiny pocket device being a sole weapon against the darkness. Plus, the batteries were prone to die with little warning. She'd hated the cellar from day one and made no secret about it to her family. But ever since that honest discussion with her mother over disturbances at the house, it had taken on an altogether more sinister significance. She unfastened the wall-mounted torch.

Craig trudged through the vaulted chambers with slow, deliberate steps. Running around down here was dangerous, even with the power on and some idea where you were going. Neither of those things applied now. The torch beam bounced off stacks of boxes and cast sinister shadows against the brickwork. He held the chunky metal light source in his left hand and rested the shotgun barrel on top for extra support. Carrying the under and over weapon made his arms ache. A heady, organic aroma filled his nostrils, punctuated only by the occasional note of methane from his own nervous farts. *Should I call out?* His mouth was dry as a desert. He was paralysed with fear, unable to speak.

"Get away from me!" Derek Griffin's voice roared from the disorienting darkness. The pitch of his voice rose from bold to terrified in the space of those four words.

In desperation, Craig finally found his voice. "Dad. Dad, where are you?" He called out and picked up the pace as much as he dared.

Amy reached the bottom of the cellar steps. Her father's wine rack stood in its pride of place. Once the source of considerable attention, now left alone. From somewhere deeper in those interconnecting tunnels, her brother's unmistakable timbre split the silence.

"Dad. Dad, where are you?"

Amy drew a sharp breath. *Why does he think Dad would be down here?* She had registered no other voices. It took every ounce of courage she could muster to press on into that claustrophobic, musty labyrinth. She tried to talk herself into shouting for her brother. At first the fear of being discovered by some fearsome, supernatural creature held her back. But then she considered that whatever this thing was, it appeared to be watching them at all times, everywhere at the Grange. "Craig." She tried to still the tremor in her voice, with little success. "Craig, it's me."

Craig came to an abrupt halt. His sister's call squeaked from somewhere behind. He spoke aloud to himself. "Amy? No, it can't be. A deception." In the back of his mind, he couldn't escape the notion that the gun he carried might prove useless against whatever lurked down here. But he had to try something. Without the weapon propping up his resolve and providing psychological comfort, the boy knew he would remain frozen to the spot with fear. Frozen and unable to move until rescued by some external force or person. He pressed on. The chamber walls became rougher. The passage opened into a larger storage area. He scanned around with his torch, the shotgun barrel moving in time.

"Craig?"

The boy spun sharp left. His light caught the base of Amy's nightgown, below the knees.

"Amy?" He raised the beam to her face and squinted. Her eyes reflected the glare.

"Why are you here, Craig?"

"I heard Mum and Dad scream. There's something not right about this house, Amy."

"I thought I told you to leave." The voice was still that of his sister, but a warning chill made the lad cringe.

"What?"

"This is not your home. If you'd used your computer again, I would have explained it to you."

Craig took a tentative step back. "W-Who are you?"

The tone of the girl's voice deepened and changed. "We've played this game before, Craig. I'm Meoria."

The boy tugged at the trigger. The safety remained on. With a click he released it. When he looked up, the figure was nowhere in sight. From over his shoulder in the chamber behind, a shrill laugh cascaded off the curved cellar roof.

Amy stopped dead in her tracks. A sinister, inhuman female laugh echoed from one storage area to the next. *Oh, my God. What was that?* The torch slipped from her numb fingers. The front of the device hit the stone floor with a dull crack and shattered the bulb. She pulled out her tiny pocket torch and turned it on. The bulb lit for a second, then dimmed and winked out. A cloak of impenetrable darkness wrapped around the terrified teenager. Amy couldn't help herself. A warm trickle of urine ran down her right leg.

Craig lumbered towards the source of the laughter. His torch caught the edge of Amy's nightgown again. He lifted the gun, but the figure vanished like a puff of smoke.

"You can't hurt me, Craig." The weird voice whispered in his right ear.

The boy twisted on the spot, whirling the beam around like a lighthouse gone mad.

Amy let out a sob. She hadn't wet herself since she was a young child. Terror and shame washed over her. From somewhere in that fathomless blanket of night, a faint pinprick of light swayed back and forth. *Craig? It must be. If I can only keep him in sight.* Hands stretched in front of her like a blind person. She staggered and clawed her way forward through the stale, empty subterranean atmosphere. With the frantic beam acting as a beacon, the girl knew she only had to carry on moving dead straight. Soon now. Soon she would be reunited with her brother. "Almost there," the words came out of her mouth in a whisper of self-reassurance.

Craig's fear turned to frustration and rage. This creature was toying with him. No way was he going to allow it to keep bullying his family out of the home they had put so much love and work into. He tensed his muscles like a cat ready to pounce. One finger hovered over the shotgun trigger. *Next time that thing pops up, we'll see how impervious it is to lead shot.*

"Craig. Craig I've foun-"

The girl never got the rest of her sentence out. The shotgun barrel swept up in a flash. One of the metal tubes discharged with a deafening roar in the enclosed space. Amy's torso flew backwards against the cellar wall. Her open-mouthed face and wide eyes stared back from where the torch illuminated her splayed body like a searchlight. Dark blood coated the white nightgown like sealing wax spread on some ancient parchment. Tears streamed down her cheeks. Her frozen form remained pinned to the wall for a second, then slid to a sitting position. A long smear of blood spread down the brickwork behind.

"Why don't you listen, Craig?" The voice whispered in his left ear.

Craig lowered the smoking barrel. The coughing, spasming, blood-soaked figure against the wall hadn't vanished. "No. No, it can't be. This is a trick." The boy hurried over, his voice heaving.

Amy shook. Her eyes focused on the pleading gaze

written across the face of her sibling. "W-w-why?" The girl struggled to get the word out. A trickle of blood ran from one corner of her mouth. Her eyes fixed in a death stare and all shaking ceased.

Craig knelt and grabbed hold of his sister. Her bloodied gown soaked his pyjamas in the gloom. The smell came thick, sickly and sweet. "Amy." The sobs began. "Amy, I'm so sorry." He cradled her head in one hand and brought it close to his own. A heartsick cry burst from his lungs. "Why? Why?" He rocked back and forth in despair. Torchlight spilt across the shotgun on the floor beside him. No reasoning or rational thought process passed through his mind. Had you been able to ask him, Craig Griffin could not have explained how he found himself kneeling over his sister. Kneeling with the cold metal barrel of his father's shotgun pressed beneath his chin. With the death of his beloved sister, all hope and purpose drained from his being in a heartbeat. In the stillness of that room, the otherworldly voice spoke one more time as his finger touched the trigger.

"Goodbye Craig."

"Derek?" Sylvia nudged her husband awake.

"What is it?" The man turned over in bed to squint at his wife.

"I'm sure I heard a 'bomp' from downstairs. In the cellar, maybe."

"The cellar? Great. What time is it?"

Sylvia picked up a bedside clock. "Three AM."

"One of those stacks of boxes must have fallen over. Do you honestly want me to go down there now?"

"No, that's okay. I've got a bad feeling, that's all."

"It's those disturbances playing on your mind. I'll take a quick look at the bottom of the cellar steps after breakfast. If it's much further in than that, it can stay 'bomped' - as you put it."

"Okay."

Derek rolled back over. "See you in the morning, Love."

* * *

"Are you sure Mr Strong doesn't mind you going in later?" Kate sipped a morning cuppa at the round pine kitchen table in their cottage.

David dropped a piece of toast back on his plate, leaned over and kissed the bulge in his wife's tummy. "Not a bit of it. He said if you had a rough night, I should take extra special care of you and come in when all was well."

"We're getting close to the same point..." She didn't finish the sentence.

"I know. Remember what the doctor said: Most women carry healthy babies to full term after a miscarriage."

Kate gulped down her tea. "I'm much better now."

A phone rang in the hall. David got up to answer it.

Kate cocked her head and listened.

"Hey Charlie, what's up?" A long pause. "You're kidding. When? Oh, my goodness. Do they know what led up to it? No, they seemed like ordinary, happy kids when I met them." His voice quietened. "In the cellar. I see. Yes, well, you could have told me when I got in. Late morning I should think. Okay, see you then. Thanks Charlie. Bye."

David re-entered the kitchen with one hand across his mouth. He pulled it away and shook off the stupor that had descended since his phone call. "That was Charlie."

Kate patted the chair for him to sit down. "That much I got. Is everything okay?"

David sat, went to pick up his half-eaten toast and changed his mind. His appetite vanished with his jovial mood. "You know that family that bought Meoria Grange?"

"The Griffins, wasn't it?"

"Yeah, that's right. Hey, good memory."

"It's an unusual surname. Suppose it must have stuck."

"Right. Anyway, the night before last, the boy killed his sister in the cellar with a shotgun."

"Oh, how awful." Kate touched one hand to the base of her neck. "Have the police got him in custody?"

"No. He shot himself right after."

The woman gasped and shook her head. "It's incomprehensible. Does anyone know why?"

"I tried to get that out of Charlie. Nobody has a clue, or at least the parents aren't saying much. They're too distraught."

Kate stroked her pregnant bulge. "I should think so. Puts our previous loss into perspective, doesn't it?"

David bit one fingernail with a distant stare, oblivious to the noise. His wife slapped the hand aside.

"Don't do that, David. It's a horrid habit."

"Sorry. Didn't realise I was. Are you sure you're okay?"

"I'll be fine. Get along to work. Tell Charlie I said 'hello,' and thank him and Claire for the 'get well' card."

"Will do." David stood, kissed his wife and fetched his jacket from a hook in the hall. "I'll call you on my lunch break. Have a good day. Love you."

"Love you too." Kate sat and listened as the front door shut. David's feet crunched up the sideway to where they parked their cars.

* * *

"Looking forward to a nice few days off over Christmas?" Charles Pembry shuffled papers on his desk.

David Holmes stretched. "Yep. But I need to stop Kate climbing on stools and ladders to put decorations up. She says I'm being over-fussy."

"I can understand why you're concerned."

"I hope *she* can. I got a right scolding the other day."

Charles grinned. "You should hear Claire whenever I leave the toilet seat up."

"How's she doing?"

"Early days. She's only two months gone. We're both excited, though. Assuming all goes well, she'll deliver about three months after Kate."

"Mr Holmes, isn't it?" A quiet, male voice cut across their conversation.

David had been so engrossed with his colleague, he didn't notice the rakish figure enter the office and approach his desk. "Mr Griffin." The agent leapt to his feet.

Charles' eyes bulged at the salutation. He recognised the name and tried not to stare at the exchange.

"You can call me Derek, like before." The once-bold and self-assured man almost winced as he offered a limp hand for the agent to shake.

"David. Won't you have a seat?"

"Thank you."

David didn't even know how to broach the topic, so he plunged in and hoped for the best. "First, can I say how very sorry I was to hear news of the tragedy at your home."

"Do you have children of your own?" Derek's eyes watered.

"My wife is expecting. We lost our first to a miscarriage, I'm afraid."

"I'm sorry to hear that. They become your world, you know. You don't realise it at first. Sometimes you even forget. But, they become your world."

David swallowed. Was the poor fellow about to break down at his desk? "Is there anything I can do in a professional capacity to assist?" He steered the topic back onto business, with as much tact as possible.

"Yes. Sylvia and I have decided to sell. I know it's only a fortnight since the- err..."

"Accident?" David offered.

"Thank you. Yes. But, we can't spend Christmas there. We will holiday with some family in London and rent a small place in the city afterwards. At least until funds from the house sale clear. How long do you think that will be?" His eyes pleaded like a puppy dog desperate for attention. An unspoken understanding exchanged between the two men.

David knew something was odd about Meoria Grange. Did the loss of this man's children have something to do with it? He'd winced when Charlie first told him their deaths occurred in the cellar. "You've done a huge amount of work to the property, as I understand it. We'll need to perform a valuation, take measurements and snap a few photographs if you decide to proceed with us."

"We'll definitely be proceeding. Sylvia and I both felt you should be the one to sell it. You represent the house well if that makes sense?"

"After a fashion. Okay. Did you have a day in mind?"

"As soon as possible." Anguish strained the bereaved father's wan face.

"Why don't I get my coat and meet you over there? I've got nothing on I can't move around or reschedule."

The relief was obvious on Derek Griffin's brow as he mopped it with a handkerchief. "Thank you so much. Okay, I'll see you in a little while."

David's Ford Escort rolled to a halt outside the

towering frontage of Meoria Grange. It was the closest he had been since that day he showed the Griffins around. Even before he entered the hallway, it became obvious they had immaculately restored this classic piece of English heritage. It was hard to imagine what the final cost must have worked out at.

Derek let him in. Sylvia hurried down the stairs and greeted the man with both hands extended. "We're so glad you could come at such short notice." Her hands trembled as David took them in his own. He delivered a subtle squeeze of comfort.

"I can already see what a magnificent job you've done on the house. Anyone with means and a desire to own a serious piece of our nation's history, will snap this place up."

Derek coughed. "Can we leave a set of keys with your office to conduct viewings in our absence? We'll keep the basic utilities running."

"That will be fine."

Sylvia pulled the agent towards to the living room. "Shall we start in here?"

That house tour reinforced David's assessment that the Griffins had conducted a thorough and sympathetic restoration of the old home. He noted down measurements and took photos as they went. Once they had covered the upper floors, the trio came down via the backstairs and wandered out to the hall. It was a striking role reversal for the bereaved couple to show the agent around instead.

David paused at the wood-panelled door to the

cellar. "We need not go down there if nothing much has changed. I can't imagine how hard this must be for you. I'm so sorry."

Derek nodded. "After they took away the bodies, and the police finished their work, the-" He slapped a hand across his face, unable to continue. David moved to speak, but the homeowner held up a palm. "It's okay." He took a deep breath. Sylvia burst into tears and ran into the kitchen. Derek glanced after her. "They scrubbed the spot clean. The only difference down there is a wine rack I added near the base of the stairs. Beyond that, all is as you remember."

David remembered far too well. Forgetting had been more of a problem. "Right. Well, I've got enough to proceed. I'll discuss the property with Mr Strong and Mr Boldwood and be in touch shortly to propose a figure."

"Could you do us two sets of figures?"

"How do you mean?"

"One for the true value and another for a quick sale. We want to get shot of the place, David. I can take a financial hit if you get a realistic buyer looking to haggle." His face darkened at his own unfortunate turn of phrase: 'get shot.'

"I'll keep that in mind."

"How will you explain our reason for selling? It's sure to come up."

"I won't lie, if that's what you're wondering. We can say a family tragedy precipitated your departure and leave it at that unless pressed. It's the truth, I'm sorry to say."

Derek extended a firmer hand this time. David shook it and turned to leave.

* * *

In the spring of 1990, Kate Warren gave birth to a beautiful, healthy baby girl. Andrea Warren-Holmes weighed in at seven pounds, five ounces. She was the apple of her mother's eye. David learnt to recognise the truth in Derek Griffin's words about fatherhood. He couldn't stop looking at the delicate little creature staring up at him.

Meoria Grange remained on the market. As David Holmes discovered the delights of early morning feeds, the grand old house hadn't received a single bite. Arthur Strong and James Boldwood insisted some of the other agents have a crack at a viewing when they got one. If Derek and Sylvia Griffin hoped for a quick sale, they would be sorely disappointed.

8

Heave Ho

"What on earth are you doing, dialling Australia? That's surely the world's longest telephone number." David twisted in his office chair to get a better look at Charles.

His colleague clasped a black Nokia 5110 mobile phone between both hands. The number keys lit up a similar colour to the small, monotone display. The man's eyebrows knitted together. His tongue poked out one corner of his mouth. It looked like it might be in danger of being bitten off by the jaw locking tight in concentration. Charles stopped to acknowledge his friend leaning closer. He let out an exaggerated tut and gave a minor head shake.

"I'm not dialling a phone number, Dave. I'm sending a text message. The number keys also correspond with letters of the alphabet. For example, number five is also j, k and l. See." He held up the device, about the size of a glasses case. "If I press number five three times, I get the letter 'l' in my message, and so on."

David frowned. "Seems like a lot of work. Can't you send whoever it is an e-mail?" He motioned to where Internet connected personal computers had replaced the typewriters that once adorned their desks. The chunky boxes with chunkier seventeen inch CRT displays occupied a lot more office real estate than the man would have liked.

"No. Claire won't be on-line until this evening. Anyway, she'll be at home making a fuss of Sarah."

"Something wrong?"

"Tummy bug, I reckon. She was out of bed throwing up all night. No way could we send her to school. I dropped Grant off on my way in. He seemed peeved his big sister didn't have to go. Anyway, I was going to tell Claire I'd get the shopping. One day we'll have mobile e-mail too, I'm sure."

"So, why don't you call her?"

"Get with the beat, Dave. When are you going to embrace mobile technology?"

David grinned. "When it saves me time and hassle. It's bad enough talking to customers who own one of those things, when the reception is bad." He thumbed open his Filofax and picked the land line handset from its cradle on his desk. He punched in six digits and paused. "Hello, Claire? David Holmes. I'm fine, how are you? Yes, Charlie said. Poor dear. Andrea? She's okay. I imagine she'll be missing Sarah at school. Anyway, Charlie wanted me to let you know he'll get the shopping today. He is, isn't he? Why didn't he call? He was planning to send a text message. But it's painful watching him key it in. I ended the misery." David listened for a moment and burst out laughing.

Charles cancelled the message, put his mobile down and mouthed the words "What did she say?" in silence.

David waved a dismissive hand. "I'll tell him. You're welcome. Bye." He hung up. "She said she loves you - among other things." David glanced at the 'day to view' paper calendar on his desk and realised he hadn't torn the previous page off this morning. The slip scrunched up in his hand to reveal Thursday 25th March 1999.

The noise caused Charles to lift his head from studying a set of house particulars. "Only nine months to the Millennium, Mate. Could it be a moment of doom - like this bloody computer date bug they keep bashing on about - or an age of peace and prosperity?"

"Considering NATO bombed Yugoslavia yesterday, I'd say business as usual."

"Oh yeah, I heard that. First time they've hit a sovereign state. You could be right. Let's see what else is going on." Charles moved his computer mouse and double-clicked the 'Netscape Navigator' icon on the computer screen.

* * *

A new, silver, Mark 1 Ford Focus hatchback slipped along the lane that followed Sydling Water. Chart hits by Britney Spears and Boyzone washed over David Holmes as he drove the last few miles home. He signalled left and pulled in alongside their cottage, behind Kate's shiny blue BMW Z3 Roadster. Ever since she saw that car in the James Bond movie 'Goldeneye' three years earlier, she'd wanted one. With her promotion to PR Executive at the local council, it hadn't been difficult to get a bank loan. In a striking example of history repeating itself, she'd also made David change his own car again. The XR3i was a little over eleven years old and had grown on him. The miles were racking up, though the car was still reliable and in good nick. But he went along with her request, for a quiet life.

"Did you speak with Uncle Charlie at work today, Dad?" A cute little girl, going on nine appeared in the hall as David hung up his jacket. Big blue eyes sparkled either side of a long, thin nose. The man suspected his daughter would be quite a heart-breaker when she grew up to become a young woman. He smiled to himself at the reference to Charles Pembry as 'Uncle Charlie' - a term of both respect and endearment, despite there being no familial bond between them. "Yes Darling, he was there. Are you wondering about Sarah?"

Andrea nodded, flicking side-parted long blonde hair over her back.

David put a hand on her shoulder. "She had a tummy bug last night and was sick. Auntie Claire stayed home from work to care for her. Didn't Mummy say?"

Andrea shrugged. "No."

"Ah well. Perhaps she was too busy to call her." He wandered into the kitchen. Kate sat hunched over an official-looking report on the table. "I'm home," David said.

His wife looked up for a second then returned to her document. "So you are." The words came out flat and lifeless, like it had been a chore to stop and utter them.

David picked up the kettle and filled it at the sink. "Tea?"

"Mmm."

"Is that a yes or a no?"

Kate put down a pen and rolled a mug round to examine its contents. Empty. "Okay then."

David regarded her, then plugged in the appliance. He lifted an airtight glass jar of tea bags from the countertop. "I remember when you couldn't wait for me to come home, so you could tear my clothes off."

No response.

He spoke again. "Kate?"

She replied without looking up. "That's when you were going somewhere. Not stuck in a dead-end job and thrilled to death about it."

David put down the jar with a crash, then hurried to check it hadn't cracked from the force of impact.

Kate picked up her pen again and studied her husband through veiled eyelids. "Hit a nerve, did I?"

David took a breath to calm himself. "What's all this about?"

"It's about getting on, David. Something other people do. Not you, though." Her tone cut crisp and curt.

"In what way am I not getting on? We live in a nice country cottage. We made it through the interest insanity of the late eighties and kept our home. Both of us earn a good wage and drive new cars. Our daughter attends a great local school, is happy and has everything she could want."

"*I* have a good job, David. *You* have the same job as the day I met you, twelve years ago."

David dropped two tea bags into a pair of mugs. Steam rose from the kettle. It also metaphorically poured out of his own ears. "Kate, I'm an Estate Agent. That's what I do. It's not like there's a big corporate ladder to climb in our world. We sell houses and earn commissions. That's pretty much it."

"So why don't you start your own firm, or become a partner in another one? You're good at what you do. There must be a better position waiting somewhere else for a man of your talents. You should at least be a regional manager for a national chain by now." The words sounded supportive, but the voice with which she spoke them did not.

"Because I like where I work. Arthur and James have been very good to me. They've been good to Charlie, too."

Kate rolled her eyes. "Charlie. There's another prize example of a crushing career disappointment."

David heard the kettle click. He grabbed milk from the fridge, milked the cups and poured on the boiling water. "Has Claire complained to you, then?"

"Claire? No, Claire's a perfect match for him. She's also still doing the same job from back when we met. I've moved up to executive. She's still taking minutes and performing lowly admin tasks. No ambition at all that one."

"Kate, she's your friend. For God's sake, she was Maid of Honour at our wedding. Our daughters are bosom pals." David squeezed the tea bags against the side of the mugs and disposed of them. "Did you even know she wasn't at work today? Sarah was sick last night, so she stayed home to look after her."

Kate underlined text in her report with a nonchalant air. "No, I didn't. I don't venture down there unless I need some photocopying done. Talking about TV soaps and cheap package holidays really isn't my bag."

David twirled on the spot and crossed his arms. "When did you become such a stuck up cow? And what's wrong with Strong & Boldwood?"

Kate wrinkled her nose at the rebuke. "How old are those two bloody fossils now?"

"Arthur and James? They're both seventy-two. Why?"

"Seventy-two? Seventy-two, David. Who carries on working at seventy-two?"

"People who enjoy what they do, I imagine. Plenty are not so fortunate."

"Or useless, lazy old farts who like to swan around, live down the pub, and pocket the lion's share of income generated by their hard-working underlings."

"And that from the executive who only goes to see her onetime friend when she needs some photocopying done."

"You don't owe them your loyalty, David. You've earned every penny they've paid you, and then some."

"I'm happy there, Kate. It's a friendly firm. Arthur told me my first day on the job he and James always wanted it to be that way. And, they've succeeded. That's why our staff stick around. Getting a position at Strong & Boldwood is like winning the job lottery.

You're set for life. A great one."

"Or they stick around because they're worried about leaving the shallow end of the career pool."

David sighed and brought the mugs of tea over to the table. He pulled out a chair and sat down. "So what's the alternative? I get a job with a slightly bigger wage? One where I'm more stressed and less happy?"

"Or less stressed, with subordinates to do your dirty work while you earn a lot more money."

"Do we need a lot more money?"

Kate's face fixed in a grimace. "What happened to you?"

David tried to change tack by way of an answer. "Look. Do you remember those books you used to read when we first got together? You even had me read one."

"Yes. Didn't sink in though, did it?"

"What is wealth, Kate? Having a lot of stuff? I'd say it's being happy, healthy and having your needs met. I'd say it's getting up each day and going to a job you don't hate with people who are kind, fun and caring. When Sunday comes around, I don't suffer that ominous feeling of dread in the pit of my stomach like many wage slaves do. That's wealth right there."

"Why is change and growth so difficult for you?"

"In what way?"

"Let's take your cars. Every time you change one, you get another Ford. No variety, no imagination, no chancing something different."

"My Dad always used to say if it ain't broke, there's no need to fix it."

"There's your problem in a nutshell. And your father is hardly the fount of all wisdom. Your home environment in Wiltshire wasn't exactly salubrious."

"Leave my family out of it."

"You brought them up."

David sipped from a mug of tea to avoid swearing at his wife. It was too hot and burned his lip.

Kate clicked her pen to retract the nib. She turned the document back to the first page and locked her fingers together, resting her clasped hands on top. "I don't want to fight right now. I've got to go away for a conference and training event next week. Will you be alright to get Andrea from school and fix her evening meal each day?"

"How long will you be gone?"

"I leave first thing Monday. Should be back Friday evening."

"Yeah, I'll sort something out. She can always come over to the office for a couple of hours and sit somewhere with her homework."

"I suppose Sarah might have her to stay there. Do a sleepover for a few nights, or something?"

"No, we'll be fine. Plus, you wouldn't want to ask her mother. What with that pleb being so beneath you."

"Fuck off, David." Kate stood up and stormed out of the kitchen.

* * *

Explosive reports from twenty cannons echoed

overhead. The cavalier mounted a sturdy black horse and adjusted his collar. His heart ached with a bottomless longing. Something called from over the hills and far away - yearning for him to return.

Stapleton's Parliamentarian cavalry thundered across Wash Common, east of Newbury. They soon cleared the Royalist pickets and the Earl of Essex started his advance across the patch of open ground. Rain from the previous night and claggy, clay soil might slow their charge. But battle would be joined, regardless.

The man brushed a finger across his moustache and goatee. He attempted to wet his dry lips, but his mouth failed to respond as if devoid of all saliva.

"Godspeed, Jacob," another horseman called to him as they assembled their cavalry guard with Prince Rupert atop Biggs Hill.

Yells, shouts and screams drifted across from nearby Round Hill. The Parliamentarians were throwing everything they had into the assault of that key Royalist position.

The cavalry guard began their engagement with a series of small skirmishes. Before long, they had committed most of Rupert's forces.

Jacob galloped his steed towards five artillery pieces on Essex's left flank. On all sides his comrades fell like wheat before the scythe. The cavalier never heard the shot that unhorsed him. His warm blood mingled with the cold mud as he lay on his back. Vision became blurred and sounds - muffled and distant. With one clammy hand he attempted to apply pressure over the musket ball entry wound. The hit was mortal, and he knew it. A tear rolled down one cheek. It wasn't from a grief born out of fear, but a love lost. With a heavy heart his eyes closed for one final time.

The vision of that fatally wounded cavalier zoomed away. David Holmes coughed and awoke. The bed alongside him had been slept in, but now lay empty. He squinted at the clock. Six AM. *Kate must have got up early and left without waking me.* Somehow this didn't feel like an act of kindness - rather one of separation. Their physical and emotional intimacy had been less frequent for several months. Even before that tense career discussion in the kitchen last week, David worried something was going wrong. He'd tried everything he could think of to engage with his wife and take the initiative. Yet Kate was always 'unavailable,' even when she was right there next to him. *What was that dream all about? No ancient Britons this time. The cavalier was familiar, somehow.* He thought about the words: 'Godspeed, Jacob.' David's mind snapped back to wiping the portrait at Meoria Grange. *Jacob Backhouse. Why would I dream about him? I'd better get up and sort breakfast before Andrea stirs. Wonder if Kate woke her? I suppose not. Ah well. Monday morning and the start of a few quiet days with my daughter.*

He climbed out of bed and fell into his usual workday routine.

* * *

"Hey Dad." Andrea opened the rear, nearside passenger door of the silver Focus and slid onto the back seat. She placed her school bag alongside and fastened the seatbelt.

David twisted round. "How was your day?"

"Not too bad. I'm struggling with the sums in maths at the moment."

"Hmm. Well, perhaps I can sit down with you after tea and have a look."

"Okay. When can we go home?"

"We should be away at about Five today. Uncle Charlie has cleared a spare table for you to work at in the meantime."

Andrea bent forward to get a better look at the interior clock. She would be at Strong & Boldwood for about ninety minutes.

David signalled and pulled away from the school gates. "You know you can go home with Sarah and Auntie Claire, rather than do this each day while Mum's away? They're happy for me to pick you up later."

Andrea looked out the window. "I know. But it's good to spend time alone with you."

It was the first sensation of comfort and affection David could remember in a long while. "That's nice."

"Are you a loser, Dad?"

"Pardon?"

"Mum's always saying you're lazy and lack drive."

David's knuckles whitened on the steering wheel. "Is she, now? What do *you* think?"

Andrea shrugged. "She likes to compare you with a

man at her office called Martin. He's a 'Go Getter' - whatever that means."

David swallowed and clamped his teeth together. "Someone who places value and importance on different things, Darling."

Andrea remained quiet for the rest of the drive into Dorchester.

"Hey Princess," Charles greeted the nine-year-old as the pair entered the office.

"Hey Uncle Charlie."

"I've cleared a space for you. Do you want a drink?"

"Do you have any orange squash?"

"Err..."

Their admin support strode over and handed him a bottle of concentrate that usually sat on her desk.

Charles took it. "Thanks Tracey."

Once the youngster settled at a side table with her schoolbooks, Charles signalled towards the rear rest area with his head. David frowned at the serious expression on his face. He followed his colleague through to the back.

Charles fiddled with his necktie. "When did you say Kate was coming home?"

"Friday night. Why?"

"I got off the phone with Claire a few minutes ago. The rest of the conference attendees are back at work on Thursday."

A flash of heat and the shadow of doubt flooded David's head. A smothering emotion followed, like someone had attempted to suffocate him with a plastic bag. His mind raced for answers. "Are you sure that's not junior staff? Maybe the senior execs are staying on for an assessment and debrief period?"

"Yeah, maybe. Thing is, Kate and her boss, Martin Anderson have booked Thursday and Friday as Annual Leave. Odd if they're working." He puffed out his cheeks. "It could be nothing. Claire said there's a lot of office gossip floating around about those two. Doesn't mean it's true. She's tried getting alongside Kate for a chat occasionally. But ever since she got that promotion, Kate's been avoiding her like the plague. Was I wrong to tell you?"

David tapped a nearby table with nervous, sweaty hands. "No Charlie. Thanks. Kate and I have been going through a difficult patch of late. Marriages have them."

"True enough. Well, if there's anything either of us can do, or if you need us to put Andrea up for a few nights so you two can sort things out..."

"You're a good mate. I'll see how things go when she comes home."

"Okay."

After they got in from work, David took Andrea for a short circular stroll around the village before dark. They turned up East Street near the hall, then headed north along a footpath that crossed back and forth over Sydling Water. It was a picturesque journey, skirting between ancient thatched cottages. The bubbling stream sang a background accompaniment. Ever since Andrea's days in a pushchair, this had been a favourite little constitutional route for the family. David had an awful feeling in the pit of his stomach. One that suggested this might be the final time he would get to enjoy it.

* * *

"You don't have the look of a man who's enjoyed a restful weekend." Charles Pembry pulled out his office chair the following Monday morning and plonked himself down. David was already at the agency when he arrived. His face appeared thin and drawn, with cheeks the pallor of death.

He stopped typing on his computer and closed his eyes for a moment. "You were right about Kate and her boss."

"Shit." The words seeped out of his colleague's mouth with a harsh hiss. "I'm so sorry, Dave. Dare I ask, or would you rather not-"

"We finally had it out over the weekend. Poor Andrea shut herself away in her bedroom for most of it, while Mummy and Daddy shouted at each other. Anyway, I packed a few clothes and toiletries in a bag last night and stopped at a hotel in town."

"You should have come over."

"I couldn't do that to you, Claire and the kids. Besides, I was in a foul mood when I checked in. Almost felt sorry for the poor woman on the reception desk."

"Well, you can't stay in hotels every night. After work you're coming home with me. We don't have a spare room, but our sofa bed is comfy. Claire's brother has never complained before on his visits, at least."

"Are you sure, Charlie?"

"I won't hear another word about it." Then, as if to cement the deal and brook no further argument, he immediately phoned his wife to relay the state of affairs. After he hung up, he clapped both hands together. "There. All done. Tonight you'll be dining at Chez Pembry on frozen lasagne, with ice cream for dessert. Then a good sleep in the family suite, complete with colour television. Well, it *is* the lounge."

David cracked the first smile he had managed in almost a week. "It's times like this when you realise who your real friends are."

Charlie nodded. "Claire and I feel awful about introducing her to you."

"No need for that. It hasn't been all bad."

"Sometimes people change, huh?"

David sucked his teeth. "Or become more of what they already were to begin with. That's the case with Kate. I knew what she was like from the start. But I didn't see all this coming. Either that or I shut my eyes to it. Wilful ignorance."

"You deserve better."

An e-mail alert pinged up on Charles' computer. Tracey waved across the room at him. "That's the new leasehold and rentals list."

"Thanks." He swivelled his chair round to face the desk, looking at David one last time. "Back to work for now then."

"Yeah." David resumed typing.

They'd been sat in near silence for about half an hour, when Charles took a sudden intake of breath.

David paused. "Found a good one?"

"Maybe." Charles pushed the computer monitor around on its turntable for his colleague to look at.

David's eyes fell upon a rental property in Cerne Abbas. The photographs were immediately familiar. "Bugger me. My old flat."

"Do you want me to make this property live, or might you already know somebody who'd like a look? I remember how special that place was to you, back in the day."

David was already pulling his jacket on. "I'll check it out. Thanks, Charlie."

It was a strange sensation, letting himself in through the ancient, studded wooden front door of the timber-framed property. He stood in the communal hallway and looked back across the road to the tower of St. Mary's Church, before allowing the portal to swing shut. Ascending those worn stairs to the first floor, reminded him of many a Friday night weighed down with shopping bags as a young man. David opened the flat door and moved his fingers to run them along the wall timbers. He touched the surfaces with the reverent affection of someone re-discovering the body of an adolescent sweetheart. The property looked smaller than he remembered. But then, your first home as an independent adult was always a palace in the rose-tinted mental images of yesteryear. David wandered from room to room in a daze. At thirty-four, he was hardly over the hill. But already, in his body, he could feel the natural changes that came with the passing years. The buff, blond twenty-year-old starting out on life's great adventure, was no more. At the barber, the first few tufts of grey were landing in his lap during a haircut. With his inimitable humour and lack of guile, Charlie said it was like 'Death' leaving his calling card. David smiled at the memory of the comment. He remembered where his sofa used to stand. Thoughts of that Saturday afternoon sitting down to watch 'Live Aid' in 1985, played out like a ghostly film on the shafts of sunlight glittering with particles of dust.

"Have you come for your stuff? I've got most of it boxed up." Kate opened the cottage door in Sydling St. Nicholas and folded her arms across her chest.

David leaned his head to stare past her into the hall. The passage had been reduced in width by half, due to a floor-to-ceiling stack of cardboard boxes. "You didn't waste any time."

"Why would I? Hanging around and not moving forward is your arena, not mine. Remember?"

David wanted to bite, but thought better of it. The sooner he was out of there, the easier this would be.

Kate backed up so he could enter. "Where are you moving to, anyway?"

"I've rented my old flat in Cerne Abbas again." David's smile immediately erased from his face, courtesy of a long eye roll and head shake from his wife. She tutted with obvious disdain.

"Why am I not surprised? Not only standing still but going backwards now, eh David?"

The man flushed and lifted the first of the boxes.

Kate walked into the kitchen at the rear of the property to peer over the boundary fence. She called back to the hallway as David reappeared for the next box. "Haven't you brought a van? You'll need multiple trips with that Ford."

"It's only over the hill. Anyway, Charlie should be here in a minute with his Volvo to help."

Andrea thudded down the stairs. She stared at her father with a face like thunder. Her brow furrowed.

David's eyes lit up as he caught sight of her. "Hey Sweetie."

The girl didn't reply.

Kate re-entered the hall. "Guess where your deadbeat Dad is moving to now?" She didn't wait for a response. "The rented flat he had when he first left home."

Andrea blinked, finished her descent and crossed the passageway to the living room. One word accompanied her stroppy journey. "Loser."

David's eyes darkened. He set his jaw at the woman before him. "What have you been saying to her?"

"Only the truth."

"Whose truth, yours?"

"There's only one truth, David."

"Spoken like a proper bigot. Damn it, Kate, she's *my* daughter too."

"And I'll expect you to honour all your financial commitments for her home and upkeep."

David grabbed another box. His eyes blazed. "You'll get your money."

A dark blue Volvo estate turned down the side of the cottage. Charles Pembry tooted the horn and brought the car to a standstill. It was a marked change from the trendy Vauxhall Astra that had once been his pride and joy. Marriage, family and new priorities mellowed Charles Pembry. The flash and ego of youth burned away to leave the stalwart friend and big-hearted human that always lurked underneath. They were qualities Claire recognised from the moment she met him. In a reverse image of David and Kate's relationship, she had appreciated, pursued and nurtured that which was *not* on obvious display.

Charles hopped out of the vehicle, opened the boot and took a box from David once he rounded the corner. One look at the expression on the blond man's face, let him know this wasn't the time for banter. He helped his colleague load the final containers in silence. They drove in procession over the hill past Meoria Grange, to Cerne Abbas in the valley on the other side of the ridge.

David observed the curious old house standing sentinel near the Wessex Ridgeway. This new one hundred and thirty-six mile footpath from Marlborough in his home county of Wiltshire, opened in 1994. How many walkers had undertaken the entire journey from Salisbury Plain across Cranborne Chase to Lyme Regis in Dorset? Of those that did, how many stopped to glimpse and marvel at the impressive historic and architectural gem nearby? That sinister home still belonged to the Griffins. Derek and Sylvia hadn't been back in the nine years since Strong & Boldwood attempted to shift it. Whenever the place provoked interest, it never got a second viewing. Arthur Strong and James Boldwood assigned the property to newer agents in the office. A chance to prove their mettle in the business. None of them enjoyed taking people around it. There was speculation that negative reports had filtered throughout the wealthy community and it would never sell. David turned his attention back to the road. He couldn't shake that familiar sensation that somehow, the house was staring after him.

9

New Developers

"Mark and Penny Chambers." Arthur Strong strode up to David's desk with a small slip of paper tucked between his fingers.

David's face went blank. "Who?"

"A nice, jovial-sounding couple that want to look at Meoria Grange."

Charles joined in the conversation with a grin. "Which young office hopeful gets the short straw this time?"

Arthur's rosy cheeks puffed out. "None of them. That place has been on our books far too long. It's time to bring out the big guns. See to it, would you David?" He placed the paper down on the desk and pressed it with one finger.

David unfolded the note and found handwritten names followed by a telephone number. Without a further word, he picked up the phone and keyed in the digits.

Arthur eased back on his heels. "Excellent. The place is as good as sold."

Charles grimaced. "No pressure then," he muttered under his breath.

"Good Morning. You must be Mark and Penny." David didn't even need to use their surnames. Arthur Strong had been right about their jovial nature. On the phone, they had already instructed him to address them on a first name basis. With Mark on one line and Penny using their extension, it had been a busy conversation. For all that, David took an instant liking to the pair. Now he saw them in person, he placed the couple at around his own age.

"David. A pleasure to meet you in person." A medium-built man with brown eyes and side-parted, short black hair stepped forward to shake his hand. David had scant time to press the plip and lock his car before the intercept occurred. A second later, the bony but feminine fingers of a tall, slender woman with wavy, shoulder-length brown hair, hazel eyes and a big smile vied for a shake of their own.

"We've been so looking forward to seeing the house," Penny Chambers said.

"It *is* special." David allowed his gaze to wander up the three-storey facade of Meoria Grange.

Mark continued. "When Pen and I studied the particulars, we knew it was the place for us, didn't we Pen?"

"Yes, Dear." She looked at the estate agent. "From what we saw on the internal photographs, we've got a few ideas for modernisation. Nothing too drastic. A new kitchen and so on. This place feels like a real gem."

David fished the house keys out of his pocket. "Well,

let's not waste another moment shall we? We offer this lovely old house as a vacant possession with no onward chain. Do you have a similar-sized property to sell?"

Penny flushed. "No actually. Our house is an average suburban semi. Mark was an insurance underwriter until recently."

"That's right," her husband added. "Packed it in after making a killing on the market. Dot-com startups, David. That's the ticket. Chuck your money in when they're new and watch the prices skyrocket. It's that easy, I promise you. I was making fourteen grand a day on new IPO's just a few months back. They're still going up."

David was no great investor, but his experience of the housing market allowed him an easy comparison with the rise and fall of others. He knew how markets worked, the good and the bad. "It must run out of steam soon."

Mark smirked and shifted his shoulders. "That's what the doom-mongers keep saying. The same types who had us all running around in a blind panic before Christmas, thinking the world would end on the first of January 2000. Here we are near the end of February, and nothing happened. As to these new Internet companies, the excitement is contagious. You should see the NASDAQ over in the States. Unbelievable."

David gave a nonchalant sway of his head in recognition of the truth in Mark's statement. "Can't argue with that. Still, an investment in more tangible bricks, mortar and land is a good way to gain a home and diversify your portfolio at the same time." The agent had learnt an important tip long ago: The quickest way to get in the good graces of a potential buyer, was to find out what excited them and pitch the sale using relevant language.

"I like your thinking." Mark snapped his fingers. "I told you he was a sharp one, didn't I, Pen?"

"You did, you did." The woman almost bounced with excitement as David opened the front door and signalled them to enter.

They filed into the massive hallway with its impressive staircase. Mark continued his reasoning without pause. "We will still use a mortgage for whichever place we buy. Good debt, and all that. It *is* first and foremost a home, so I'll keep most of our capital in investments. My realised returns will allow us to put down a killer deposit and fund the monthly payments. No sweat."

David wasn't concerned about how they paid for the house as long as they bought it. Although, it would be nice if it stayed off the market for a change. Meoria Grange had become something of an albatross around the neck of Strong & Boldwood. He cleared his throat and began the tour.

Penny became as giddy as a schoolgirl, the more they saw. Each room got lavished with superlatives, or complimented with thoughtful suggestions about the changes she might make. The sudden arrival of previously unimaginable wealth was making her head spin. "This floor, you see. I would definitely want to change it, Mark." She swept the back of her hand through the air above large, olive green tiles that covered the kitchen. "I thought as much from the pictures, but they're worse up close."

"We can do that without a problem." Mark weighed up the size of the job. "Shouldn't take me that long at all, once we've got some new materials."

Penny gripped David's arm. "Mark is an absolute whizz at DIY."

"Bonus." David nodded.

Mark regarded the agent with a warm but calculating expression. "So, I have to ask the obvious question."

David tried not to grimace. *Not again. Okay, here it comes.* "What's that, Mark?"

"What's wrong with it?"

"Wrong?"

"Oh, come now, David. I know for a fact this place has been on the market for some time. I may have only made my money recently, but that doesn't mean Penny and I didn't used to dream. Every Sunday morning we'd sit up in bed and look at magazine adverts for houses in places we'd like to live. This one's been around for ages."

"I see. Well, I've only recently been re-assigned to the property. I dealt with the previous sale some years back. As far as I'm aware, there have been viewings but no offers. None that went through if there were."

"So what is it: Deathwatch Beetle, the whole place needs underpinning, collapsing roof, plans to build a rail line through the garden, what?"

"Nothing like that, I'm sure. A full structural survey

would show most of that up, anyway."

"The owners must be minted if they can keep this as an extra home. Wonder what their primary residence looks like?"

David didn't answer.

Mark stuck his head through the parlour door to where they had descended the back stairs during their viewing. "Speaking of underpinning, this place must have a cellar, no?"

David swallowed hard. It was like history repeating itself. "A veritable labyrinth. No minotaur, but you could probably squeeze one in."

"So where is it?"

"This way." Blood pumped heavily in the agent's neck. His shirt collar gripped much too tight, like a strangling hand.

They reached the panelled door in the main staircase. David opened it and retrieved a torch mounted on the wall. The unit had received a replacement bulb and lens housing. He clicked it on, but the device was dead. "It *has* been a while. Don't worry, I always keep my own pocket torch to hand." He attempted to disguise his waning confidence and rising discomfort with an awkward smile. The pocket torch lit at the first flick. He turned it off again and clicked on the cellar lights. "There are no sources of external illumination from above, down in the cellar. Always worth keeping that in mind. You could get lost or suffer an injury attempting to grope your way back to the steps in the dark if the power went out."

"Gosh. Is it that large?" Penny gulped.

David raised one eyebrow. "Prepare to be amazed."

The rest of the tour saw a significant alteration in Mark's wife. Her demeanour quietened to a whisper. She remained passive and still, frightened of disturbing something down there in the vaulted gloom. Something that should be left well alone to rest. It was a space not to be intruded upon.

Mark gave her a squeeze. "You've gone silent, Pen. Everything alright? Goodness, you're cold and trembling."

"I don't like it down here, Mark."

"Don't be silly, Love. Oh, it's not a place I'd want to spend a lot of time either. But it's only a cellar. They all feel like this, to a greater or lesser extent. This one's worse, because it's massive. Nothing to worry about. The house is so large, we'd be unlikely to run out of storage space upstairs. Probably wouldn't ever need to come down here, anyway. Wouldn't you agree, David?"

"For certain. People often ask to be shown around the cellar. It's one thing that puts them off, I imagine. Unfortunate both for the current owners and ourselves as agents. But, you're right. Why would you even need this space? Someone built it in a different time for folk with different needs. Plus, they had staff living on the top floor in those days. No attic storage, etcetera." The fear was plainly evident in Penny Chambers' eyes. David knew that if he mentioned the shooting of Amy Griffin and her brother's suicide, or the supposed murder/suicide of their predecessors, it was all over.

Such revelations would take this agitated woman over an unnecessary emotional cliff edge. All the positive excitement she exuded earlier in the viewing, would be for nought. And over what? A big, creepy old cellar and some awful but personal tragedies? The only problem was, David still couldn't forget the voice and sensations experienced down here alone, all those years ago. He felt a heel, but masked the guilt with the consideration he was being 'professional.'

Mark mouthed a silent 'thank you' to the estate agent. Despite not emoting as much as his wife, Meoria Grange had engaged his interest. A sale might be in the offing. "There you go, Pen. Let's head back up into the light. We can forget this collection of morbid, dusty rooms filled with bric-à-brac." He turned his wife on the spot and guided her back the way they had come. "We could even block the cellar door off and seal it up, if it bothers you." This calmed Penny a great deal. When the stairs came back into view, her mood ascended once again with her steps.

David lingered a moment longer in the gloom at the foot of those stairs. From the tunnels beyond, a sweet fragrance blew into his face. It was fresh and pleasant, like the aroma of agitated lavender. *Where did that come from? There's no access to the outside air down here.* He turned and shuddered. A soft touch like a gentle, loving caress slid across his right shoulder. His uneasy hands reached for the cold stone wall. He climbed back up to the hallway.

"You sold it? Dave, you realise your reputation amongst our younger staff is about to reach 'God-like' status, don't you? Nobody thought they'd move that house, ever." Charles Pembry shook his colleague by the hand. "Wait until Arthur and James hear. I detect a long lunch down the pub approaching."

"Thanks, Charlie."

"That's two for two on Meoria Grange with you in charge. They should have let you deal with it a decade ago. Bet it would have gone in under six months."

"Well, I don't know about that."

Charles paused in thought for a moment. "How about some more good news? Or, sort of good."

"Is Claire expecting again?"

Charles laughed. "No. Not sure that would qualify as good news. We love our two to bits, but three might push things too far. Glad I talked her out of a third."

"What then?"

"Kate broke up with Martin Anderson."

"Oh." David didn't quite know how he felt about it at that exact moment. "Any idea what went wrong?" He had his own thoughts.

"Not sure. Only thing Claire heard was that he patched things up with his wife and moved back in. Are Kate and Andrea still at the cottage?"

"Yeah. She was looking to get a place with her fancy man, last I heard. He used to divide his time between staying there and some other pad he bought."

"While you continued to pick up the bills? Ouch."

"For Andrea. Kate's on the clock and she knows it. Once Andrea hits eighteen…"

"The gravy train ends?"

David shrugged. "No way am I going to hurt my daughter. I want the best for her and a secure home without worries or distractions during her exams. If she goes to Uni, I may revisit my contributions to the house."

"All that, even though Andrea treats you like crap these days?"

"Yes Charlie, even with that. Jesus, she's only a kid pushing ten years old. But, once the divorce goes through... Anyway, Kate will have moved on by then. If she hasn't already got another-"

"Victim?" Charles offered.

David smiled. "*Person* in her sights, I'd be very surprised."

"Do you think we should find out who it is and warn him? You know, like an act of mercy or public service?"

"We're estate agents not guardian angels, Mate."

"Speaking of which." Charles signalled to Arthur Strong as he emerged from James Boldwood's office. "Arthur, he did it. He only bloomin' did it."

Arthur beamed and rubbed his hands together. He craned his neck back around the door frame. "Grab your jacket, James. Young David sold Meoria Grange." He ambled over with a limp brought on by occasional gout. "Come on, you two. Lunch and drinks on the firm."

Charles considered mentioning that he had done nothing to bring about this windfall, but thought better. If there was no such thing as a free lunch in normal life, why spoil a break from normality?

David tried to conceal his smile. Arthur often referred to him as 'Young David,' through force of habit more than anything else. At thirty-five, it gave the agent a warm glow inside.

*　*　*

Mark and Penny Chambers moved into Meoria Grange in short order. They left their own house on the market. The Griffins couldn't have been more eager sellers. Formalities were soon taken care of and 'new money' found an old home.

"Bathroom or kitchen?" Mark posed the question while tucking into a boiled egg and soldiers one morning.

Penny spread marmalade across a slice of hot buttered toast. "For starters? I've been pondering that exact question. Kitchen."

Mark held up a soldier, dripping with the golden egg yolk. "Okay. Why?"

"Simple. It's the room we both spend more time in. Oh, it will be nice to cheer the bathroom up a little, but it's serviceable for now. In here we're fixing three meals a day, plus assorted housework and relaxation periods."

"Sensible." Mark inserted what was left of the egg-soaked slice of bread into his mouth. He hadn't finished chewing when he spoke again. "I'd better rip some of these floor tiles up for starters, to see what I've got to work with. Did you want to keep the range?"

Penny frowned at him talking with his mouth full. She cast a glance at the large, old cooking appliance standing against one wall. "Yes please. It's such a nice focal point for the room. I'm getting the hang of using it now. It might be good to have a conventional hob installed as an extra once we get round to changing the cabinets and worktops. Something with enough gusto for a stir-fry and things of that nature."

"Good idea. Well, if you can cope with preparing food in a mess, I'll start this end of the kitchen near the parlour door."

Penny bit into her toast and rubbed crumbs from one hand between her fingers.

Even in such a spacious house, the noise of Mark chipping away at the floor tiles with a hammer and chisel carried. He began at the eastern wall of the kitchen and worked the opposite way.

"Penny?" The man's voice became the only noise as all work reached an abrupt halt.

"Did you want something?" Penny appeared in the kitchen from the orangery.

"Look at this."

Penny joined her husband, leaning over his form squatting on the floor. He levered up another tile to add to a pile of chipped and broken ones nearby. Underneath, he had revealed a portion of some circular piece of wood.

"What is it, Mark?"

"I'm not sure." He chipped away at another tile and soon moved it aside. "It looks like a cover of some kind." The man knelt and stuck one ear against the wood. Inverting his hammer, he tapped against it with the base of the handle. A hollow report came back. "Do you know what? This must be an old well. Crumbs, the place has history. What other secrets is it hiding?"

Penny took a few steps backward. "Isn't that dangerous? What if the wood is rotten? You're kneeling on top of it and have no idea how deep the thing is."

"We'll soon see. Don't worry, I'll be careful."

"Wouldn't we have seen that down in the cellar?"

"Doubtful. I should think it's a sealed shaft, tucked away behind the walls and bored deep underground."

Penny cast one uneasy glance through the hallway door to the panelled cellar entrance. It seemed advisable to remain in the kitchen. She perched herself on a chair where she could keep a watchful eye on her husband's safety.

A short time later, Mark stepped back from a fully revealed, circular wooden cover about the size of an agricultural tractor tyre. A couple of hinged, wrought iron lifting rings were set in recessed nooks on either side. With a little persuasion, he shifted the hefty stopgap and slid it clear.

"Wow, it's deep alright." His voice bounced off the circular stone walls, down into a black pit like the throat of hell.

"Steady." Penny rose to her feet but hesitated about

coming over. She didn't fancy getting closer to the gaping hole, any more than she wanted to venture back into that uncomfortable cellar. Even the thought that she'd been walking back and forth across the pit for goodness knows how long, sent a shiver down her spine. She half expected long, slimy tentacles from some forgotten beast of antiquity to slither out and grab hold of her husband at any moment. Slither out and drag him down to feast on his panicked, flailing body.

Mark's eyes sparkled with excitement. "You know, we might install an industrial strength glass or Perspex cover over this and make it into a feature. Like looking down from the CN Tower in Toronto, only underground."

"Not a chance!" Penny almost choked in shock.

Mark's face sank. "Just a thought. Take it easy, Pen. I'd better get a specialist in to make this safe, though. If the well is dry, they might fill it. Otherwise it can be blocked off." He caught the mix of anguish and trepidation on his wife's face. This would become a psychological stumbling block if he didn't nip it in the bud. She already hurried past the cellar door whenever she went from the kitchen to the main part of the house. "Look. Every day you walk down streets and step on all manner of manhole, junction box and drain covers. Many of them are a lot skimpier than this big old beastie here. And that's before we get a modern solution in play for the well. If you knew what was underneath those covers in town, it might startle you. When was the last time you heard of someone disappearing down one by accident?"

Penny sighed. "That's true."

"Don't worry, Love. All part of working on an ancient house. Once upon a time, they'd have been delighted with a source of water to draw from, right here in the kitchen. In the days before plumbing." He nodded at the taps and winked.

Penny cracked a faint smile. Her shoulders unwound a little and her face softened.

Mark retrieved the - now functional - torch from the top of the cellar steps and returned to shine the beam over the lip of the shaft. "Looks like it's still got water down there somewhere." He picked up a broken chip from one of the olive tiles and dropped it over the gap. There was a long pause followed by a faint plop. "Yep."

For the rest of the day, Penny made a point of pressing herself against one of the kitchen walls and sliding out into the hallway. Even though Mark had put the wooden cover back in situ for now, she still didn't trust it. Her deliberate distance from the well at all times, reflected an inner struggle and growing uneasiness. The house was beautiful; no doubt about it. And yet, it almost felt as if it didn't want them here. How silly was that? How might she even broach such a topic with her husband?

It wasn't long after sunup when they awoke.

"Would you fix us a cuppa, Pen? I'm going for a leak. I'll get on to those structural people first thing and see when they can come out." Mark got up out of bed.

Penny slipped a dressing gown over her nightwear and trudged onto the landing. She paused at the painting of the cavalier, halfway down the stairs. It was funny: Despite her growing unease about a nameless, faceless fear hanging over their new home like a cloud, the portrait didn't bother her. That was the most unusual part about it all. Somehow, ghosts or spirits of former occupants didn't spring to mind when the fears came. She didn't look over her shoulder, half expecting to find some civil war phantom or vaporous apparition of a murdered scullery maid. Looking over your shoulder seemed pointless at Meoria Grange. When the sensation hit, it was everywhere at once like a smothering pillow. The woman turned at the bottom of the main staircase and stopped in her tracks. The cellar door stood open. Her muscles went taut, like a puppeteer bringing a marionette to attention. She thought about calling out, but Mark was in the bathroom. Half-closing her eyes like a child afraid of a beast in their bedroom cupboard, she pushed the door to and slid a small brass bolt across. *Mark hardly goes down there. He wouldn't have left it open.* A disturbing thought. Penny was still pondering the discovery when she reached the kitchen doorway and froze to the spot. Her mouth opened, but no scream came out. She didn't even manage a murmur. Panic rose like steam to the whistle of a stove-top kettle, yearning for release. Immediate pressure on her bladder also yearned for release. It took every ounce of self-control the woman possessed, not to wee all over the kitchen floor. And that was the point. When they went to bed, there *was* no kitchen floor. Mark had been industrious throughout the day. By the time he finished, all that remained was an uneven mess of rubble and uncovered, battered flagstones no longer fit for purpose. That and a pile of damaged olive green tiles that once covered the spacious room. Now the floor looked better than the day they moved in. The olive green tiles were back. Shiny, as if from a fresh scrub or coat of polish. The pile of damaged coverings were gone and the deep, sinister well and its cover lay obscured once again. Penny almost imagined David Holmes wandering around with a camera, taking pictures for a sale. The muffled sound of the toilet flushing upstairs, provided enough momentary distraction for Penny to release her scream.

Mark's footsteps pounded along the landing. He raced downstairs, almost losing his footing and grabbing the newel post for stability. He made his wife's side, several seconds later. What he saw negated any need for her to explain the outburst.

"Oh, my God. How...?" His mouth remained open.

Penny shrieked and sobbed. "I can't stay here, Mark. I'm worried sick."

"Pen." He found it impossible to continue. What could he say?

She sniffed. "Did you leave the cellar unlocked last night?"

"The cellar? No. I don't go down there unless I can help it. You know that."

"It was wide open when I got here."

"Do you think someone got in? I wonder if there's another entrance underground we don't know about?"

"Got in and re-tiled our kitchen with what appears to be Victorian floor tiles?"

Mark knew he'd asked a stupid question. His rational mind grappled for answers, like a spider fighting for grip to climb out of a slippery bath. "Okay. How about if I seal that door up? Do you remember how I said I would when we came to look at the house?"

A gentle whimper emanated from his wife. Mark took her in his arms.

"Listen. I'll set the handle in a closed position. Then we'll secure the bolt and I'll screw a makeshift piece of wood across the frame near floor level. We can do a proper job later. But at least it'll keep the cellar door shut. Nobody will be able to open it from either side."

Penny held on tight and pressed her head into his chest as if attempting to smother herself. Thoughts of what had happened in the kitchen did little to persuade her that a set handle and piece of screwed timber might stop whatever was doing this.

*   *   *

David Holmes tossed and turned in bed. It had taken an age to get off to sleep, though he couldn't place the exact topic that prevented his mind switching off. Now he hovered on the cusp of wakefulness and dreams; a state providing little rest. Images pushed their way into his subconscious. There was a man. Not some ancient tribal Briton nor civil war Cavalier this time. He didn't recognise the image staring back at him from a silver mirror. Once again he experienced a bizarre nocturnal adventure in the first person. Or rather, a series of adventures. Nothing drastic or exciting for a change. The fellow seemed engaged in various home improvements. While he may not have recognised the owner of the eyes through which he peered, the house was unmistakable. From the dress and equipment of the period, David placed it somewhere during the reign of Queen Victoria. An upstairs storage room was converted into the first of a series of bathrooms. Pipes and plumbing were being added to Meoria Grange by a crew of workmen. The man himself panelled the lower portion of the bathroom walls with loving hands.

In the kitchen, a worn flagstone floor got covered over with the olive green tiles David knew well. On one side of the room, several workmen hauled a hefty wooden cover across a circular opening. A young lad - one of their apprentices - jumped up and down on it to test for sturdiness. At last they laid the olive tiles to rest across the lid.

The next image appeared to be a few years later, during the Edwardian period. The man's hair looked greyer than before. He wore no ring on his finger and still appeared devoid of a wife or family. The first installation and wiring of electrical conduits took place under the master's watchful eye. Incandescent bulbs lit the old manor house, replacing the gaslights David had noticed in earlier scenes. Throughout the whole montage, the homeowner experienced a profound sense of love and appreciation. It was as if he were lavishing affection on some radiant beauty and receiving her undying passion in return. So strong was the sense of completeness and wellbeing, it permeated David's soul and flooded endorphins into his physical body.

The last image felt very different. The man struggled to push his broken torso from beneath a horse that had fallen on top of him. He reached for his riding crop with blood-stained hands. It was his own blood, and he knew it, however accidentally drawn. Across the rolling Dorset landscape, he could see the Grange some miles distant. Focus blurred, and the world tilted from side to side. The man's eyes closed to the accompaniment of a crushing heartbreak, as David's opened with a start.

10

Old Developments

"Are you certain, Bill? No pay-outs at all?" Mark's face turned ashen. He paced back and forth in his upstairs study, cordless phone clamped to one ear. Vacant, panicked eyes flitted to the view down the drive. Trees lining the approach to Meoria Grange bent in a blustery gale. "What about my other holdings? Worthless. Won't anyone buy them? I see." He listened intently to the solemn voice on the other end of the line. Resting on the desk before him, a newspaper headline announced further collapses of the Dot-com bubble. People were getting stung left right and centre. Mark Chambers was one such casualty. It was tempting to state the obvious: 'How am I going to pay for the house?' But, that was hardly his broker's problem. A faint waft of fried, smoky bacon drifted along the landing and teased his nostrils through the ajar door. Penny was whipping up a full English to restore their spirits. The shock of yesterday's discovery and a restless night left them both lacking in energy.

In the kitchen, Penny plated up some cooked mushrooms and tomatoes. She placed them in one of the range ovens to keep warm. Mark had sealed the cellar door yesterday as promised. He'd left the kitchen alone for now. Walking across the old olive tiles didn't bother Penny so much this morning, even knowing that a deep well lay beneath. Whatever bizarre force had acted upon the room, it seemed determined not to expose the shaft. The chances of her tumbling in there, were remote. Plus, when they came down first thing (Penny insisted Mark go with her) the cellar door remained sealed; the new wooden bar screwed in place across the bottom to secure it. Could it be that peace had been restored? When Mark went back to work on those tiles, they'd find out for sure. She cracked two eggs into a pan of black pudding. Several slices of bread sat ready to be fried in the final few minutes of preparation. The woman nipped out into the hallway to call up from the bottom of the main staircase. "Mark? Breakfast will be on the table in about five minutes. Mark?"

"Okay." The voice that answered came short and sharp.

Penny frowned. She muttered to herself. "No need to snap like that. Whatever can be wrong?"

The sound of splintering wood grabbed her attention. A crack crept along the beam at the base of the cellar door. It moved in jagged spurts like one of those spreading earthquake crevasses, when land masses shear apart in action or disaster films. It may have only been a piece of timber four feet long, but the effect on Penny's nerves felt no less dramatic.

"Mark?" the word came out in a whisper that nobody would hear. "Mark?"

The bracing bar shattered into a cloud of vicious wooden shards. They flew past her body like a swarm of blowgun darts. Lacerations appeared on her face, arms and legs. Tell-tale streaks of crimson oozed in fibre-thin lines from the incised flesh. Penny screamed at the top of her lungs. It was a cry cut short as her wide eyes observed the brass bolt slide back of its own accord. A clunk rang out from the internal latch where Mark had set the handle. Now the knob turned and the panel door swung open with a faint creak.

Mark slammed the phone down on top of the newspaper at the first cry of distress from his wife. His head still reeled from the news he'd lost everything. That would soon include this grand old house that had once been their dream. What horrors awaited him at the bottom of the stairs to compound his misery? The salty taste of blood daubed his palate. His neck was sweating, warning of a possible fainting spell at any moment. As he raced to the top stair, his left ankle twisted. It went out from underneath him. He dived headlong down the first flight, smashing a hole in some wood panelling at the right-hand turn in the staircase beneath the portrait. But the impact couldn't overcome his inertia. His body continued its downward tumble, hitting every step before his twisted torso came to rest in the hallway. Mark Chambers let out a cry of agony. Fingers on both hands tensed into quivering talons. Pain seared through his body. Bones stuck out of his right forearm above the wrist. They presented the appearance of a gnawed chicken drumstick. Thick gobs of blood dripped from the wound like syrup.

"Mark." Penny's blood-stained countenance appeared above him. Tears mingled with the red produce of her own cruel, facial injuries. "Oh my God, Mark." Nothing appeared through that open cellar door but a blast of cold air. Now Penny had more pressing worries to distract from that fearful, supernatural encounter.

"Mrs Chambers?" A middle-aged doctor with cropped, ginger hair caught Penny's attention. She had been sitting in A&E at Dorchester for several hours. A nurse attended to her injuries. Now she drummed her fingers on restless legs, waiting for an update from medical staff on her husband's condition. She stood on uneasy pins, grabbing the back of a chair in front for support.

The doctor motioned her to sit again. "How are you doing? The nurse told me you suffered cuts from some splintering wood."

"I'm okay."

"How did it happen?"

Penny thought for a moment. The last thing she wanted was a psychological evaluation. Telling the doctor 'a beam of wood exploded at the hands of an unseen force,' would not help any. "It's a long story. Accident because of DIY. We've been doing up an old house."

"I see."

"How is my husband?"

"He's stable. I'd like to say comfortable, but he's in quite a bit of pain. They'll be taking him through for surgery in a little while."

"Can I see him?"

The doctor stroked his chin. "You could, but we've given him a lot of painkillers. He might not make much sense."

"Sounds like Mark on any normal day." She attempted to smile.

The doctor grinned. "Good. A little humour helps. It eases the stress and worry."

"I'd like to see him. What was the damage?"

"Considering his tumble, not as bad as it could have been. A sprained ankle and some fierce bruising to his lower body. We're more concerned about the right forearm injury at present, because his bones fractured and poked through the skin. If infection takes hold that can be bad. It's a genuine risk, so he's on an antibiotic drip to prevent it. The ulna and radius - that's the two bones in the forearm - were both broken in the fall. The surgeons will push the bones back beneath the skin and wire them together. That should hold them in place and help everything knit." The doctor glanced over his shoulder. "I can get you in for five minutes, if you like. Follow me."

"Penny?" Mark struggled through a fog induced by a cocktail of pain and the medication administered to ease it.

"How are you?" His wife shook back a tear.

"I've been better. How are you doing?"

"A few cuts. Nothing serious."

"What happened?" The man tried to sit up. Penny placed a gentle hand on his chest to restrain him.

"Easy. Don't worry about it now."

His own eyes reddened. "We're going to lose the house, Pen."

"How do you mean?"

"Bill Theakston called. The investments have collapsed."

"What, all of them?"

Mark nodded. "I'm so sorry."

"I'm not." She caught the pained and confused expression on her husband's face. "Oh, I'm sorry about the loss, Darling. But I'm not sorry about the house. I don't want to stay there."

"How did you get cut?"

Penny tried to shake the question away with a waggle of her trembling chin.

Mark's eyes narrowed. "Something happened with the cellar door, didn't it?"

"Yes." She attempted to change the subject. "They're taking you through for surgery soon."

"I know. I had to sign a consent form. Couldn't manage it with this." He lifted his right arm. It bore a bandage and temporary plaster cast. "Used my left hand instead. The signature looked like something I would have written when I was five. If it all goes wrong and you end up in court; when they ask 'is this your husband's signature?' you'll understand what I mean."

Penny's facial muscles strained. "Don't say that, Mark. After your operation, everything will be fine."

"They're hopeful I'll be home in under a week. But, it'll be a long road to recovery. And with a skint, jobless husband and repossessed house. Are you going back there tonight?"

Penny shuddered. "I don't want to. I'll run in and fetch a few essentials. Mum and Dad will put me up in Bournemouth. I can still come over to visit."

"That's a thirty mile drive each way."

"I'll get the train to Dorchester South. Three quarters of an hour. I used to do it when I visited friends here as a teenager."

A doctor and a nurse entered the room with a hospital porter.

Mark squeezed his wife's leg with his left hand. "I love you, Pen."

"I love you too." She watched them wheel his bed away.

*　　*　　*

The house was almost brooding, hunched over to examine her as Penny Chambers pulled up outside. At least, that's how it appeared in her imagination. Dark rain clouds were gathering fast on the horizon. The threat of thunder and lightning hung on the air with near palpable certainty. Her shoes crunched on gravel leading up to the front steps. The cold iron key felt like an ice cube in her hand as she inserted it into the lock. The heavy wooden portal swung inward. The smell of bacon still lingered. Penny had pulled the items from the stove and dumped them to one side as the ambulance arrived for her husband. No time to clean up. She stepped through the entrance. The door swung shut with a resounding crash that echoed along the atrium. Penny edged forward to the foot of the stairs. Splatters of blood from Mark's forearm injury were still visible on the shiny wooden floorboards. The cellar door stood closed and bolted. A jolt whipped through the woman's frame with the first spectacular flash of lightning. A crash of thunder added a sinister note to her realisation she hadn't touched the door since it opened at the moment of Mark's accident. She put one foot in front of the other, never taking her eyes off the cellar door as she approached the kitchen. Nothing happened. Two minutes later she had deposited the spoilt food in a bin liner and dumped it in a can outside. The rain began in earnest, hammering against the large windows in relentless sheets. Another flash of lightning flickered. Penny held tight to the banister and climbed the main staircase. At the half landing she stopped where Mark had smashed a hole in the panelling. It was perfect. Mended and with no sign of damage or repair. Penny's blood rose. For the first time since their arrival at Meoria Grange, anger replaced fear. Another flash illuminated the cavalier portrait. She snatched it from its hooks and broke it over the newel post, tearing and impaling the canvas. With a shriek of feminine rage and frustration, she cast down the remains of the picture into the hallway. The frame broke on impact with the floor. A mild aura of self-satisfaction mingled with the adrenaline that pumped through her system. "See how you like that," she bellowed across the atrium.

An echoing moan and whisper resounded along the corridors. "You shouldn't have done that." A weird voice arose from everywhere at once. It bore a timbre like that of a young woman and aged crone blended together in some discordant cacophony.

Penny grabbed the banister. Her pulse pounded like an engine with the throttle open.

The voice spoke again. "Why did you have to hurt me?"

Penny ran up the next flight of stairs and didn't stop until she reached their bedroom.

Wherever she went that voice was present. "You won't get away, Penny. Nobody ever attacks me and gets away. You're mine now."

Penny tugged a bag from underneath the bed and flung it onto the mattress. She tore open the wardrobe door and her eyes bulged. Bladder discharge ran down her leg and her bowels let go at the vision of a weird, disembodied face that met her eyes. All she did was cry out. "Nooo!"

"Has anyone tried to call the ward?" Mark sat up in his hospital bed and poked at a tray of food deposited by an orderly. A nurse pumped the rubber bulb connected to an aneroid sphygmomanometer, secured around his good arm. "It's unlike my wife to not even phone. She was planning to stop over with her parents in Bournemouth, but intended to visit me."

The nurse tore apart the Velcro fastenings and removed the blood pressure device. "I can double-check with Sister if you like, in case there is a message waiting they've forgotten to give to you."

"Please." Mark watched a family of four arrive for a visit. They gathered around the bed of an old man opposite, who had one leg in traction. His wrinkled, grey face lit up with pleasure and relief at some respite from the monotony and misery of time spent in hospital.

A few minutes later, the nurse returned. "I'm sorry, Mr Chambers. There are no messages for you." Her patient's face fell. "Can we call your wife's family in Bournemouth? You know, to check everything is okay with Mrs Chambers and give them an update on your condition?"

"No. Thank you. I don't have the number and they're ex-directory."

"What about someone else? Do you have other relatives nearby?"

"I'm afraid not."

The nurse winced, searching for answers. "Sister thinks the consultant will sign your release papers in the morning. You'll need to come back and have the wires removed in a few weeks. They'll perform a wound inspection when you do. You'll get a fresh, lighter cast or sling and some advice on physio. But otherwise he's satisfied you're safe to walk out of here under your own steam now. That was the principal goal. Reception can call a taxi for you if we haven't heard from Mrs Chambers first thing."

Mark put down the small plastic tub of lime jelly he'd finished. "Thank you again." Then to himself. "I'm glad Pen had the presence of mind to chuck a few fresh clothes in a bag for me when she followed the ambulance here."

Morning came, and the consultant signed Mark Chambers' release. There was still neither sight nor sound of Penny. The man dressed in his spare clothes and thanked the ward staff. Hospital reception phoned for a taxi and Mark slipped into the rear seat, being careful not to bang his fresh cast. He pulled the seatbelt across with his left arm and clicked it home. The cab pulled away. Mark didn't notice much of the journey until the driveway of Meoria Grange swung into view. He paid the driver and tipped him. The man held the vehicle door open. The car trundled off down the tree-lined approach and Mark watched it go. In his jacket pocket, the chunky outline from one of the house's spare keys announced its presence. He swallowed hard and retrieved the cold metal object. Penny's car still sat parked out front. That didn't bode well. *Might she have been delayed with a situation at her parents' and stopped off on the way to visit?* Mark was clutching at straws and he knew it. Once his wife got the things she needed to leave, there was scant chance she'd come back here of her own volition. She also would have phoned the hospital every day from Bournemouth if she couldn't visit. He set aside freakish, paranoid worries that Penny had suffered some kind of car accident. But dispelling such a horrific consideration brought the injured and agitated man little relief. If her car was here, then so was his wife. His own motor sat parked alongside it, so she hadn't taken that instead.

Mark inserted the key into the lock and let the solid door swing open. The house lay silent, still as stone. He stepped into the hallway, ears straining for any sound indicating another human soul. "Penny?" The call rang out unanswered. He tried again with more gusto. "Penny, are you here?" No reply. He reached the cellar door. It stood closed and bolted. The wood he had screwed into the bottom, was nowhere in sight. From up on the half-landing, the cavalier portrait - in perfect condition - appeared to have a new lustre. Better than the man last remembered it. A faint, gentle creaking noise whispered down from above. It formed into a slow rhythm that reminded him of summer holidays swinging on a hammock in sunnier climes, cocktail in hand. Something dripped onto the top of his head.

"Leaking roof, on top of everything else," Mark grumbled, considering that at least it would no longer be his problem once the bank repossessed the place. Another drip impacted his crown. He reached up his left hand to wipe the drops away. They felt sticky and viscous. When his fingers came back round to eye-level, they were smeared with blood. Mark took another step to crane his neck upwards for a better view. His feet slipped on a puddle of fluid and he crashed to the floor, cradling his plastered arm for protection. The smell of the goo he landed in reached his nostrils, causing the floundering figure to retch. It was a foaming patch of blood, urine and goodness knows what else. The creaking noise came louder. A large, dangling object swung into view. Moving back and forth from a high beam in the atrium, Penny Chambers' torso hung secured about the neck with a noose. Her bloated body, green and coated with peeling skin and fluid-filled pustules acted like a pendulum. Whether from escaping gas caused by leaking enzymes or some subtle breeze above, the lifeless mass remained in perpetual motion. Mark's vocal eruption registered somewhere between a gut-wrenching howl of agony and scream of abject fear. Mouth wide, he let fly where he sat in the puddle of evacuated decomposition juices. Something hit him in the eye. It was solid this time, not blood or puss. Another object landed in his mouth. It was about the size and shape of a piece of engorged rice. He spat the thing out: A maggot that wriggled in situ on the stinking floor between his thighs. His gaze returned to the fat, gas-inflated mass of decaying flesh that had once been his wife. A seething collection of flies pushed and fought their way out of the dead woman's nasal cavity. Mark cried out again. What remained of the eyelids flicked open. The sockets had sunk in. A heaving mass of maggots replaced them. Her jaw lowered and formed into a hideous grin. With a click of bone, the mouth opened. A cloud of green gas escaped, followed by sounds formed into poor but distinguishable words. "Time to leave, Mark."

The man on the floor went stiffer than the rigor mortis locking the joints and muscles of the deceased. The only movement visible was a tiny quiver of the lower jaw. His screams came in an endless series of waves, like breakers crashing on a rugged shore. He didn't know how long he remained there.

By the time Mark Chambers staggered from the structure and keyed '999' into his mobile phone, his voice was hoarse. It had been a desperate act, conducted almost on auto-pilot. The emergency operator at the other end got little sense from him. At last, police and ambulance services arrived in tandem. They found the gibbering former shadow of a man, curled up on the ground in the foetal position outside his palatial home.

* * *

"Charlie, David, get your jackets, we're taking you both to lunch." Arthur Strong stomped up to his two favourite employees, followed by James Boldwood. Despite having no blood-ties to each other, the business partners were so alike in appearance as to have oft been mistaken for twins. Puffy red cheeks, bushy white sideburns and cherub-like bellies marked the two out in a crowd. That and their rich, booming voices thick with satisfaction from lives well-lived, as they considered it. Their jolly demeanour was legendary among the local property community, in this popular and picturesque corner of England's green and pleasant land.

"Blimey and at one o'clock on a Tuesday too." Charlie secured his computer and fumbled to unhook his jacket from the back of the chair.

"We're not getting the elbow, are we?" David grinned at his jovial employers.

James Boldwood rapped his knuckles on the desk. "I don't think we'd be taking you to lunch if you were getting your cards."

David smirked. "Kidding." He frowned at Charlie and moved to help him find the arm of his suit. "Offer you a free lunch and you're all fingers and thumbs."

Charles straightened his clothing and regained his composure. "Thanks, Mum."

The pub in question was a five-minute walk from the office. Arthur and James had been patrons there for time out of mind. The four sat down to a fine lunch. As they were polishing off dessert and considering coffee, Arthur leaned across to David. "Any movement on Meoria Grange?"

David swallowed a last mouthful of sticky toffee pudding. "Not a peep. Still, it's only been back on the market for a year. Not unusual for that house, I'm afraid."

James Boldwood sipped his pint. Far away in thought, he looked like a philosopher pondering life's great questions. "That place has suffered a tragic history. What was it last time, David?"

"The husband lost everything when the dot-com bubble burst. He returned from hospital after an accidental tumble down the stairs, to find his wife had hung herself. Emergency services discovered him raving in the driveway. I suppose the combined loss caused his mind to snap. Awful." If David had other thoughts of a more sinister and unbelievable nature about what else might have been involved, he didn't let on. "Anyway. With the housing market heating up, the mortgage lenders aren't putting us under any pressure to get rid of it. They can afford to wait."

"Terrible course of events." James took another pull on his drink.

A waitress arrived with her pad, ready to take the coffee order. She shifted and fidgeted on the spot.

"Everything okay?" Charles Pembry moved his head from side to side, to get her attention.

"Sorry," the young woman's cheeks burnished with a hint of cherry. She pointed to where a few punters gathered beneath a TV in the main bar area. "A light aircraft collided with a building in New York, or something."

"The perils of fog," Arthur Strong mused.

David followed the woman's gaze to the TV set. "Doesn't look like it. It's a beautiful morning there. Check that blue sky."

Charles scratched his right cheek with a ponderous index finger. "That can't be an accident or pilot error. Engine failure?"

James coughed. "We'll have a look in a moment." He nudged his business partner. "Time to get down to brass tacks, Arthur."

Arthur nodded. "Let's give coffee a miss." He raised a finger to the waitress. "A bottle of champagne, if you please."

The waitress put her pad back in one pocket of her

dress. "Is Moët okay?"

"That will be fine. Thank you."

Charles raised an eyebrow. "Are we celebrating something?"

Arthur cleared his throat. "As you know, James and I are both seventy-four now. We've had a long chat and finally decided to call it a day at the firm."

The colour drained from Charles' cheeks. "You're selling the business?" His face was a picture of horror. "Who to? Are we going to get bought out by one of those impersonal national chains?"

James Boldwood held up both hands. "Whoa, Charles. Take a breath and don't panic. Arthur and I have decided you and David should run the show."

David sat back in his chair. "But Charlie and I can't afford to buy the agency from you."

Arthur plucked one bushy eyebrow. "Yes lad, we realise that. That's why James and I intend to remain silent partners. We'll retire on a small regular stipend to supplement our pensions. Nothing that will stop you both doing nicely out of the arrangement though. When we shuffle off this mortal coil, Strong & Boldwood will remain in the hands of its surviving general partners: Charles Pembry and David Holmes."

Charlie's mouth fell open.

David was first to speak. "I don't know what to say. You could sell the firm and make a killing."

Arthur stuck one hand in the pocket of his tweed waistcoat. "Perhaps. And live long enough to see the happy outfit we've worked so hard to create, torn apart. Destroyed by one of the soulless conglomerates

Charles is so frightened of. No. We trust the two of you to put your heads together and make good decisions. Both could have gone elsewhere years ago, for better money and prospects. We realise that. But you haven't."

Charles broke his involuntary silence. "That's because it's such a happy place to work."

"Exactly." James Boldwood slammed a flat hand down on the table. "You understand and appreciate the ethos of what we've built."

Charles blinked and swivelled to gaze at his younger colleague. "Claire will shriek like an excited madwoman when I give her the news."

David licked his lips. "Put her on speaker phone back at the office. Should be good for a giggle."

Charles appeared to be weighing up the idea. "Well, that's one in the eye for Kate. Here you are, about to become a partner at thirty-six."

David shrugged. "It wouldn't impress her. Nothing's good enough for Kate. I could own the whole bloody housing market and there'd be some way I'd have come up short."

"What was that phrase you told me she used to justify the break-up?"

David sighed. "She said I didn't make enough money for the life she wanted to live."

Charles shook his head. "Ouch. Well, enough about 'Bitch-face.' This is a moment for celebration."

The waitress returned with a tray containing four champagne flutes and a large, chilled green bottle of bubbly. Her face hung ashen, devoid of colour and life.

Charles' buoyant mood slackened at the sight of her. "More developments?"

The woman set the tray down. "It was a commercial flight that collided with one of the World Trade Centre towers."

"Good heavens." Arthur's face sank.

The waitress set a flute before each man. "A second one just hit the other tower."

James Boldwood opened the champagne in silence. David offered a quiet toast to 'Strong & Boldwood' once they had charged their glasses. The men sipped their drinks and wandered over to the bar. On the TV screen, dark black smoke rose against a deep blue sky before a cityscape on a continent far away.

11

Oblivious Occupiers

"Didn't think we'd ever see the day." Charles' face bore an uncharacteristic mask of sombreness as he entered David's office. His attire was also more subdued than the flamboyant, high-sheen fabric that hallmarked his normal professional life.

David reclined in a high-backed, luxury leather chair and pushed himself away from the desk. "I still find it odd, working in Arthur's old den. Even after seven years. Is everything in hand?"

"Yeah. Tracey ran off a note to put in the window when we close up at lunch. Thought you might want a gander, but I think it looks good." He handed David a piece of A4 paper, still warm to the touch from the laser printer.

David scanned the document.

'Strong & Boldwood are sorry to announce that we will be closed this afternoon, for staff to attend the funeral of Arthur Strong. The last surviving founder of our agency, Arthur passed away last week aged eighty-one. His jolly and positive influence made him a local legend in the Dorset property market and a cherished character in our beautiful town. He shall be sorely missed. Business will resume as normal in the morning. In the meantime, please contact us via e-mail so we

can address your queries as soon as possible. Thank you for your patience.'

He handed the paper back to Charles. "That about covers it. Funny. James first and then Arthur only three months later."

Charles raised his eyes to the ceiling. "I hope God has the bar well stocked upstairs. That will be one hell of a long lunch with those two."

David got up from his seat and stretched. "Did you hear we've got a viewing for Meoria Grange?"

"Tracey mentioned it. Another one, huh? The last few didn't yield much. Anybody we know?"

"Some local chap called Darren Drake. I'm taking him round the place in the morning."

"Never heard of him. Can't be short of the odd copper if he's thinking of buying a house like that. Time waster?"

"Haven't spoken with him enough to get a sense of what he's like."

"What's it going for now?"

"The last re-evaluation we did considering current trends, put it a little under five million."

Charles whistled. "Not that I want to see us out of business or anything, but I hope the long-overdue property market price collapse comes soon. Sarah and Grant will never afford their own homes at this rate."

"Yeah, I've been thinking the same about Andrea."

"She's eighteen now, Buddy. Time for you to stop pouring every penny you earn into Kate's pockets for the girl's support. She quit her job, you know. Kate, I mean. I've no idea what she's doing for money now, or where she's working. Do you?"

"No. I didn't know she'd left. We only speak when we have to. Anyway, it's not like that."

"Oh, come on. How much did that private school Kate insisted she go to, cost you each term?"

"You don't want to know. She's my daughter. I'm happy to give her a good start in life."

"Shame she doesn't appreciate it. Dad works his butt off to provide everything while languishing in a tiny rented flat."

"I don't *languish*, Charlie. God, what a one you are for exaggeration."

"Do you think you'll buy a place now?"

"Guess I'll wait for the market to deflate and then snap up a bargain. I'm doing fine. I can still get a mortgage at forty-three."

"Especially if you work until you're seventy-four, like our late benefactors."

"We owe them."

"That we do. Come on, Dave. Time to shut up shop and take a trip to church. Don't forget you're delivering the eulogy."

* * *

There was an uncomfortable knot in the pit of David's stomach. Arthur's funeral the day before had been a moving affair. David knew enough to realise few people had the luxury of working for a boss who inspired such affection. Many might happily drop something unpleasant into their tea if they thought nobody would ever find the body. Barring the usual niggles, he and Charles now enjoyed a carefree existence. They were owners of a turnkey property business with a great reputation. As long as the sales kept rolling in, they had little to worry about. The global financial crisis of the last year, caused them to become more watchful. Starting with the US sub-prime mortgage market in 2007, it was sending ripples of havoc and devastation across the international finance sector. On the whole though, as a prosperous outfit 'in the black' with no debts, they got to sleep at night with little difficulty. No, this knot was about something else.

The roof line of Meoria Grange poked above the treetops. David turned off the road to start his approach. *Might the house be giving me what feels like an irritable bowel?* He wasn't scared. Somehow the old place rarely frightened him, even with its worrying history and the odd things he'd experienced. But today, there was a definite sense of internal foreboding he couldn't ignore. The reason soon became apparent.

A brand new, metallic blue BMW M3 sat parked outside the steps to the grand residence. Its windows were tinted almost black. As David's Ford Focus slowed to a halt, the BMW driver's door opened. The man who emerged from the interior appeared less than thirty years old. He was built like a muscular male model. Toned torso, ripped and solid, thick neck and short brown hair with a buzz cut at the sides. It was all there. His skin had a certain sheen that spoke of creams, moisturisers and fake tan. David performed a mental sizing up of the potential buyer as he did at every viewing. *Model? Lottery winner? Toy boy? Trust fund kid?* They were all possibilities. He got out of his own vehicle and closed the gap between them to shake the man's hand.

"Darren Drake?"

"Good morning. You must be David Holmes."

"Deadbeat Dave," a woman's voice cut across their greeting from inside the Beamer. The coupe's passenger door opened. A flick of shoulder-length, side-parted mousy hair appeared above the roof level. The owner rotated to look back across the top of the vehicle and lock her familiar, large blue eyes onto the estate agent. "I see you're still driving a Focus. That's a newer model though, isn't it?"

"Hello Kate." David's smile disappeared.

His ex-wife bent down to tilt her seat forward. A heart-shaped face with pronounced cheekbones rose from the rear of the sporty car. The eyes were heavily shadowed, but almost identical to her mother's. A straight nose and small mouth completed the attractive facial aspect, accentuated by side parted blonde hair cascading over her shoulders in long waves. The eighteen-year-old was slender with a fulsome chest. A pretty young lady, and aware of the fact. "You should have at least picked a different colour from the last one." The girl wrinkled her nose at the silver Ford behind her father.

David hadn't seen his daughter since her special birthday earlier in the year. That was an unpleasant and boisterous party at a hotel which he had put his hand in his pocket to help fund. He put his hand in his pocket again to pay for the damages some of her private school chums had inflicted upon the joint, during what turned into something of a raucous orgy.

Kate smirked at Andrea's comment. "Let me guess, David: If the colour's not broken, why fix it? Change and advancement don't get any easier for you, do they?"

The agent folded his arms across his chest. "What are you doing here, Kate?"

The woman laughed. "I should think that's obvious, even to you. I'm here with Darren and Andrea to look at the house."

"You didn't tell me Andrea had an older boyfriend." His face was empty of emotion, the tone of his voice calm. Inside, David Holmes pushed down a tumult of boiling anger and frustration that threatened to erupt like a geyser.

Kate's eyes flashed and her jaw tightened. She strode around the front of the BMW and drizzled an arm around Darren's waist. It ran up and over his firm pectorals to stroke the man's neck and angle it towards her. Their lips met in an open-mouthed kiss. Kate made certain to display her tongue sliding in and out for her ex-husband to observe.

David shook his head.

Kate ended the intimate exchange by nuzzling Darren's designer stubble.

The estate agent unlocked his car and turned to walk back round it.

"Where are you going?" Kate's tone dug into his back like a throwing knife finding its mark.

He wheeled about. "To get on with some work. I haven't got time to waste. Charlie and I run the business now."

The woman put a hand across her mouth, mimicking a silent laugh. "Oh yes, the mighty 'Strong & Boldwood.' You two couldn't even bring yourselves to change the name, hey?"

David knew it was pointless to defend their decision. 'Strong & Boldwood' was an established title. It meant something to many people, including him and Charles. But then, Kate knew that too. She was simply enjoying whatever narcissistic power trip today had afforded her.

Kate glanced back over her shoulder, up to the stepped gables far above. "Don't you want to sell us a house, then?"

"This place is now five million Pounds, Kate." David almost spat the words.

"Then I imagine your commission will be a handsome one." Her voice came flat and serious.

David looked into those piercing blue eyes. She wasn't kidding. No way would that woman pretend to have the money to buy this place and then suffer the humiliation of admitting she couldn't afford it. He moved his attention to the man beside her. "Do you mind if I ask what you do, Darren? I'm sorry, it's a precaution when we're taking people around a place with a price ticket this large." It wasn't true, but no way did he intend to make this easy. "I had someone last month unable to afford a bedsit. It transpired he believed he'd magnetise the place into his ownership with feel-good energy. You know, like those daft, get-rich-quick self-help books." He allowed his attention to shift momentarily onto Kate as he delivered the deliberate slight from their shared history. The woman appeared unmoved, but spoke for her partner. "Darren is a personal trainer. He's building a fitness empire of exclusive gyms, having gained a new backer. Should you insist on a financial statement, my bank can arrange it. I wish you'd have mentioned it on the phone to Darren, though. We also don't have time to waste, thank you."

Behind the BMW, Andrea stood biting her nails. It was a habit David observed his daughter begin around the time he and Kate started having trouble in their relationship. A comfort blanket of sorts, he thought. He locked his car again. "Okay. You want to look around, let's do that. We'll begin with the cellar. That's always good for a laugh."

"No thank you," Kate said with firm disapproval. "We'll begin with the ground floor. Unless you'd rather we look someplace else instead?"

David bit his lip and pondered her statement. *No chance of you going to look at anything else. You intend to buy this house and enjoy rubbing my nose in the fact you got it.* He thought about calling her bluff, but overcame the temptation. Finally he spoke. "Fine. Let me fetch the key." He reached into his bag and pulled out the cold metal object.

In every room, Kate voiced her admiration and disapproval in equal measure. Each was 'great' but would become so much better once she'd enacted her superior good taste upon its decor, furnishings, fixtures and fittings. She swanned around as if already holding the deeds. From time to time the strutting woman walked over to Darren and squeezed his hand, shepherding her toy boy around like an obedient poodle. He bowed to her every whim.

"I suppose you're wondering how Mum will pay for this?" The quiet question from Andrea caught David off guard. Kate was waxing lyrical to Darren about how magnificent she would make the orangery. The agent and his daughter remained near the kitchen door. It was the first honest statement - delivered without attitude - from Andrea he could remember in a long time.

"The thought had crossed my mind."

"Great Uncle Bernie passed away. He left her his fortune."

"What, *all* of it?" David remembered Kate's investment banker relative 'Uncle Bernie' well. Principally because he was always held up as an example of everything David wasn't (in terms of financial success), during their marriage.

"Far as I know. She left her job when the money came through."

"And hunky dunky?" David angled his head towards Darren.

Andrea's face softened. Her eyes misted and lingered on the attractive man's form. David observed her lips moisten. She was eighteen and nubile. Darren was around thirty and handsome. Infatuation? She blinked and looked at her father. "Darren's a trainer at Mum's gym."

"What about his fitness empire and those backers? Wait, let me guess. The backer is your mother with Uncle Bernie's millions?"

Andrea hesitated then nodded. "He's a nice guy. Bit of a loser, like you. But quiet and attentive. Properly fit though." She stared at the Adonis a moment longer and licked those moist lips. "He's always staying over at the cottage."

Bit of a loser, like you. For the briefest moment, David thought something of the adorable child he once knew had survived into adulthood. But it was not to be. If a chink had appeared in her armour revealing emotional vulnerability, it was only because of momentary arousal. She may have inherited some of David's genes, but the apple hadn't fallen very far from the maternal tree when it came to her personality. David pointed around the room. "So what do you think of this place?"

Andrea shrugged. "It reminds me of school a little, but in a good way. We could throw some wicked parties here."

"Do you know that the cellar system goes way back under the hill?"

Andrea frowned. "What is it with you and the cellar in this house? I imagine it's dark, dusty and full of spiders. God, Mum was right. You're such a retard."

David closed his eyes and let out a sigh.

Kate and Darren returned to the kitchen. Kate gave the room another once-over. "Okay David. What's next?"

The agent's plan to lead them into the far murky depths of the cellar network and so put them off purchasing, failed in spectacular fashion. With anyone else it might have been a sure-fire winner. The space delighted Kate almost as much as the upstairs. She showed no discomfort at all. Andrea bubbled with excitement and ideas about creating her own personal nightclub. A place for her and her spoilt friends to get wasted and engage in all manner of debauchery. Darren remained silent, mostly. David didn't like the way his eyes caressed Andrea whenever her mother turned her back. Oh, this chap wouldn't rock the boat. The guy knew he was on to a good thing. He'd ride the crest of the wave until it finally crashed ashore either at his own instigation or Kate's - David had no doubt. But the jilted husband and faithful provider felt these people shouldn't own Meoria Grange. They didn't deserve it, somehow. His disclosed details of the tragedies that struck the previous occupants, also had zero effect on this trio. Andrea even remarked how 'cool' it was that a young boy had shot his sister and taken his own life down there. She would enjoy spooking her pals about it during a 'Basement Halloween Rave,' as she put it. The idea of a lingering supernatural, malevolent or spiritual presence went straight over their heads. They felt nothing; saw nothing, other than how parading around and showing-off this party pad might bolster their egos and well-concealed fragile self-esteem. The cellar even felt different to David today. That familiar, pervasive sense of being watched was there. For him, it never went away. But whatever lay behind it also seemed confused about the visiting guests. Something was different with this viewing. If the others had unfolded like it, the house might have sold long ago.

*   *   *

David didn't know how or why he ascended Weam Common Hill that Sunday afternoon. It wasn't unusual for him to take a weekend stroll. He'd conducted his typical circular constitutional before getting lunch on: A route from the abbey remains near his home, over Giant Hill and back through his personal meadow. Maybe it was because of the fine weather. That and a slight bloating from the excellent braised lamb shank he'd sat down to devour alone in the flat. But in his heart of hearts he knew there was more to it than that. Kate, Darren and Andrea were buying the house. He smiled at his own term: 'the house.' Had Meoria Grange become such a part of his existence now he'd filed it away in his mind under that odd but familiar heading? David considered things at a deeper level. Kate was buying the house. Darren would live there until she tired of her plaything or he got whatever he wanted and ran. Andrea would doss around, confident that - thanks to her mother's fortune - she'd never need to work. Kate might shape her into some withering man destroyer, like Estella in 'Great Expectations.' A pet project to occupy his ex-wife's now abundant time and attention. Something to pass the days as her looks faded and bitterness replaced any pretence of civility. The 'family' were due to move in next week. That's why he found himself near the stile in the woods that provided a view of the curious, sandy-coloured ancient residence. He wanted a moment alone with the old place, even from a distance. A moment before Kate destroyed it with her self-declared, superior good taste in interior decoration. His fingers rested on top of the stile. He remembered Kate's slender young digits in the same position over two decades before. That moment of stolen passion that led to the conception of poor baby Paul. David shook back a tear at the thought of his miscarried son. As ever, the Grange shone in the sunlight on such a splendid day. The man reached into his back pocket and pulled out a smart-phone. He'd resisted mobile telephony for a long time. But when the first Apple device came out the year before, Charlie finally convinced him of the benefits. He unlocked the unit and engaged its camera feature to click an image of the house as a memento. He had various pictures from over the years back at the office. But this was different. It wasn't business this time. The picture was personal. A token he didn't understand but knew he needed.

*   *   *

"David seemed surprised we bought the house. Isn't that odd for an Estate Agent?" Darren Drake lowered a box of Kate's fine china onto a kitchen worktop at

Meoria Grange. The removal crew milled around, lugging crates, containers and furniture items of all shapes and sizes.

Kate let out a sigh of relief as her boyfriend slid the cardboard box to a secure spot against a tiled splashback. "Odd should be David's middle name."

Darren thought for a moment. "Then his initials would be DOH." He stressed the last word with a slap to the forehead, like someone who'd made a stupid mistake.

"Quite." Kate didn't enthuse but was amused by the quip. "The truth is, I suspect jealousy. He's always had a thing for this house. But not the talent or drive to go out and do what he needed to acquire it."

"Five million pounds is a big ask for anyone."

"It didn't used to be that price. Only since the boom."

"Even so-"

"Look, are you defending David's lack of verve? I hope you've got plenty of your own. You will need it to get your chain of gyms established. Even *with* a strong financial safety net. Don't turn into a younger David Holmes, please. He was cute too once. Useless, but cute. I need something more than that in my life."

Darren pulled Kate close and gazed into her eyes. "I was making a simple observation. Nothing more. Once he took us down in those cellars and began with the death stories, I was curious. I've never been an estate agent, but it seemed a bizarre way to go about selling a house you want to get rid of."

"Exactly. His ruse to scare us off didn't work though,

did it?"

"Nope. This place is perfect."

Kate scanned around the kitchen with a cynical raised eyebrow. "Well, not yet. But it will be by the time we're finished with it. I'd better check on the removal men." She made for the hallway.

Andrea passed her mother and leaned over some boxes to tug at the brown parcel tape stretched around one labelled 'Glasses.' Darren watched her shapely buttocks wrapped in tight denim, designer jeans. The motion of her exertions allowed the coarse material to stress every curve and intimate crevice of the teenager's attractive form. She twisted her head round and flicked back the long blonde hair that had fallen forward in her way. The sight of Darren's eyes bulging with intense concentration caused the corners of her mouth to rise. An obvious stirring in his crotch raised them further. "Can you help me with this? I'm gasping for a glass of water. Must be all that dust."

"Sure. Gets in your throat, doesn't it?"

Andrea watched the muscular man rip the top of the box open like it was made of rice paper. "Yes. The only things I want down my throat are the ones I allow there." She placed one delicate hand on his shoulder blade and bent forward to retrieve two tumblers. The girl rose to stare unblinking into his dark, deep-set eyes. "Want one?"

"Huh?" Darren's mind was a fog, ushered in by Andrea's sweet perfume and suggestive manner.

"A drink of water. Would you like one?"

"Oh. Yeah, that would be great. Thanks."

Kate returned from enjoying her role as boss to the removal crew. Several of them now wondered if this had been such a smart career choice. She found Darren and Andrea leaning with their backs to the sink. They were laughing and sipping water, next to an opened box. "Is there a spare glass for your mother?" She adopted a martyr face that caused Andrea to fish another tumbler from the container. "Here we go, Mum."

The day passed in a flash. When you're moving the contents of a small cottage into a spacious, stately home, multiple trips and vehicles are seldom a necessity. Meoria Grange felt big and empty. Kate couldn't wait to fill it with all manner of stylish, expensive furniture and objet d'art from the bounty of her late uncle's generosity. Some furnishings came with the house, like the grand double bed in the master; several desks, tables, chairs and assorted antiques. Then there were all those curious storage boxes down in the cellar. What rare and marvellous finds might she discover once cataloguing began? Something to make the news? Not that she needed the money, but a spot on a TV antiques show would make her feel on top of the world. A chance for Kate Warren to craft a big name to go with her big fortune.

* * *

"Hey Gill. Yeah, we're in at last." Andrea paced back

and forth in her new bedroom, a mobile phone clamped to one ear. It was a spacious chamber with dual aspect windows. One looked south, down the drive. The other offered a panoramic bay facing east. A bay in which a young boy had once written programs on his home computer. Andrea sat down on the side of her bed, nose wrinkling at a question from one of her school friends on the other end of the line. "I don't know. He saw me bending over today. I swear to God it gave him a hard-on. He's so fit, Gill. What? I know, I know. Living with him will be like torture. I can't believe Mum gets to shag that every night. She's in her forties, for Chrissake." Andrea listened and burst out laughing. "Gill! If only. In my dreams anyway. Can you imagine if we did and Mum found out? Huh? I don't know. Disowned, I should think. Mum has been good, but she's a serious bitch. It's one thing I love about her." Andrea listened again. "Hey! I'm not. Well okay, maybe a little. But she's the real pro."

There was a gentle knock on the door.

"I've got to go. Shit, did you know it's one-thirty in the morning? Oh, you did. Well get some sleep, crazy chick. Soon as you can make it over, we'll go out on the piss. By then I'll be gagging for some wine and a decent bit of rough to clear my head. Love you too, girlfriend. Bye."

The knock sounded again.

Andrea opened the door a crack to reveal Darren standing in a pair of grey shorts and nothing else. Her mother liked to enjoy his ripped torso, every chance she got. Small wonder the guy wore those to sleep in.

The girl had only seen him without a top on a few times. The breath caught in her throat. She ached to play with Mummy's toy. "Hey Darren. Everything okay?"

"Your Mum's fast asleep, but I couldn't drift off. New house and all that. Got up for a leak and saw your light on under the door."

"Is she snoring? Mum sounds like a pig after she's had a few glasses of red. She was hitting the Merlot pretty hard earlier. Talk about celebration." Andrea enjoyed degrading her mother with a genuine observation. Especially to the impressive hunk of a man at her door.

Darren snorted.

Andrea pointed at him. "Yeah, like that."

The man laughed again. "I thought - since you're up - you might fancy a chat. How's your room? Are you settling in okay?"

"Great." She let the door open further to reveal her silken, skimpy nightwear. A low-cut, mint green teddy. Waxed legs crossed in a seductive slither. "Did you want to come in and have a look? Maybe you can help me sort a few things out. I'd love your input."

Kate awoke with a grunt. She had been sawing the wood pretty well with her snores. The bed alongside lay empty, mattress and pillow creased from where Darren tossed and turned in an effort to lose consciousness. Kate slipped from beneath the duvet and staggered across the hallway to the bathroom. She clicked on the light and grimaced at the dark wood panelling. "The sooner we rip this crap off the walls, the better. Yuck." She relieved the pressure on her bladder and washed her hands at the sink. Straightening up to the mirror, her eyes caught sight of Andrea's reflection standing in the open doorway. Kate spun in surprise. "Did you want to use…" There was no sign of her daughter. She strode to the door and craned her neck around the frame, onto the landing. No-one in sight. "Odd. I must be a bit worse for wear still. Where can Darren have got to?" She extinguished the light and tramped to the top of the stairs. Further across the landing, a glimmer of artificial illumination crept around the edges of Andrea's door. The portal was only pushed to.

Darren's head arched back where he stood. Intricate plasterwork on the decorative ceiling rose couldn't take his attention away from the epic sensation down below. Andrea had allowed something else into her throat. Deep in. She released the item from her mouth with a gentle pop and stood with half-closed, sultry blue eyes. Her innocent, eighteen-year-old face belied a wanton harlot - horny and wet. The pair tumbled in a naked embrace onto the girl's mattress.

Kate approached the door with deft steps. Andrea emitted a gasp, followed by a long groan. Her voice dripped with pleasure. "I love a big snake between my thighs." A giggle came after. The middle-aged woman's heart pounded in her chest. Her world span. She had enough lucidity to work out what was going on. There could be no other explanation. Her mind screamed at her to cover her ears and wish those sounds away. If you could magnetise things into your life, could you also magnetise them out of it? She reached forward with trembling fingers to give the door a soft but definite push. One that would be enough to make it swing wide and reveal any activity taking place on her daughter's bed, perpendicular to the entrance.

Light from the room flooded onto the landing. Kate squinted. Straddling the reclined and masculine torso of her lover, Andrea bounced up and down like a child enjoying a ride on her first Pogo stick. Her eyes closed, hair flicking behind like a golden pennant. It waved in time with a faint squelching noise from between the teenager's legs that interspersed her soft moans. Andrea's impressive breasts - a source of envy for Kate ever since her daughter hit puberty - jostled with the motion, nipples erect. On the face of the muscular man below, Kate saw an expression of joy she had never witnessed during their own intimate encounters. She could hold in her yell no longer.

12

Settlement

"Andrea, how could you? After all I've done." The statement erupted from Kate's lungs on an emotive scale somewhere between a wail and a roar. Her nostrils flared. One claw-like hand grabbed hold of her daughter by the hair, fingers twisted with rage. A vice-like grip yanked the girl off balance and she tumbled to the floor. Darren sat up in shock. His mind wheeled from their sudden discovery. The thud of Andrea's body hitting the wooden boards, deflated any last vestige of arousal. Andrea let out a shriek. She tore at her mother's hands while the woman dragged the naked teenager along the landing by her golden locks.

"Kate, stop it. You're hurting her." Darren launched off the bed to stand looking out of the doorway.

Kate moved her gaze from the fitness instructor's dark, pleading eyes to his pathetic, flaccid penis. She spat into the air. "You have exactly until I finish dealing with my trollop of a daughter to get out of this house, or I'll call the police." Kate fought back against the eighteen-year-old's desperate scratching. Anger and adrenaline at the double betrayal, infused the woman's muscles with a power beyond their normal range. She reached the top of the staircase and bundled the girl down it with a shove. Andrea bumped on each step, pushed and prodded by her mother like a disobedient and wilful dog. Kate still kept a tight hold on the leash - her beautiful blonde hair.

Darren pulled his shorts back on and hobbled out to grab hold of the top banister. He leaned over the edge in time to see Kate unbolt the cellar door. She tugged the flashlight from its housing and cast it out into the hallway.

"Get in there and spend some time in the dark, thinking about what you've done to me." Kate's mouth twisted into a sneer. She threw her weight against the girl and let go of her hair. Andrea went head over heels down the cold stone steps into the blackness below. A shriek of pain was cut short by the slamming cellar door. Kate slid the bolt back across and strode to the nearby wall-mounted electrical fuse panel. Brows knitted together, she read the typewritten labels until she found one marked 'Cellar Lighting.' The fuse came out of its socket with a definite tug of the angry woman's hand.

In the pitch black, Andrea winced and sobbed. Her left ankle burned with a relentless intensity. Naked in the darkness, the flagstones chilled her tender buttocks. The sensation caused her to tremble further. It was a shivering cocktail: two parts agony, one part shock and dismay, and a good dash of low physical temperature. If you found it at a bar, the drink might have a bizarre but descriptive name like 'Ice Cold Flaming Screamer.' She felt for the wall and slid her back against it. Disoriented and tasting blood in her mouth, she pushed against the stone for support. Her backside never made it more than a foot off the ground before her ankle bit back with a savage stab of agony. It must have broken somewhere on the way down. Andrea put a hand over her face as the tears fell. The sound of her weeping bounced back off the arched walls like a mocking playground bully.

"Andrea." The voice came like a whisper from somewhere deep within the cellar network. The girl stopped crying and froze. "Andrea." The sound echoed closer this time. She peered into the blackness. It seemed hopeless. With zero illumination, there was little chance of her eyes tracing the outline of even the nearest box of junk. From a chamber to the north, a soft, rhythmic padding split the silence. Robbed of sight, the teenager's ears identified the sound as that of bare feet on stone. They were coming closer at a slow but steady rate. The girl's bottom lip quivered. She took a deep breath. "Who's there?" Her query rang with fear and lacked conviction. For all that, the vaulted ceilings amplified her statement like a sounding board. There was no response. Still the bare feet approached. A cold, faint glow shone from one passage. It was no stronger in power than a single candle, but steady and constant with no living flicker. Andrea's breath came fast and panicked. The urge to hyperventilate rose like an insistent torrent that wouldn't subside. The small light grew stronger. Andrea gasped. The figure of a naked girl strode into the chamber. The surface of her skin glowed like the chemical reaction of some rare, underground lichen. Long blonde hair hung before her lowered face. She stopped and turned to regard the teenager who winced in pain and fear a few feet away. As the spectral head rose, and the hair flicked back, Andrea realised why the form bore a certain familiarity. She was staring at a facsimile of herself. The facsimile stared back, but with white, empty eyes devoid of pupil or iris.

Andrea whimpered. "Oh my God." She splayed one hand across her mouth.

The glowing apparition tilted its head to regard her with an aspect that blended disdain with curiosity. The voice that came out was old, coarse, definite. "I am not your God."

"N-no. What?" Andrea grappled with her senses. Pain and terror threatened to snap the fragile thread of her sanity at any moment.

The creature spoke again. "You're his seed, aren't you?"

"Who?" Andrea shook her head. "My father is David Holmes."

"Bastard child." The figure took a step to one side, walking in an arc before the teenager.

"I'm not a bastard. My parents were married when they had me."

"Bastard child." The repeated phrase was uttered with greater force, venom and volume this time.

Andrea remained silent.

The sinister, glowing mirror image of the girl's form stood square on to her. This time the voice altered to sound exactly like Andrea's. "I love a big snake between my thighs." It giggled. The tongue flicked out and transformed into a forked, reptilian one. Mouth open, the front teeth stretched down like serpent fangs. The creature slunk its hips and took slow steps forward. With each movement the body morphed into the slithering shape of a giant snake. Its head stretched and deformed to match the metamorphosis.

Andrea pushed her back against the wall again. Screams burst from her lungs. She spread her legs further apart, to prevent the anaconda-like monstrosity from touching her even one second longer. Her cries fell silent, mouth stretched wide in soundless horror. The head of the serpent plunged into her intimate female cavity, forcing her womanhood to distend like a mother giving birth. Andrea's head spasmed and jerked, knocking back against the cold brickwork as more of the beast entered her body. Her short, quiet gasps came to an abrupt halt. The cellar remained in darkness. Only a mild glow was visible. It seeped through the skin of an eighteen-year-old girl, rigid and lifeless at the bottom of the steps. Her torso bulged here and there as if something rippled beneath the surface. A burrowing creature on a mission. Andrea had still been alive for those last few seconds when the serpent feasted on her internal organs.

*   *   *

In the kitchen, Kate Warren sat at a long wooden table. One hand held a tumbler of whisky before her. She supported the forearm with her other hand, resting it beneath the right elbow. A bottle used to replenish the glass already stood half empty beside her.

Darren appeared in the kitchen doorway. He had pulled a t-shirt over his chest to go with the shorts.

Kate didn't even look at him. Her eyes stared into space. "I thought I warned you to get out."

Darren folded his arms. "Kate, what are you doing? She's your daughter."

"All the more reason she should know better." Kate took a slug of her whisky without coughing.

Darren half-turned to the hallway. "Andrea might be injured down there. She's butt naked, for God's sake."

"And don't you know it." Kate poured herself another glass, not stopping until the spirit spilt over the brim.

"She'll catch her death of cold."

"Good." The word came out through clenched teeth.

"That's it. I'm fetching her up." Darren moved to go.

"Don't you dare." The menace in Kate's voice stopped the fitness instructor dead in his tracks. "If you interfere with my daughter and I any further, I will make it my mission to ruin you." By the time she reached the last few words, Kate was on her feet screaming each syllable.

A series of additional screams blended with those of the half-cut woman. Darren twisted his head around. At first it sounded like some weird echo. Then the source became clear. "Kate, she's frightened and in pain."

"She's a drama queen and a player." Kate took her seat again. All noise from down below ceased. "See?

Not getting any attention, so she's given up." She knocked back half the refilled glass. "I'll leave her there until morning to stew." This time she looked at Darren. "And you'd better not still be here by then."

Darren watched her a moment longer. He knew Kate well enough to realise the events of the night had been terminal to their relationship. Was there anyone with whom they wouldn't be? In fact, he'd be lucky if she didn't strike at him in some other spiteful fashion, once she'd had time to scheme and ponder. He lowered his head to stare at the floor for a second, then wandered back upstairs to pack a few clothes.

Kate sat there another ten minutes, drinking spirits to fill the cavernous void in her heart. The alcohol numbed her senses, but offered little else in the way of comfort.

Darren reappeared wearing jeans and a jacket, clutching a holdall. He dropped it in the kitchen doorway and strutted to the worktop opposite where the woman sat. His arms spread either side of his body like an a-frame. He leaned, staring at the wall as if attempting to summon one last speech. Kate kept her attention fixed on the whisky glass. She didn't acknowledge him.

The man cleared his throat and spoke. "You didn't deserve David."

"That's a pathetic attempt at a comeback, even for an idiot like you." Kate reached behind her and picked up the cordless phone. "I will give you until a count of ten to get your sleazy butt out my door. Then I'm calling plod."

Darren drummed his fingers on the worktop. His head rose to fix on a wooden knife block within grasping distance. "Did you ever love David, or were you using him the whole time for your selfish ends?"

"That's it." Kate dialled '999' and lifted the phone to her ear.

Darren's right hand extended and grabbed hold of a broad-bladed chef's knife. It gleamed and flashed as he withdrew the fearsome piece of cutlery with a jerk.

A faint crackle on the phone speaker said "Emergency - Which service please?"

"Police." Kate's voice lost some of its confidence at the sight of Darren retrieving the blade.

Darren whirled on the spot. His mouth distorted into a spitting maw of fury. His eyes were pure white, like two bulging cue balls. When he spoke, the voice sounded female yet harsh and powerful. "It's time for you to leave *his* house."

Kate dropped the tumbler. It shattered on the table. She pushed her chair away and stumbled to her feet, reeling from shock and the effects of alcohol in her bloodstream.

The Darren creature hissed. "It's time for you to leave - for good." The knife blade arched into the air with a swish.

Kate screamed into the phone in a desperate plea for aid. She spoke the only words that came to mind, which would summon the police in a hurry. "Help. My boyfriend is trying to kill me. Come quick. Come Qui…"

The fearsome, distorted figure of her former lover lunged forwards. Kate ran for the doorway. In her woolly head, time appeared to slow down. Each step was like running through treacle. And then the sensation came: Falling. Falling headlong into a deep, dark pit. Like those dreams where you know you are asleep and pray you awaken before your body hits the bottom. She prayed for the falling sensation to end. When the impact came it was cold and wet. Her body plunged into freezing water. The shock to her system stung like being stabbed by a thousand tiny needles, but it sobered her in an instant. Kate kicked in a frenzy to tread water. Her face snapped back to a circle of light far above. Her cry for help rang back off the circular stone walls of the yawning, dark shaft.

* * *

In the master bedroom, Darren stuffed clothes into a holdall with angry vigour. *I've well and truly blown this one. God, I hope Andrea is okay.* He took one last look around the boudoir that could have been his - for a while at least. The bronzed Adonis was smart enough to realise his relationship with Kate Warren had a definite 'sell-by' date. But he'd envisioned enjoying the ride a little longer and ending it a wealthier man.

A distant, echoing shout called for help from somewhere down below. It was Kate's voice, not Andrea's. Darren grabbed the bag and marched for the stairs. *Don't say she's got paralytic and hurt herself.* He pivoted on one heel after attaining the downstairs hall.

In the kitchen doorway an identical holdall rested on the olive green floor tiles. Darren looked down at the one in his hand and then back to the door. The duplicate had vanished. It was then he noticed a circular, cavernous dark opening in the kitchen floor. A whole section of tiles were missing. He dropped his bag where he stood. Kate's voice cried for help from somewhere far below, booming out of the pit. "What the hell?" Darren paced forwards and dropped to his knees at the rim of the shaft. "Kate?" His voice rang down into the darkness. A splashing sound grew in intensity.

"Help - Police" Kate yelled.

"Kate. Kate, it's Darren." He squinted in the low light, but couldn't see more than a few feet into the gaping hole.

"Help - Police" Kate called again. She seemed to ignore him and grow more agitated.

Something butted against Darren's shoes. He swivelled on his knees. "Oh, my God. What the fuck?" The missing olive floor tiles were re-appearing. They materialised like a growing leaf canopy, played back with time-lapse photography. The man staggered aloft and stepped a few feet away from the manifestation. Around the rim of the hole, a wooden cover spread across the gap. It emerged with a fluid, almost organic beauty.

In the water below, Kate watched the circle of light shrink. Her limbs froze, fatigued and heavy like dead wood. She couldn't kick much longer. Straining lungs forced out one last curse. "Darren, you bastard." She followed the final word with a long wail, cut short as the shaft entrance became swallowed up in the kitchen above. Kate's numb hands clawed at the slippery sides of the well. There was no purchase to be found in the darkness. Nothing to pull herself up with and hang on in faint hopes of rescue. Her energy expired, and she sank beneath the surface. All fight burned out of her frame. The freezing water flooded her airway with little resistance.

The pulse pounded in Darren's head like a tribal drum. He stared at the olive green floor, as perfect, innocuous and unremarkable as it had always looked. "What just happened?" He spoke the words as if half expecting someone or some*thing* to answer. *It sealed Kate up down there.* His mind wandered to the cellar. "Andrea." He raced to the panelled door and drew back the bolt. The steps descended into darkness. He flicked the switch. Nothing happened. *That's right, Kate pulled the fuse.* When he reached the panel, the empty socket was clear. *Must have it in her pocket.* He considered ripping one of the other fuses out and swapping it over, when his eye caught sight of the discarded torch lying on the floor. Darren swiped up the unit, clicked it on and hurried down the steps. His pace slowed as the electric beam fell across Andrea's lifeless form. It slumped against one wall, close to the flight of stone stairs. Her torso gave the appearance of an inflatable beach toy with the air let out. She was thin and saggy, like a banana skin missing its contents.

Blood pooled between her legs. A smear of crimson ran away as if from the stroke of an artist's palette knife. The trail suggested something had slithered off. Darren sank to his knees beside the wretched sight. He placed the torch down on the flagstones and cradled the blonde head in his hands. Blood from her body squelched into his clothing and over his arms, but the man didn't care. He squeezed her rag-doll figure tight and screwed up his eyes from the overwhelming emotion. Quivering lips kissed the top of her head.

From somewhere deep in the cellars, an authoritarian voice rang out. It was feminine, but not human. "Get out, Darren. Get out while you still can."

Darren's muscles locked up. He rested Andrea's head back against the wall and fumbled for the torch.

The voice called out once more. "I won't ask you again."

The man backed away, feeling for the steps behind him with one hand. He scanned the torch beam from side to side as if some hideous creature might emerge from a tunnel at any moment. Whatever did this to Andrea and made that hole appear and disappear in the kitchen - swallowing Kate - was beyond his abilities. It didn't matter how much weight he could bench press. Muscles and body strength were of little use against such incomprehensible power. He staggered out of the cellar, letting the door swing free behind him. Casting the torch aside he delved into his pocket and grabbed hold of the BMW car keys. Seconds later he was in the driver's seat, peeling away from the front of the house with smoking tyres. He couldn't bring himself to look in the rear-view mirror, until the driveway was far behind and he hit the open road.

*   *   *

The door buzzer chimed in David's flat. He put down his briefcase and pressed a button to talk on the intercom. "Yes?"

The speaker crackled. "Is that Mr Holmes?"

David frowned. He'd just returned from a busy day at the office and was in no mood for salesmen, politicians or religious zealots. "Who wants to know?"

"Dorset Police, Sir."

David paused and thought for a moment, weighing up if this might be a scam. He pushed the button again. "Hang on a moment, I'll be right down."

The chunky wooden communal front door of the Cerne Abbas flat crept open. As soon as David clocked the uniforms of the man and woman in the street and noticed the parked police car, he opened it wide. "How can I help?"

"You *are* Mr David Holmes, the father of Andrea Warren-Holmes?" the male officer began.

David placed one hand unconsciously across his chest. "That's right. Has something happened?"

The female officer's eyes glistened. "It might be best if we step inside, Sir."

About ninety minutes later, David pushed open the double-doors of the hospital mortuary. He plonked his backside down on a nearby bench and rested his head between his knees. Both hands clutched the rear of his cranium, fingernails digging into the flesh. No father should have to identify the body of their child. No child should be subject to the inhuman brutality inflicted upon his daughter. How would his mind ever forget the visceral scene his eyes witnessed in that cold and clinical room, smelling of disinfectant?

The male police officer, PC Willis, sat down beside him. An Airwave radio clipped to his stab vest lit up.

A narrow bandwidth voice crackled. "Is my read-back correct, over?"

"Correct, over."

"All received. Out."

A series of clear-to-send beeps punctuated the disembodied exchange from other officers.

PC Willis flushed and pressed a button to mute the unit. "Sorry. Forgot to do that when we came in."

His female colleague, PC Shea, emerged through a doorway with a plastic cup of water from the cooler. She sat down on the other side and offered David the drink. "This might help a little."

David released his head, sat up and took the water. "Thank you."

PC Willis cleared his throat. "I'm sorry you had to see that."

David shook his head. "How could anyone do such a thing?"

The male copper grunted. "Every once in a while we

meet someone in this job who is a wrong-un. There's something about them and you know it won't change. Prison won't rehabilitate them. They're born wrong, simple as. Evil - you could say."

"*Definitely* in this case," his colleague added.

"Is there any sign of my wife - err I mean, my ex-wife?"

PC Willis shook his head. "Not at present. Our teams are searching the house. I understand the basement where they found your daughter is a sizeable space with lots of nooks and crannies."

"Yes. It goes back a long way."

"If she's in there, we'll find her. Plus, our colleagues are interviewing Darren Drake as we speak. I can't tell you any more than that."

PC Shea chipped in. "I know the guys in traffic who pulled Drake over. He was burning down the A37 at a rate of knots when they stopped him. Covered in blood and babbling like a lunatic, they said."

PC Willis murmured under his breath. "Slam dunk, even if he doesn't cough to it, I should think." He remembered his place and raised an eyebrow at David. "Not that you heard it from me, Sir."

David took a sip of water. "Thanks for your support."

PC Shea stood up. "Would you like us to run you home, or do you have friends or other family coming over?"

"I'll call my business partner. He's the closest thing I have to family around here. I appreciate your time."

PC Willis joined his colleague. "We'll keep you

appraised of any developments. Take care of yourself now."

*   *   *

The unmade leafy path to the doorway of St. Nicholas church was always a haven of tranquillity. The building rested on a slight incline at the end of a quiet no through road, in the village where David and Kate bought their first home. This parish church had a pleasing aspect with an elegant tower. If it lacked the amount of stained glass one might expect, this was only because of Cromwell and his Parliamentarian thugs. The structure stood surrounded by deciduous trees, now red and golden in the autumn light. A gentle dusting of leaves from the same formed a scant carpet, like petals thrown by a wedding flower girl. But today was no wedding.

Inside, near the altar, Charles Pembry sat with his wife Claire, daughter Sarah and son Grant. All were clad in elegant black garments. Sarah lost touch with Andrea after David and Kate's divorce. When it came time to attend 'big school,' Kate further separated them by sending her daughter to an expensive private educational establishment. Still the girl had fond memories of her childhood companion. Her heart ached at the news: Kate Warren's younger boyfriend had murdered Andrea and her mother. Despite attempts to keep the gruesome details secret, some of it still came out in the local press.

A cortege of funeral vehicles drew up outside. David

Holmes followed pall bearers carrying two coffins into the church. He joined Charles and family in their pew. Claire squeezed his arm and kissed his cheek. Her eyes welled up with tears.

On the opposite side of the aisle, Kate's parents ignored their former son-in-law. This wasn't a new experience for David. He was too lost in his own grief to care. They'd have to speak to him eventually, as Kate left her fortune to them in a will. A document crafted with malicious intent to exclude David from any benefits after the woman's sudden windfall. Unless they planned on living at Meoria Grange, the family would sell. David knew only too well that no other agency would touch the property, except theirs.

The vicar took his place at the altar and the congregation rose in quiet unison.

"I feel like I should say something, but there aren't any words. Not ones that don't sound patronising or flippant, anyway." Charles stepped up to stand at his colleague's side near the open grave. The other mourners had withdrawn and only the Pembrys now remained at a respectful distance.

"I can't believe they're gone, Charlie." David's voice was calm but faint. "I thought at first the police might find Kate wandering in the grounds, or tied up in the attic or cellar. But she and Andrea both…"

"At least they've got the bastard. He'll be going away for a long time. I know that won't bring Andrea and Kate back, but justice has been served. Bloody psycho. How did he do such a good job on those tiles? Fancy dumping your own girlfriend in a well and sealing it up. How did they find her again?"

"Police dog. It made such a fuss in the kitchen, plod dug into the floor. That's when they found the well and Kate's body." He hung his head.

Charles put a hand on his shoulder. "I'm sorry, Mate. That was tactless of me."

David patted it. "Don't sweat it, Charlie. I'd go mad without someone to talk to about all this."

"I notice Kate's family didn't even acknowledge you. Which of them will come into the office when they want to put the house on the market, do you think?"

David shrugged. "I suppose they could go down the public auction route."

Charles shook his head. "You and I have both been in this game enough years to know there's two hopes of that happening."

"Yeah, that's true. Meoria Grange won't go at auction. Not a chance."

"Wonder how long we'll sit on it this time? Murders and suicides. What is it about that house that sends people to violent destruction?"

"I don't know. Darren Drake is still pleading his innocence."

"Fat lot of good that will do him. Cases don't come much more cut and dried. Prat must think we're all gullible, claiming the floor opened up and swallowed Kate, then grew back over her."

David pondered similar but milder comments others had made in relation to the Grange over the years. He knew he was upset and not thinking straight, so let the musings go. They were no use to his ex-wife and daughter after the fact.

Charles twiddled his thumbs. "I know it doesn't look like it now and we're not in our twenties anymore, but you'll make a fresh start in your own way. There was that equity from your share of the cottage sale. A new chapter could be right around the corner."

David bit his lip. "The thing of it is, I'm not sure I'm finished with the old chapter yet."

"How do you mean?"

The grieving agent stuck both hands in his trouser pockets and turned to stare up at the ridge. "I don't even know the answer to that, myself."

13

Digging Deeper

David strolled along the narrow footpath that ran beside Sydling Water. From the indistinct, sunny soft-focus appearance of the scene, he realised this was a dream. But it was a dream he didn't want to end. At least, not this first part. A small girl in a white, feminine, puff-sleeved dress clutched tight to one of his hands. With her other she held onto Kate. It was a halcyon depiction of the couple around thirty, taking a favourite family walk. The bouncy blonde child beamed at her father. He was her hero; a man who could do no wrong. Kate threw back her head and laughed with hearty abandon. Not the critical, sarcastic, patronising laugh of later years, when their marriage fell apart. This was a simple expression of joy and contentment. Did the rose-tinted playback spawn from a corner of the man's mind, unjaded by later events? It was an amalgamation of memories from many such walks, moulded into an expression of how special they made him feel. Whatever happened to that happy family? He lifted the child's hand in time with Kate, to swing her tiny infantile legs a short way off the ground. Both parents uttered an 'aah' sound to stress the fun aspect of their game. The little girl squealed with delight. She giggled and beamed.

David shifted in his bed but remained unconscious. This sequence had become something of a regular occurrence. It always played out in the same way. His body tossed and turned at what his mind knew was coming next.

The cellar door at Meoria Grange drifted open. David found himself walking towards it. All sound became muffled as if somebody had stuffed his ears full of cotton wool. Movement unfolded at a slower rate than normal - if not total slow-motion. A tool that allowed his catatonic self to experience every nuance of each moment with striking emotive force. He would miss nothing. The cellar sat in darkness, yet the wall outlines remained clear. With every step downward, a curious, deflated human form faded into sharper focus. It lay near the bottom, resting on the floor of the first chamber. A female corpse, propped against one wall. David hadn't seen Andrea where she lay at the point of her demise. But identifying the body of his eviscerated daughter left his mind with a rich palette of imagery to paint from. That and graphic descriptions of the scene and injuries, delivered during the trial of Darren Drake. David listened to every word in court, like a bewildered child discovering for the first time that the world might be unkind. He reached the bottom of the steps and knelt at his daughter's side. Her face, pale like fine porcelain, bore an expression of peace. He suspected this was not representative of the true state in which police discovered the murdered girl. But, he had only seen her lying on that hospital table. The eyelids fluttered and rolled up. As he gazed into her countenance, it morphed back into the child's face from earlier in his dream. The little girl spoke with a cute but anxious voice. "Why did I have to die, Daddy? Why didn't you stop it? You had the power to stop it. You had the power but did nothing."

The cellar walls contracted and David felt himself falling. Stones formed into a circular shaft. He crashed into ice cold water and gasped from shock. Something bumped against his back. The man twisted and kicked to bring himself around. Kate's lifeless body bobbed near the surface, jostled by his impact into the well water. David spluttered. The woman's head rose and opened bloodshot eyes to gaze at him with lifeless hatred. Kate's bloated corpse coughed up a trickle of fluid and delivered a rasping accusation. "You never loved us."

It was at this point the restless dreamer always awoke. Today proved no exception. David took a few long, slow breaths and shifted himself up to rest against the headboard. It was a bright and sunny Saturday morning. He'd overslept, but felt less than rested for it.

After breakfast he checked the post and found a typewritten letter with a Worcestershire postmark, addressed to him. Inside, its letterhead bore the title 'HMP Long Lartin.'

* * *

David drove from Dorset in almost total silence. As

his Ford Focus dipped into the Vale of Evesham, he clicked on the radio. More news reports from a devastating explosion at an oil drilling platform off the coast of Louisiana; plus further details of how volcanic ash from an eruption in Iceland was causing havoc with air traffic. He jabbed the off button and signalled at a turning for South Littleton. It was a week since that letter confirming his addition to Darren Drake's visitor list. David had never visited anyone in prison. He'd not even known someone banged up for a minor conviction, let alone a 'Category A' offender.

Strolling away from the visitor's car park, he reached into his jacket pocket to feel for passport and driving license - his two forms of required identification. HMP Long Lartin had the capacity for six hundred and twenty-two adult men. David checked his watch. One in the afternoon. He'd made good time to clear security, before visiting started at two. What must Darren Drake be thinking? How would he react during a visit from the father and ex-husband of his two murder victims? The meeting got scheduled and approved without incident. Darren was using one visiting entitlement for this, so he must at least be curious.

David entered the visitor centre and presented his identification. He pulled a pound coin out of his trouser pocket to use on a locker for his valuables. Watch, mobile phone, keys and his pocket handkerchiefs were all placed inside. With search and X-ray procedures completed to satisfaction, David donned a visitor's wristband and received an ultraviolet hand stamp. He entered the visits hall and sat down at his allocated table.

A door opened on the far side. Darren Drake sauntered through. He had lost none of his bad-boy good looks, but the confident swagger had vanished from his gait. Those dark eyes caught sight of his visitor. He hesitated and swayed on the spot before approaching the table at a slower pace. David regarded the CCTV cameras and patrolling guards. A couple of official heads turned as he stood and extended his hand in a stiff gesture. The man wasn't sure why he did it. If this conviction was sound, the prisoner before him had gutted his daughter with ruthless efficiency, then drowned her mother. Darren was taken aback. He scanned the man's hand, as if the estate agent might have concealed a shiv to exact personal revenge upon him. A moment later he reached out, and the two exchanged a limp and momentary shake. David sat back down with Darren opposite. The prisoner attempted to read the face of his unexpected guest. His mind wrestled with - but gained no purchase on - a satisfactory reason for the visit. He allowed the awkward silence to continue for a moment before speaking in a stilted burst of words. "I- I err, was wondering why..." He paused and collected his thoughts. "David, why are you here?" His head shook in tiny movements, eyes narrowing to shiny slits.

David sat back in his chair and studied that expression. There was no such thing as the face of a typical killer. If TV documentaries had taught viewers anything, it was that the most ordinary visage can conceal rage and violence beyond comprehension. "Because I want you to tell me what happened." The sentence was quiet, masking more hope than he let on.

Darren put a thumb beneath his chin. "Weren't you at the trial?"

"Yes. I was there."

"Then you've heard it all before, haven't you?"

"Have I?"

Darren folded his hands. "The judge described me as a cold and calculating killer. The only reason I'm not on a high-security psychiatric wing, is because the shrinks declared me compos mentis. That only poured oil on the fire of sentencing after my guilty verdict. They deemed me to be in full control of my faculties. That means I must be an evil person rather than a nutter. No doubt that's why I got sent down for the rest of my prime."

"And yet you protested your innocence to the end."

"Which only made things worse. His Honour then took the view I was making a mockery of his court. What with my insistence on floor tiles that re-grew themselves and disembodied voices ordering me to leave the house. He thought I was taking the piss; laughing at him and everyone else."

"I can't get them out of my head, Darren. Kate and Andrea, I mean."

"That makes two of us." He sighed and frowned. "So why *are* you here? Are you looking for closure? Hoping to listen to my wild fairy-tale again, on the off-chance you might now believe it and find peace? Jesus, how long has it been?"

"Getting on for two years."

Darren leaned forward. "Has anyone else moved into the house?"

David shook his head. "No. It's on the market. Not unusual for that place to stick around for a decade, with no offers."

"You tried to scare us away at the viewing, didn't you?"

"Yes."

"I remember that now. God, I wish we'd listened. Kate thought you were jealous because you always liked the place. That's what she said, anyway."

"*Liked* might not be quite the right word. It's an impressive home. Meoria Grange has been a background feature of my career for the last quarter century. I'm drawn to it, though I couldn't tell you why."

"So why did you try to scare us off?"

"You heard the stories I told you."

"Yeah, I heard them. No bullshit then?"

"No bullshit. Those awful things really happened."

"And you suspected there was something wrong with the house?"

"That's one way of putting it."

"Like ghosts and shit?"

"I had a few odd experiences there, once or twice. I don't know about ghosts. I'm no expert on the subject. But the encounters were weird and disconcerting. With the history of tragedy at the Grange, I didn't want my daughter living there. Nor my ex-wife, despite the obvious cracks some people might make."

"Kate was a handful alright." Darren looked around at one guard. His eyes glazed over. "She was wild in the sack. Classic example of an experienced woman with a healthy libido." He turned back and caught the uncomfortable look in his visitor's eyes. "Sorry. She was around your age, I guess. I didn't mean to go off on one. When you've been inside a long time... Well, I'm sure you catch my drift."

David leaned forward and studied the prisoner's face with greater intensity. "I'm not a detective, but you don't strike me as a cold-blooded killer, Darren."

"That's because I'm not." He glanced down at the table for a moment then made eye contact again. "So you want to hear it all?"

"I need to. No court rooms. No Agendas. No prejudice or pre-judgement. I want to sit across the table, look you in the eye and decide for myself what's true and what isn't."

"It won't get me out of here."

"No, it won't."

"Are you going to use it to take action over that house?"

"How do you mean?"

"Like an exorcism or something. Nobody will believe the word of a convicted murderer. But if you can take the truth and use it to stop another girl like Andrea suffering the same fate, then for God's sake do it."

"No promises. I keep having these dreams. I've got to do something or they'll haunt me until the day I die."

Darren swallowed hard. "Okay then. Here goes. It all took place on the one night. We'd just moved in. Kate kept me up snoring for hours. She'd been hitting the wine hard to celebrate our new home. Shit, that woman could put it away when she wanted to."

David blinked and pressed his lips together. He remembered those snores.

Darren rocked on his chair. "I couldn't get settled, so I took a leak. Andrea's light was on. When I approached the door, she was chatting to a school friend or someone on the phone. Anyway, she let me in. That beauty was wearing this skimpy nightwear and acting all provocative." He flushed. "David, are you sure you want to hear this?"

"Not the intimate anatomical details, thanks. But I need to get an idea of events and where you were, in your own head."

"Okay. Well, one thing led to another. You know, we-"

"Yes, okay."

"Anyway, Kate burst in when things were getting vigorous. She freaked out and hit the roof. No surprise there. The woman went nuts: dragged Andrea off the bed and onto the landing by her hair. I yelled at her to stop. She ordered me to leave."

"Then what?"

"I took a gander over the banister. She bullied that kid all the way downstairs and threw her into the cellar. Tossed the torch in the hallway and pulled the lighting fuse too. Even locked the bolt back in place."

"That sounds like Kate's spiteful streak." David's

eyes watered.

"I got downstairs to find Kate knocking back whisky in the kitchen. Andrea screamed in pain from down below. I decided I'd unbolt the door and check on her."

"Did you?"

"No. To my eternal shame and regret. Kate threatened to call the cops if I didn't leave. She'd have made something stick too, not that it matters now. Her mood was ice cold. Would have turned me to stone like a bloody Medusa, if she could have, I'm sure. Andrea's shrieks stopped, so I headed upstairs to pack a bag. Then I heard Kate screaming and shouting. At first I thought she'd got drunk and hurt herself. I grabbed my bag and hoofed it back to the hall." A light of realisation flashed in those dark eyes. "Hey, I just remembered something I didn't mention during the trial."

"What's that?"

"When I reached the bottom of the stairs, there was an identical holdall on the kitchen floor. I did a double-take on my own, because it's quite unusual and I've never seen another. When I looked up, the other bag had disappeared."

David's brow creased.

Darren's voice rose in volume. "I'm not making it up. The bag was there one moment and gone the next."

"Sorry. I'm trying to picture it all. I'm not calling your account into question."

"So the bag disappeared. It was then I noticed a bloody great hole had *appeared* in the kitchen floor. Kate was calling for help from somewhere down this deep shaft. There was a noise like water, too. Now I've been party to police reports about the well, it makes sense. A little sense."

"And that was when the tiles re-grew?"

Darren regarded the agent's face for a second, as if determining whether his far-fetched story was once again the subject of ridicule. "That's right. The tiles and a wooden cover over the well. I stood up and stepped aside. As God is my witness, David, those floor tiles spread back into place like they'd never been removed. Presumably they opened in the same way, for whatever reason. I was still stunned when my mind turned back to Andrea."

The storyteller was now sweating in profuse rivers of perspiration. His voice stammered and his fingers shook. Whether the tale was true or not, Darren Drake believed it to be so. He had nothing to gain from spinning the same web of lies, almost two years after his conviction. David was hungry for more. "Go on, Darren."

The prisoner's words came with difficulty now. "I walked down those steps with the torch. Near the bottom, I found her." With reddened eyes he locked his gaze on David. His expression was one of pure incredulity. "I've never seen anything like it. She was-"

"I identified her body at the hospital." David stepped in to save the man relaying in words what his mind clearly still pictured as if it were yesterday.

"I cradled what was left in my arms. That's how I got her blood all over me. But what with Kate's drowning and 999 call - the one where she told the operator I was trying to kill her - the police were never going to buy it."

"And the voice?"

"Yeah. It came out of nowhere. Or somewhere in those cellars. The noise was weird. Sort of like a woman, but in an out-of-tune musical tone. Whatever it was, it didn't sound human. That much I'd swear to."

"It ordered you to leave?"

"That's right. Then said it wouldn't ask me again. That thing wasn't messing around. The evidence lay in my arms. I felt angry, but what could I do? How do you fight something like that? Can it even be hurt or killed? Sometimes I still wish I'd tried."

"I suspect you'd have ended up like Kate and Andrea."

Darren studied his surroundings. "And how would that be worse?"

"Well, you cou-"

"Listen David. My life is over. It was over the moment the judge passed sentence. By the time I get out of here, my useful, productive working years will be behind me. Nobody is going to employ an ex-con with my record. I've lost my home, my income, my future. Wherever I go, I'll be *'The Meoria Grange Monster,'* as the press dubbed me. There's no hope of reprieve or appeal. I'm innocent, but I also know what happened. The police aren't going to discover new evidence to quash my conviction. And they won't go out and arrest the real culprit because the real culprit isn't a person. At least, not as we understand it. I'm screwed."

One of the guards frowned at the prisoner's raised tone.

Darren barked across at him. "I said screwed, not *screw*. I wasn't talking about you."

The guard's face remained unmoved. "Just keep it down."

David regarded the inmate and took a deep breath. "I'm sorry."

Darren looked him over. "That's the last phrase I ever expected to hear from you, after everything that happened. You believe me, then?"

"I think so. I don't believe you killed my ex-wife and daughter, at least."

"Well, apart from my distraught parents, you're about the only one. Listen. I'm no saint. I've never pretended to be. I realised things with Kate wouldn't last and so did she. We kept up the pretence while it was still exciting and juicy. A mature, experienced woman and a virile younger man. It's the age-old story; old as the hills. I never intended to fall for Andrea, either. That's not my game. Her mother was an exciting fling, with the possibility of lining my pockets. A chance to share in a little of her good fortune, then move on once we'd both had enough. Mutual separation. Not the stuff of romance novels, but hardly a crime either. So maybe I *am* a player, but I'm no murderer. Flights of fancy and imagination aren't my deal either. The shit I've described to you is real. It happened. God help me, it happened."

"Okay."

"So, what are you going to do now?"

"There are still some surviving occupants who once owned the house. I'm hoping to track them down for a frank discussion or two. See if I can learn anything else of use."

"Then you're heading back to the place?"

"Looks like it."

Darren blew out his cheeks. "Rather you than me. I wouldn't want to get within ten miles of that ridge."

David pushed his chair back on the floor with a scraping noise. "Thanks for seeing me, Darren. There's nothing much I can do for y-"

"Don't sweat it. It was good to clear the air between us. I hope you find the answers you're looking for, and some peace. For me the nightmare goes on. I wake up screaming in my cell to little relief." He stood and was first to offer a hand this time.

David shook it. "Take care of yourself."

"Bit late for that. Watch your back at the Grange. Good luck."

* * *

"So your relationship to Mark Chambers is professional?" A plump man in late middle-age with horn-rimmed spectacles, leaned back to prop against his sumptuous oak desk. One hand idly swept across his shiny forehead where once hair had grown. Now all that remained were a few white strands at the back of the head and over his ears. Except the veritable bush of hair that sprouted from inside his ears. David had often considered that hair retreated inside a man's head and poked out of nose, ears and any other available orifice, once he reached a certain age. It was already forming part of his own experience, albeit early days.

"That's something we have in common then, Dr Beecham." David played with the knot of his tie as he squirmed on a low-backed leather chair in the psychologist's office. Despite the comfortable, private surroundings, visiting a psychiatric hospital set him on edge.

"Mr Chambers has been a long-term resident here, for his own safety. He has a tendency to self-harm. What was the nature of your connection?"

"I sold him the manor he lived in."

"I see. You're an estate agent?"

"That's right."

"Were the two of you friends or acquaintances, outside of that transactional relationship?"

David's shoulders sank. This wasn't looking good. "No."

Dr Beecham crossed his arms. "Odd you should want to visit him, isn't it?"

David grimaced and went for broke. "The thing of it is, Mark Chambers could help me find answers."

"Oh? What kind of answers?"

"Owners of the same house have suffered a series of horrific incidents, before and after him. My former wife and daughter were both murdered there. I have a suspicion he might know something to help with my search."

The doctor unfolded his arms and drew up a chair alongside. David wondered whether it was wise to continue, lest he find himself detained against his will.

Dr Beecham leaned closer. "The Meoria Grange affair. I remember seeing it on the news. I'm sorry for your loss, Mr Holmes. But I'm curious. In what way do you think a mentally ill patient like Mr Chambers might assist you?"

"I want to know what happened to him."

"Do you think it has some bearing on why your wife and child were killed?"

"I believe so."

"How?"

David swallowed hard. "There's something unusual about the place. Something paranormal."

Dr Beecham chased away a kind smile with one hand. "Are you an amateur parapsychologist?"

"No."

"But you want to ask Mark Chambers to re-live events that sent him over the edge - mentally speaking?"

David gritted his teeth. "Aren't your type always encouraging people to talk about their problems?"

The doctor stiffened. "My *type* - as you put it - encourage people to answer specific questions. Ones designed by qualified staff after years of training, and to aid a patient's recovery. It seems to me that you want to pump Mr Chambers for information to resolve your own difficulties." His firm tone and taut facial muscles eased a little. "Can I ask if you're sleeping, Mr Holmes? Are you getting any rest after a hard day's work?"

"Off and on."

"Do you have troubled sleep? Dreams about the deceased?"

"Yes."

"Have you spoken with a medical professional about them?"

"No."

The doctor stood and walked over to a filing cabinet. He opened a drawer labelled 'A - C' and pulled out a thick file. "Therapy isn't a dirty word. I urge you to seek help." He sat down at his desk and unhooked a memory stick pinned in the file's flap. "It's good you are looking to resolve your issues, but speaking with Mark Chambers will confuse *you* and agitate *him*. I'm afraid I can't allow that. It would be unethical and wrong."

David pressed his hands together either side of his nose and let out a subtle huff of frustration.

Dr Beecham continued. "However. In the interests of your recovery, I will use my professional discretion and play you part of an audio file." He inserted the memory stick into a laptop computer on one side of his desk. "Ordinarily such a recording would fall under the heading of doctor/patient confidentiality. But I want you to hear a snippet of his rantings about the house. When you do, it will show you how fruitless a discussion today would have been in helping you move on. For that reason, I'm allowing this." He scanned some typed notes of a transcript and fast-forwarded the audio file to a key marker. The computer speaker crackled to life. Dr Beecham's voice could be heard, speaking in a warm, reasoned tone. "But how could the kitchen floor be perfect again next morning, if you removed the tiles the day before, Mark?"

David's ears pricked up.

Another voice answered. It stopped and started with a pitch that rose and fell in unpredictable waves. One moment the words came soft. The next they soared with a crescendo that almost distorted the recording. "There was a well. A well under the floor. I found the well. Penny didn't like it. Oh, no." At the mention of his wife, Mark sobbed. His tone altered to match the cute lilt of a small child acting coy. "Ding, dong, bell, pussy's in the well. Who put her in? Little Tommy Flynn."

Dr Beecham's voice followed again. "Do you want to talk about your wife, Mark? Is that what you want?"

The crying began afresh. "Penny. Penny was afraid of the cellar. I tried to close it up, but it wouldn't stay shut."

"Could a draft have opened it?" the physician reasoned.

Mark Chambers shrieked and shouted. "Draft. No! Swing, swing, swing. Swinging in the draft. Maggots in her eyes. No. She's telling me to leave, but it's not her. Penny! P-E-N-N-Y." Dr Beecham shut the recording off as the screams reached fever pitch. "I think that's enough, don't you?"

David nodded. "What was the nursery rhyme all about?"

"A coping mechanism for a traumatic experience, I would say. Happy memories - often from days of safe, childhood innocence - sometimes surface like a shield raised for protection. He claimed to have uncovered an old well beneath the kitchen floor. Next morning the tiles were back as they had been when the couple bought the house. A time they didn't know the feature existed, if I understood him right."

"That's correct. There was no well when I showed them around. I didn't even know a well existed beneath the kitchen until the police pulled up the floor and found my ex-wife's corpse in it."

"Hmm. That *is* curious. Mixing up events on a time-line isn't unusual for a man in Mark's condition. Unfortunately, it adds to their confusion. The linear events of our day-to-day experiences fall out of logical sequence." He paused. "So, there was no open well at the house when it came up for sale again? You honestly had no clue about the feature?"

"No. If there are dangerous issues at a vacant possession property, we'll get contractors in. They make everything sound for a viewing and we bill the responsible party. But the floor looked perfect to us. The same way I remember it."

Dr Beecham tweaked an eyebrow. "Well, I don't know what to say about that. But, as you can hear, Mark Chambers will offer little help with your quest for answers. Didn't they convict someone for the murders?"

"Kate's boyfriend."

Dr Beecham made a clicking sound with his tongue.

"You're from Dorchester, aren't you?"

"Thereabouts."

"Let me give you the details of an old colleague and friend over there. He specialises in bereavement therapy. Your subconscious mind is wrestling with difficult emotions and questions. Some of them may relate to unresolved issues with your broken relationship, causing you to reach out for anything to hang it all on. Martin can help you uncover those questions and process the emotions in a safe and helpful environment. He's not cheap, but no charlatan either. I encourage you to consider paying him a visit." The physician scribbled down a name, address and phone number on a pad and tore off the top sheet.

David took it from him. "Thank you for your help, Dr Beecham."

"Pleasure. Go and get some rest, Mr Holmes. You can't burn the candle both ends and remain in good health. Have a safe journey."

*   *   *

Charles Pembry raised a glass in the pub, surrounded by the collected staff from Strong & Boldwood. "Here's to Tracey - an institution at the office and the legs we stand on. Happy Birthday."

The assembled crowd repeated the last two words of his toast.

David Holmes pushed open the front door and appeared from the dull illumination of streetlights warming up outside.

Charles called out. "Here he is. The happy wanderer returns."

David gave their senior admin officer, Tracey, a reciprocated kiss on the cheek. "Happy Birthday."

"Thanks David." The woman clutched a glass of white wine in-between thin, ageing fingers.

Charles slapped his business partner on the back. "So, what are you having, the usual?"

"Please." David followed him over to the bar.

Charles waved a hand at the barmaid and nodded in David's direction. He didn't even need to speak before the server whipped out a straight glass. She pulled a pint of the man's favourite tipple.

David propped up the bar.

Charles joined him. His sociable smile sagged a little. "You seem tired, Mate. Busy day in the city, was it?"

"Yeah."

"Mind if I ask what's going on? You've not been yourself lately. Not that you've ever been loud or brash, but there's something on your mind."

David thanked the barmaid and sipped his pint with deliberate hesitation.

Charles nudged him, causing the man to almost spill his drink. "Come on, Dave. Tell me."

David put the glass down. "This morning I visited the hospital where Mark Chambers is a long-term resident. This afternoon, I paid a call on Derek and Sylvia Griffin. That's what I was doing in London."

"Those names sound familiar."

"If I told you I travelled up to Worcestershire to see Darren Drake last weekend, the penny might drop. Get the picture yet?"

Charles almost choked on his pint. "You're not serious? You had a sit down with that psycho?"

"I don't believe he *is* a psycho."

"What? Dave. What about Andrea and Kate?"

"I'm doing this for Andrea and Kate, Charlie. And myself, I guess."

"Doing what?"

"Trying to understand whatever influences people to go mad at Meoria Grange."

Charles thought for a moment. "Okay, now I know where I've heard those names. Previous occupants of that creepy old pile, right?"

"Exactly. The surviving ones, at least." "They convicted Darren Drake of murder, Dave. This search - or whatever you're up to - won't bring the girls back. I realise you're hurting. Kate bought a big, spooky house. Her gym instructor boyfriend went postal on her and your daughter. It was a shit time and you've had the biggest dose out of anyone. But what good can come from talking with those people? We all suffered from hearing Drake's nonsense at the trial. What did you even ask the others?"

"I wanted to discover what happened. All about their experiences."

"And they told you?"

"In a roundabout manner."

"So how does that help? Do you think the place is haunted then? That old excuse 'the Devil made me do it' is now true?"

David went to taste his drink again then put it down

instead. "How many times have you been to a house in our line of work and couldn't wait to get out again, Charlie?"

"Yeah, okay. Listen, I don't have an issue believing in ghosts, poltergeists, or whatever you want to call them. But we're not talking about furniture that moves or strange knocking sounds here, Mate. Kate was dumped in a well and sealed up. Andrea... I'm pretty sure we need not revisit that one. Are you telling me a ghost did all that?"

"No. But a force. An entity of sorts. I'm not sure. I had some weird stuff happen there, way back at the start. Voices, sensations, the whole deal."

"So what are you going to do?"

"I want to go down into the cellars at Meoria Grange. Go down there and face whatever comes out to meet me. Or wait until something does. I've been putting this off for far too long."

A vein stuck out on Charles' neck. "That doesn't sound smart. Or sane."

"I've got to do it, old friend. Until I overcome the hold that place has on me and confront it, I won't find a moment's peace." David's eyes fell on a newspaper some patron had left behind on a nearby table. The headline read: *'Meoria Grange Monster takes own life in prison.'* The man closed his eyes and lowered his head.

*   *   *

"Okay. Thanks Love. I'll give Dave a call." Charles Pembry wandered into the hallway at his home, clutching his wife's address book. He keyed in a number on the phone and waited for an answer.

"Dave? Charlie. Listen. I was talking to Claire about your plan for the house. Yes. Whoa, hold on a minute, I'm not tryi- Dave, will you let me finish? Okay, I know you're a tenacious old bugger and will go through with it, whatever I say. Anyway, Claire's got this contact they once used at the office. Some psychic or mystic woman. A freaky but effective weirdo apparently. I don't know - one of those new age types. Could be a tie-dyed pothead. When they refurbished an old building for their IT call centre, some of the new staff refused to move in there. Insisted something was haunting it. Then they found tea mugs stacked in bizarre places, chairs in odd arrangements and so forth. People quit their jobs or went on long-term sick. Claire's manager suggested they get somebody in to have a nose around. You know, an expert who might find out what was behind it and resolve the matter. All on the quiet, you understand. The press would have a field day with a story like that. So, they hired this local woman called Sable Masters. Very discreet and spiritually sensitive. To cut a long story short, it worked. So, Claire was wondering if you'd like to call her. Couldn't hurt, could it? I know I'd feel better if you weren't plunging around in the dark down there on your own. The number? Yeah. Got a pen and paper handy? Right, here goes."

14

Spiritual Support

David wandered down a tight alley in an almost forgotten part of Dorchester. A rusty metal sign screwed high on the wall declared the thoroughfare to be 'Private.' On the phone, Sable Masters told him to ignore it and follow the dark passage to its end. Shafts of sunlight stabbed down at odd angles through a narrow gap between rooftops above. Dust motes hung in the rays, lending an atmospheric ambiance to the estate agent's unusual journey. After twenty-five years selling property in the area, David thought he knew every nook and cranny of the old town. But, he had never been down here. His left shoe dipped into a puddle formed by a blocked drain. He shook the damp away from his foot and caught an ammonia-heavy scent on the breeze. They probably used the dark alley as a public toilet, those revellers stumbling around after kicking out time. At the end of the alleyway, a morbid green wooden door with peeling paint greeted the man. It was the tradesman's entrance to some old junk shop in the arse end of town. A battered, grey plastic intercom screwed to the wall nearby, bore two handwritten labels. One read 'Shop,' the other '1A.' David pressed the second button and waited for a response. A woman's voice crackled with static over the speaker.

"Hello?"

"Sable Masters?"

"Yes?"

"It's David Holmes."

"Okay. I'll be right down."

A few seconds later, footsteps sounded on a creaking wooden staircase beyond the portal. The door latch clicked and a square-faced woman in her late thirties with grey eyes and a tiny mouth opened it. Dark, centre-parted hair reached down to her shoulders in ill-managed tangles. The large, Aviator framed glasses she wore would have looked disproportionate on many faces; but a broad, smooth forehead absorbed some of their dramatic impact. She wore a floral dress that revealed an hourglass figure - curvy without being fat. The flowery print balanced on a knife edge between kitsch and full-blown 'summer of love.' Her pupils dilated as she looked the caller up and down. Was it because of the dark alley and lack of interior illumination from the hallway?

"David. Hi. Nice to meet you." The woman's voice was quiet and calm.

David took hold of a well-manicured hand with long nails that floated through the door in greeting. It seemed the only part of her appearance to have received much care and attention.

"Hello. I've never been down here before."

Sable kept hold of his hand and drew him into the tiny dark hall. A short corridor led to a door which probably belonged to the shop. The narrow wooden staircase rose in a steep curve to a battered white door above. Sable closed the alley entrance. "I hear that a lot. It takes new postmen a good ten minutes pacing up and down on the street out front, looking for my address. They end up asking in the shop and get directed round back. Either that, or old Mr Gregson the shopkeeper takes the letters in for me."

"I'm amazed he keeps his doors open in the current climate."

"Business rates are low in this part. I rent the flat from him. Makes up any shortfall on his costs. He lives elsewhere in a bungalow with his wife. Think he runs the shop for something to do. Told me he'd sit in a chair and fade away, otherwise. The guy could almost sell buttons and break-even round here."

"I can appreciate that."

David followed the well-padded but shapely backside of the scruffy woman up the rickety staircase. She pushed open the flat door. A heady aroma of sandalwood incense beckoned them inside.

Sable stopped for a moment. "I've never done any work for an estate agency before. Usually you guys are happy if houses keep coming back on the market. More commission, I assume. Troublesome hauntings must be good for business." Sable put an old, azure stove-top kettle on a dirty hob ring and lit the flame with a spill. "Would you like tea or something else?"

"What are you having?"

"Redbush. No caffeine and high in anti-oxidants. I find it gentle on my sensitive stomach."

"Okay. I'll give one of those a shot, if you can spare it."

His concern was heartfelt. You could barely swing the proverbial cat in this poky hovel. Her kitchenette held one person. It opened onto a chamber filled with a small, round dining table. To one side, an ajar door revealed a bathroom. At the rear of the principal living space, a bead curtain semi-masked a metal-framed double bed. Not a bedroom as such, more a partitioned-off section of a two-room bedsit. She'd crammed dog-eared books of many shapes, sizes and colours into every available space. A few pastel-dyed silks hung here and there by way of decoration. Candles and incense sticks jostled for position on a dresser that looked as if someone had sawed it in half to fit the room.

"Do you make your living from this kind of work?" David leaned over a box containing gorgeous, illustrated cards depicting angels or fairies - he wasn't sure which.

"Mostly. I do a little card reading, clairvoyant sessions and so forth. I also write articles for several websites on those themes. It's not much of a living. I could earn more down the local supermarket, but it would crush my soul. I don't know how people stick at a job like that, year in year out."

"This is a passion then?"

"Very much so. Please." She indicated one of several wooden chairs tucked around the central table.

"Sounds like you're in it for the right reasons." David sat down.

Sable fished two mugs out of a cupboard and dropped a Redbush tea bag into each. "It's more than a vocation. It's who I am. I'm not in this to bilk or manipulate vulnerable, upset people for cash, like some do. This is my journey. With every experience I grow and connect to something deeper. That world beyond, yet present. One day we'll all cross over and understand it in its fullness. I suppose I'm impatient and want to know more, without having to kill myself first."

"Did you ever connect with something you wish you hadn't?"

"Like a negative energy? Sure. I used to do some trance medium stuff, but had several bad experiences. I don't offer that service anymore. Being open to messages is one thing. Allowing something to take over your body - another entity - is quite different."

The stove-top kettle whistled. Sable lifted it from the hob and filled the mugs before extinguishing the gas flame. She retrieved a stainless steel teaspoon from a murky bowl of washing up water in the sink. Wiping it on a towel, the psychic raised one eyebrow at her visitor. "So I'm guessing this place of yours is suffering some serious activity?"

"What makes you say that?"

"The questions about connecting with a negative energy. The fact an estate agent phoned me for help with an unconfirmed spiritual presence. What are we dealing with here?" She squeezed out the tea bags and tossed them in a bin. "There you go." She handed a mug to David and sat down opposite. "So, is the house in Dorchester?"

"Not too far. A short drive. Do you have a car?"

"No. Not my style. Plus, they're expensive to run."

"We can go in mine. The house lies up on the Wessex Ridgeway between Sydling St. Nicholas and Cerne Abbas."

Sable's face whitened. "Are you talking about Meoria Grange?"

"You know it?"

"By reputation and experience."

"You've been there?"

"Only along the track, never inside the house. Oh, my days. I've always wanted to take a walk through its halls."

"You're one of only a few, in my experience."

"It scares me too."

"That would be a more common response. In what way does it scare you?"

"Well, the stories for one. Tragic deaths. Murder/suicides. That guy who killed his girlfriend and her daughter."

"My ex-wife and child." David sipped his tea. In the back of his mind, he wondered if this psychic should have already sensed an important detail like that. Weren't they supposed to receive spiritual impressions from contact with people? Was she genuine after all, or just a well-meaning fruitcake?

"Your second child. But the only one to survive birth." The words came out of that tiny, thin mouth with a soothing, tender reverence. She smiled at the look of shock, writ large across his countenance. "The longer I'm with you, the more I'll pick up on."

David put the tea down with both hands, as if he might drop it using one. "My wife, Kate, suffered a miscarriage with our son. He would have been our firstborn."

Sable reached over and squeezed one of David's hands. "Paul loves you. He wants you to know you did everything you could."

David snapped his hand away and swept back his blond hair, eyes reddening.

Sable watched him with sympathetic eyes. "I'm sorry. I know you didn't come here for that. There are layers of distracting energy around you, confused and vying for attention. If we're going to Meoria Grange, focus will be essential. The energy clouds your aura with heartbreak and turmoil."

"How much do you know about the place, beyond news reports and local gossip?"

"Nothing concrete. There's scuttlebutt in the community about geomantics. Not surprising, given its location. But the house is private and stands on private land. I got a sense that whatever flows out of that site, is ancient. Buried somewhere in space and time, I suppose. I don't know. These are the impressions of a girl who hiked past once or twice. Nothing more."

"That makes sense. What's geomantics?"

"Geomancy derives from an ancient form of divination, using the earth. Geomantic Energy is a term sometimes used to describe an interconnecting pattern of spiritual networks that hum with occult power. They typically follow ridges, hilltops and other geographically significant or interesting features."

"You mean Ley Lines?"

"Exactly."

"But that's energy, not a presence."

"Like I said, I've read a few things and received some impressions nearby. Until we get in there, I won't know much else. Would you mind describing anything pertinent you've experienced in relation to the place? It doesn't have to be something that happened while you were at the house itself."

"My own encounters have always centred around the cellars. They go on for a long way under the hill. Extra tunnels were dug in later years." He relayed everything he could remember: Voices and sensations from the house. His weird dreams about a tribal ritual and subsequent battle. The images of Jacob Backhouse from the civil war and those later pictures of a man who loved the house and died in a riding accident nearby. Sable didn't interrupt or ask another question until he had finished.

"When can we go?"

David drained his tea and pulled a large, old key from a jacket pocket. "Right now."

* * *

"This is for you." David retrieved a chunky, handheld battery torch from the boot of his car. He pulled out a second one for himself. "There is electric lighting down in the cellars, but not beyond a certain point. Once we hit the tunnels, these will be our only source of illumination. Unless your powers extend to night vision."

Sable turned from examining the tall house and took the torch with a smirk at his mild sarcasm. David must know she wasn't a fraud by now, but this world lay far outside his comfort zone. She studied his fit frame. He'd maintained himself well for a forty-five-year-old man, with no beer belly or middle-age spread. The quiet estate agent gave off an attractive, innate sensuality, to which he was oblivious. Sable had spent her youth in pursuit of the spiritual at the expense of all else. Raised in foster care, she had no family to speak of. Once she left school, friends drifted away to do their own thing. That, or because her alternative lifestyle meant she didn't go out on the piss or pair up with boys. Now at thirty-seven, her neglected physiology reminded her she was also a healthy woman, as well as a voyaging soul. She checked the light and watched David close the car boot. "It would be nice if my abilities extended to night vision. Think of the electricity bill savings. What a treat."

The pair walked into the hallway and atrium without a word. Sable gazed around, eyes wide in awe. Was this a response to the impressive building or something invisible that she sensed? The woman took a few steps further and reached the bottom of the main staircase. "That's Jacob Backhouse?" She pointed at the portrait.

David nodded. "The very same. Did you want to look around the place first before we descend into the pit - so to speak?"

"Yes. That might prove helpful."

David brushed past her and made for the kitchen. In the doorway he paused and stared at the floor. The wooden well cover lay in place, revealed by uncovered floor tiles stacked against one wall. Nothing had changed since the police investigation. When Kate's parents came around to putting the property back on the market, they decided not to have any work done on the floor. A prospective buyer could see the well for themselves and decide what they wanted to do with it. Having their daughter's fortune in the bank, basic tax and utilities on the unused manor didn't make a dent in the balance. David suspected they weren't fussed if it sold or not. The less they got involved in the house, the happier they seemed. He thought about Darren's assertion that the tiles grew back. Memories from his first day on the job re-surfaced. He remembered dear old Arthur Strong teasing Ted Deeks the contractor after he swore the fire-damaged stairs repaired themselves. "Does it only happen when others are here?" He didn't mean to vocalise his thoughts.

"How's that?" Sable appeared at his side.

"I was thinking about those claims of Darren Drake that the floor tiles grew back. It reminded me of the day I started work. The Grange had suffered fire damage. My old boss got a guy in to do some makeshift repairs. He swore blind that parts of the house repaired themselves. Also said it made him feel tired."

"Psychic Energy Transference." Sable adjusted her

glasses and paced in a slow, deliberate circle around the kitchen.

"What on earth does that mean?"

"We know certain types of psychic manifestation draw energy from present hosts to bolster their actions."

"Like some sci-fi energy vampire?"

Sable's eyes twinkled and laughter lines creased the edges. "I suppose that's one way to understand it." She indicated the exposed well cover. "I assume nobody has been back in the house for any length since..." Her voice trailed away at the realisation she might be about to raise the spectre of grief in her companion.

"No. Nobody has been here."

"David, I'm sorry I-"

"It's okay. Come on, I'll take you round the rest of the joint."

The remaining tour went much like a viewing, except Sable kept quiet and didn't ask annoying questions. From time to time she paused and shut her eyes. In the bathroom, the quirky lady was almost overcome with horror and sadness. David couldn't ignore the sincerity on her face. This was no showgirl putting on a performance. If anyone could help him get to the bottom of the mystery surrounding Meoria Grange, it must surely be Sable Masters.

"And now we come to the heavy stuff." David hesitated at the panelled door to the cellar.

Sable touched him on the arm with delicate fingers.

"Take as long as you need. If it's too much, we don't have to go down there."

"I'll be okay. Thanks." David tapped her hand then slid back the bolt and opened the door. The only fix he'd performed on the house when the property came to the office again, was the installation of a replacement lighting fuse for the cellar. He flicked the switch and dim illumination glimmered from the darkness below. "Here we go then. I can hardly believe I'm doing this. Not before time."

Sable took one pained last look back up to the high ceiling above. Her grey eyes narrowed and her head moved from side to side as if watching something swing.

The pair descended the steps into the chamber where Andrea Warren-Holmes met her terrifying end. Sable gripped David's hand. Her knuckles whitened, and she shook. The pain of her grasp washed the man's mind clear of images relating to his daughter. He fixed his gaze on the frozen psychic. "The same goes for you. We don't have to do this if it's too much."

Sable gasped and caught her breath. "I'm okay. Sorry." She let go of him. "Whatever attacked your daughter was powerful. And old."

David stepped around the spot where the police found Andrea's body, as if she still lay there in spirit. His voice stammered. "D-do you... Is s-she here?"

"Andrea?"

David nodded.

Sable's eyes misted, and she shook her head. "No. Andrea's not here. But the echo of her last moments remains, like a spiritual footprint. Fear. Pain. Shock. Sorrow. It's like having an emotional bomb go off in your hands."

"I wish I could feel it too."

Sable stepped closer to him. "No, you don't. This isn't how you want to connect with Andrea or remember her, David. Come on, show me more."

They moved north through several of the vaulted chambers. A few minutes later, Sable stopped again. She almost dropped her torch as if slapped by some unseen hand. Tears flowed down both cheeks. She hurried to crouch by a wall. David realised where they were, but remained silent to see what the woman brought out.

"Children. A brother and sister." Sable sobbed. "He didn't mean to kill her. He was trying to protect his family. Love. He can't go on without her and face what he has done in the light of day." She darted her head back round to a patch of ground nearby as if watching something fall. "They hold hands. Not their bodies - the eternal essence of each. They hold hands and ascend to the light."

David almost fancied he could see that light as the woman rose with her head angled upward. She wiped away the tears and shuffled across to where he stood watching.

"We're nearing the tunnels, Sable."

Sable sniffed and checked her torch was functioning. "How far have you gone in the past?"

"Only a short way in, like I described. This will be a

first for me too."

"Let's go."

A pair of broad, white electric beams scanned from side to side in the darkness. The further the spiritual investigators went, the rougher the walls and floor became. Eventually things narrowed to a long, claustrophobic passage that opened into a small chamber about the size of an average master bedroom. It stood stacked with old crates, much like the ones from the earlier part of the cellar. David stopped short and huffed. "What? That's it? All that flippin' great long passage for a small junk room? I don't get it."

Sable shone her torch across the stack of crates. She shivered. "There's something back there."

David spun on his heel. "Can you feel it?"

The psychic nodded. She clasped the light with both hands to still her quivering arms.

David put his own torch down, with the beam illuminating the tallest stack. "Here. Help me lift some of these out of the way, would you?"

Sable joined him. After they had removed three crates, a jagged crevice became visible in the wall behind. They cleared the remaining obstructions. David pointed his light through the narrow opening. "Looks like a cavern of some sort. Come on, we'll have to shimmy through sideways. It will be a tight fit."

A minute later, David and Sable stood in what appeared to be a natural rock chamber formed beneath the ridge far above. Whether by the action of underground water erosion, human intervention or some other mystical force, it had been hollowed out around an angled rock sprouting from the earth floor. The man's light swept across swirling organic patterns that adorned the feature. He recognised it at once. "Oh, my God. That's the thing I saw in my dream about the tribal ritual, all those years ago." He drew closer and extended his right hand. As his fingers came in contact with the object, the patterns illuminated like blue neon, filling the cavern with pulsating sapphire light. A dull hum pulsed from the object, throbbing through the mortal bodies of the humans and causing their stomach muscles to tense in unison.

Sable let out a panting breath. "Can it be?"

David looked over at her, his face taut with confusion. "What? Can it be what?" His entire body flooded with an intense joy. Connecting with this bizarre light was pure ecstasy. It thrilled and terrified him in equal measure. "Sable. What the heck is happening here? What is this place?"

A wind rose out of nowhere. The chamber lay sealed, with no external draft able to penetrate its depths. A howling blast whipped around David's torso, then drove straight into Sable's chest, knocking her against the wall. The woman winced and let out a cry. An echoing, eerie female voice boomed around the rock face. "He is not yours. You do not belong here." Sable tried to take a step sideways. The wind walloped her again. She tumbled to the ground.

David's face darkened. He stared across at the rocky walls that shimmered from the illumination of supernatural power. "Stop it. Stop it, you're hurting her." He let go of the stone menhir. The blue light faded until only their torch beams remained. "Sable. Are you okay?" He dragged her into a sitting position.

"I hurt my arm. It's not broken. Painful, but unbroken."

David hooked his hands underneath her armpits. "Come on, let's get you up. We're outta here. I've had enough of this place." With a considerable effort he squeezed the injured psychic through the narrow crevice. Cradling her bruised arm in the other, she recovered enough strength to stumble back through the tunnels and cellar. At last they made the manor hallway. David went to shut the door. A sweet fragrance blew up from the darkness below. In the distance, he almost fancied that he heard a soft weeping. The man's heart walloped against his ribcage. He secured the panel and pulled out his car keys. "Do you want us to stop by the doctors?"

"No. It's not serious. I've found my second wind now. David, we need to get back to my flat."

"Oh?"

"There's a book I must show you."

"Will it explain any of what just happened?"

"It might."

"Okay. Come on."

*   *   *

"Here we go." Sable opened an old book on the table in front of her. She inverted it and slid the item across for David to examine.

He scanned the open pages. They were adorned with photographs of swirling symbols and patterns carved into a stone object. "Hey. These are like the ones on that angled stone in the tunnels." He read the header title. *"Geomantic Energy Wells.* What the hell are they?"

Sable poured herself a glass of tap water from the kitchenette and sat back down. "Geomantic Energy Wells are extreme concentrations of Ley Line energy. At least, that's what some researchers have concluded. The rock patterns you're looking at came from tribes who transferred their culture orally. No writing to speak of. People like the Romans sometimes recorded observations of vanquished, indigenous populations. Solid information is scant at best."

"So what do these researchers think they are?"

"Here's where it gets interesting. Some tales describe concentrations of energy so high in certain places, the ancients discovered they had become sentient."

"Intelligent energy?" David struggled to disguise the disbelief and sarcasm in his voice.

Sable offered an upturned palm toward him. "And what are we?"

"How do you mean?"

"What are we, David? You and I, what are we?"

"We're people."

"Meat and bones. That's it? Why did you ask me if Andrea was present in the cellar? Her meat and bones weren't there."

"Sable!" David frowned.

"I'm sorry to be blunt. What were you thinking?"

"I don't know. Her soul, spirit, essence. Something, I

guess."

"And if you go right down to the subatomic level, what are we?"

"Okay, I'll bite. We're energy."

"Yes. The table, the chair, you, me, all a mass of vibrating energy."

"Jesus, this sounds like the *get rich quick* books Kate used to read. Are you saying there's something in all that directed energy stuff after all?"

"I don't know about the books. But, energy with free will and purpose isn't so far-fetched, when you think about it with an open mind."

"So where do these supposed experts think the intelligent energy came from?"

"It's believed that it was here since creation. Not like you and I. This energy is earthbound. It doesn't drift off into the afterlife or exist there. The ancients also believed the energy was feminine in nature."

"Mother Earth?" David never thought he would use the term.

"You could say that, though without all the dogma associated with that label. The ritual you described sounded like an old wives' tale. Or that's what I thought it was until you touched that stone today. Tribal shamans sought a perpetual soul to act as 'Guardian' for an energy well. Always a male. Sort of a betrothal, if you will. If the candidate survived the ceremony, it bound them to the well for all time. Although the energy was raw and intelligent, it could also be unpredictable. It was said the presence of a guardian brought balance to the site and blessing to the area. A yin and yang situation. Myths record that when the guardian died, he'd ascend like the rest of us. In time, the soul would re-incarnate afresh and be drawn back to connect with the well source."

"Jacob Backhouse?"

"Could be. He built the house there and remained unmarried. Maybe it was him who dug the tunnels and found the stone. Before his death fighting the Parliamentarians, anyway. Or, perhaps it was the other fellow you dreamt about."

"You mean the chap from the riding accident who updated the property?"

"Yes. There might have been many others over the years."

"So what has this got to do with me? Why do I keep dreaming about all those people? Why am I drawn to that house and what made that stone light up when I touched it?"

Sable lifted her glasses off her nose and wiped them on her dress. "Have I got to spell it out for you?"

David slammed one hand on the table. "No. No, that's not possible. And even if it were, I want nothing to do with that creature. It's evil, pure evil."

Sable put her glasses back on and shook her head in slow, definite movements. "No, it isn't."

"What are you talking about?" David leapt to his feet, fists clenched. "All those people ruined or murdered. Men, women, children, my own beautiful daughter for Chrissake."

Sable remained seated. "It's neither good nor evil. Not light or dark, David. It just *IS*. A Geomantic

Energy Well doesn't have morals or ethics, a code of right and wrong. It's pure energy and emotion. All it knows is love and longing to reconnect with its guardian. Its soul-mate. Its spouse. Polite society and the niceties of respectable twenty-first century human behaviour mean nothing to it. When the guardian re-incarnates and draws near, no action is off the table. In its desire for union with that long lost and eternal love, anything goes. Or so the stories say. Maybe they're not just legends after all." Sable touched her throat and gagged.

David's hands relaxed, and he leaned forward. "Sable, are you okay? I'm sorry, I didn't mean to get angry."

The woman's eyeballs bulged. "She's coming."

"What? Who's coming? You mean that thing? But we're back in Dorchester."

"Her range doesn't extend far. She's weak here, but I can't stop her."

David's pulse raced. "What should I do?"

Sable threw her head back and let out a long, rasping moan. Both hands thrust downward, pinning David's arms to the table. Her pupils rolled up into her head, leaving only the whites of her eyes visible. In a familiar, inhuman but female voice that mingled with her own, the psychic spoke over and over. "I am Meoria, we are one. I am Meoria, we are one. I am Meoria, we are one." The woman coughed and slumped down on the table and went limp.

David pressed two fingers to her jugular. There was a pulse - faint but solid.

*   *   *

Sable pressed a button on a tiny CD player with built-in speakers, nestled atop a beaten old side table. It was the kind of stereo that looked like a mainstream manufacturer made it, but featuring cheap components and a name nobody had ever heard of. A synth pad of sampled vox sounds drifted across the room. Recorded bird song and the gentle tones of a soft, woodland breeze among treetops accompanied it.

When she awoke from her traumatic and involuntary medium session, David Holmes had been there to see if she was okay. In the days that followed, Sable thought about the curious estate agent at ever decreasing intervals. He had an intoxicating power amidst all that helpless confusion.

A message alert tone chimed from a mobile phone resting on the central table. The woman picked it up and saw the name 'David Holmes.' She opened the correspondence and read:

'Up at the house. Can you get here? I need you.'

Sable bit down a smile. Her eyes twinkled. She keyed in a reply, reached for her jacket and pulled out a folded local bus timetable. Despite the overwhelming and powerful ancient presence that enveloped her at Meoria Grange, she couldn't stop thinking about David. If he needed her, she would be there for him. Somehow she felt safe in his presence. Might the obliviously attractive businessman feel something for her too?

An experienced walker, Sable Masters was no stranger to puffing uphill. She got the bus from Dorchester to Cerne Abbas and made a hasty, energetic climb to the house on the ridge above. Rain lashed down in thick sheets from a leaden sky. Her pulse raced with exertion and nervous anticipation.

As she approached, the chunky wooden front door swung wide. She almost skipped across the threshold, heart aflutter like an excited schoolgirl on her first date.

The portal swung shut with a resounding echo. Nobody heard the screams that followed.

*   *   *

"Morning Tracey." David pushed open the front door at Strong & Boldwood. He remembered to switch on his mobile phone - it remained off at night, until he got to work each day - then put it away again.

"Hi David. How are you?" The admin lady responded once she had his attention again.

"Not too bad, all things considered. It's raining cats and dogs out there."

Charles Pembry poked a cocked head from inside his private business lair. "Thought I heard you. Hey, when you've got a minute I'd love to hear how that thing worked out last week. You know, the one Claire helped you arrange."

David smiled at Charlie's attempts to be discreet. His mobile phone vibrated, and he pulled it out of his pocket to read a delayed message. "Speaking of which," he said aloud after noticing the name 'Sable Masters.' David flicked the digital envelope to its open position.

'Will be glad to help. I'll catch the bus to Cerne Abbas and walk up. Can't wait to see you. Be careful at the house.'

David frowned. "What the...? Has she picked the wrong contact?" He considered the text with greater care and his mouth dropped open.

"Everything alright, Dave?" Charles took a step out of his office.

"I've gotta go. Catch you later." David wheeled about and almost tumbled into the street.

"How long had you two been seeing each other?" A female police officer with fair hair tied back in a neat bun, regarded David with emotionless eyes.

David lingered in the upstairs hallway of the manor while the officer's colleagues attended to a body in the bathtub. He had arrived at the house too late. A cursory search of the rooms led to the discovery of Sable Masters' corpse. She reclined in the empty bath, lifeless eyes bulging beneath a clear plastic bag wrapped tight over her head and neck. A scribbled suicide note lay on the lowered toilet seat lid. She addressed it to David and described how she couldn't go on living without him. The man regained his focus. "We weren't seeing each other. This makes no sense. Sable is a psychic... Was a psychic. She was helping me deal with post-bereavement issues relating to this house. My wife and daughter were killed here."

"Yes, I remember." The officer scribbled down a few lines in her pocket notebook, still unmoved. "Did the lady have a history of mental illness that you knew of?"

"What? No. I don't know. I met her for the first time last week."

"I see. This house doesn't belong to you, does it?"

"No. I'm the agent in charge of selling it. I brought Miss Masters up here the other day, to see if she could help with my issues."

"Useful, having access to the property."

"We hold a set of keys. The vendors live elsewhere and leave all business regarding the sale to us. We come and go as needed."

"And you say you arrived on the scene and found the lady like this?"

"Yes. Why do you think I called?"

The woman stared at him as if in her own attempt at psychic mind reading. "How did the deceased gain access to the house then? Did you give her a key?"

"No. I don't know how she got in. I received a message from her to say she was on her way up. Thing is, I never asked her to come here."

"We'll obtain phone records for you both under RIPA as part of our enquiries. Can anyone vouch for your movements prior to attending the house?"

"Yes, the staff at our office in Dorchester. I arrived this morning and received Sable's message. I raced over here at once."

"Why?"

"Pardon me?"

"Why did you *race* over here? Was there a problem?"

David flushed. If he explained the truth of his suspicions regarding the death of the psychic, he would most likely find himself in a hospital room next door to Mark Chambers. "Because she didn't have a car and was walking all the way from Cerne Abbas."

"Odd reason to race."

"My phone stays off overnight. I switched it on and received the delayed message at work. I knew she'd already be here and get drenched hiking up the hill. Didn't want her hanging around outside and catching her death." He winced at those last words.

The police officer scowled at him as if he were making light of the tragedy, or gloating like a murderer who has covered his tracks. "And you didn't come to the house before going to your office?"

"No. What is this? Are you fitting me up for a murder or something? Sable was a decent girl. No way would I hurt her."

"Calm down."

A voice called from inside the bathroom. "Mary?"

The police officer turned. "Excuse me for a minute, Sir." She left David standing there while she conferred with a pathologist.

David couldn't say it pleased him that the final verdict on the death of Sable Masters was unassisted suicide. Nor did he believe it. But, it was good to be out of the frame at last. The poor woman got portrayed as a frustrated, lonely hearts, mentally disturbed nut-case who developed a fixation on him and took her own life. Phone records received from the service providers and digital forensics performed on Sable's device, yielded no trace of a message sent by David. As far as the evidence went, no such communication ever existed.

15

Marina

The front door buzzer sounded in the Cerne Abbas flat. With annoyed effort, David turned his head away from watching the London 2012 Olympics on TV.

He poked a squinting face out one of the open lattice windows to peer down into the quiet street below. It was a warm summer day. A portly man with thin, greasy black hair fidgeted on the communal doorstep. The fellow was Jake Billings, the farmer from whom he'd bought the tiny patch of quiet meadow.

"What's up, Jake?" David called down.

A pair of steely eyes rose to meet his own. "David. Such news. Can I come up?"

The estate agent was more than a little curious now. Jake was a nice chap. They exchanged greetings from time to time and shared the odd pint in the local. But nothing much ever made him emotional. "Okay. Hang on, I'll let you in."

"Are you serious? Will they make the topsoil good afterwards?" David sat perched on the edge of his sofa.

"Of course. Once it's grassed over again, you'll never know the archaeologists were there. Could take a year or two for us to receive any income from the finds, but..."

"Well, this calls for a beer. I still can't believe it. Tell me again while I fetch a couple of cold ones from the fridge, would you?"

Jake chuckled. "It's simple. An amateur metal detecting buff located something on the boundary between our two land parcels. I let him have a dig around on my patch and he turned up some iron age bangle or other. The university came out to do one of those geo-thingies-"

"Geo-Phys. A survey using underground sonar of some description." David popped the crown caps off two bottles of craft ale.

"That's it. Turns out there's a whole bloomin' hoard sitting beneath our land. Right across the boundary if you can believe it. They want to excavate the site. You and I get a share of the proceeds as landowners after the Treasure Valuation Committee finish their assessment. From the excitement this bangle has caused, we could be looking at a tidy sum once they get the rest up. That's what the fella told me."

David handed him a bottle. "When I bought that parcel as an investment, this wasn't quite the dividend I expected. I wonder what's down there? Bet you wish you hadn't sold me the plot now?"

Jake shrugged. "I'm not greedy. You did me a good turn at the time. I needed cash. All I know is, history boffins and academic types want to be our best friends at the moment."

An Olympic medal ceremony flashed across the TV

screen. A British athlete stood tall to receive one of twenty-nine golds the nation would take home. David clinked his bottle against Jake's. "Here's to gold."

* * *

"Let me see it, then." Charles Pembry burst into David's office.

His colleague laid a newspaper down on the desk, open at an article about the Conservative majority win in the 2015 general election. He rummaged around in a pocket of the jacket that hung on the back of his chair and pulled out a DL sized business envelope.

Charles hovered close to him, bobbing like an excited school child waiting for a magician to pull a rabbit from his hat.

"Here we go." David passed him a slip of paper wrapped in a letter.

Charles held it up to the light and whistled. "I've never seen a cheque for a sum that large. Worth the three year wait to get your reward?"

"Absolutely. Not to mention all the other years since I bought the meadow."

Charles shifted on the spot and fidgeted with his tie. "Yeah. About that. I've given you some real stick over the land purchase since we first met. If you want to rub my nose in this, I must have it coming."

"Don't be daft, Charlie. First thing I'm going to do is write a few cheques of my own for my sister Mandy and her kids. Then I'm taking you and Claire out for a top meal."

"You're all heart, Mate. It would be nice to see you take a chunk of that and do something for yourself, for a change. You've been in limbo since the divorce."

"Have I?"

"That's how it looks from the outside. No offence."

"None taken. Okay, maybe I will."

Charles handed back the cheque and headed for the door. "I'll ring Claire and tell her about the meal. That should brighten up her working day."

David finished his newspaper and folded it on one side of the desk. A gentle knock sounded from the doorway. He looked up to meet the gaze from a pair of large, female emerald eyes set in a rectangular face. Bouncy brown hair in volume curls, tumbled down to tease bare shoulders accentuated by a low cut, mango coloured top. A broad, winning smile with a hint of subtle cheekiness held him transfixed on both her countenance and slim, shapely figure. David pegged the woman at around thirty-five. It was some time before he spoke; a delay which caused his cheeks to redden.

"Can I help you?"

"Are you the person I speak to about buying a house?"

The voice rang with a gentle lilt. The agent couldn't quite place her accent. It sounded like a strange blend of southern Irish and rich west country English.

David chased away a smirk with his index finger. "Anyone in the office can help you there. Did you have a specific property in mind, or are you looking?"

"I'd like to tour that large manor pictured in one side of your front window."

David's neck became hot. He tugged at his shirt collar. "Then I *am* the person you need to speak to. That place is my responsibility. Please, won't you sit down, *Miss...*?" David couldn't believe he was chancing his arm by stressing the 'Miss' in an effort to gauge her marital status. Was the sudden financial windfall making a new man out of him, like Charlie once suggested it might?

"George." The woman stepped inside his private room, never taking her eyes off the flustered man. He rose to greet her and extended a hand. She took it with a slender grip that ended in perfect, manicured white nails.

David sat back down and waited for the visitor to join him. "We have a range of other upmarket properties too. If you like, I'll bring up the details on my computer for us to have a look at?"

The woman thought for a moment. "I'd rather look at the manor." She licked her lips with a delicate, subtle sweep of the tongue.

"Very well. But, should you change your mind, please let me know. It's no bother."

"Okay. When can I see it?"

Her confident, direct approach took David aback. *No preliminaries? If only all our customers were as focused and certain.* "We can go there now if you want to. Are you parked in town?"

"I came on foot. Would you drive me there and

back?"

"Yes. No problem." David was on his feet again in an instant. He couldn't remember the last time he'd received such an injection of verve. Never mind that this pretty woman might be nothing more than a nosey time waster. It seemed the arrival of that cheque and this attractive lady - around fifteen years his junior - were doing him a power of good. He motioned toward the door. "Shall we? Oh, please call me David, by the way."

"Marina." The woman looked over her shoulder with a flash of ivory white teeth and a sparkle in those enchanting green eyes. She sauntered back into the main area of the building. The pair paused by the front door.

The estate agent felt a pressing urge to say something more. "Marina? Reminds me of the girl in that TV show 'Stingray,' I used to watch as a kid. Also reminds me of my Granddad's old car from the seventies. But that might be a less flattering comparison." David was waffling like a nervous beau and he hated himself for it.

The woman giggled. "I don't think I know either of those."

"Ignore the daft old git. Sorry."

"Old? Not you."

"Fifty. My business partner tells me it's the new forty."

Marina shook her head for an instant. "It's a number - nothing more. What does it mean?"

David shrugged. "That I rarely go the whole night

through without taking a leak." He winced at the unprofessional response. "Oh, I forgot the key. Wait here a minute and I'll fetch it."

"Everything alright, Mate?" Charles craned his neck round the door frame. David retrieved the large, cold key for Meoria Grange from a locked cabinet.

"Yeah. I've got a viewing request for the Grange. Off up there now."

"Someone on the phone?"

"No, that woman who came in a few minutes ago."

Charles shifted on the spot. "Thought I saw you having a good old chat. Are you going to put her off if you can?"

"Put her off?"

"Ever since that incident with the psychic, I could swear you're protecting potential buyers from making offers."

"Why would I do that?"

"Because you're a decent chap and you're worried someone else might go mad or get hurt."

"We'll make our commission on it eventually, Charlie."

"Oh, I'm not worried about the money. In fact, there's a delicious irony about dragging this sale out as long as possible. The owners *are* Kate's family after all. They always treated you like crap."

David locked the cabinet again. "Makes me feel less guilty about compromising my professional integrity. Yeah, you're right. I suppose I don't want people to buy it. I definitely don't want Marina to buy it."

Charles' eyes widened. A teasing grin spread across his lips and lifted the corners of his mouth in a movement that seemed to go on forever. "Bit nice is she?"

David lowered his eyes.

Charles grunted. "Nothing to be ashamed of, Dave. That's great. At least you're *thinking* about women, if nothing else. How long have I been on at you to start seeing someone again?"

"Too long. I'd better go, I'm keeping her waiting."

"Be careful up there. I know that place doesn't spook you like it does others, but-"

"We'll be fine. Now why don't you get back to work and earn us some money while I try to stop the firm getting a pay-out on this one?" David dropped the key in his pocket and made for the door.

Charles stood looking after him. "Sure," he said in a soft, distant voice.

* * *

David was taken aback by how well Charles nailed his treatment of prospective buyers for the old house. But then, they had been friends and colleagues for thirty years. Each time a new person, couple or family with money showed up, David did his level best to scare them off. He always kept the cellar until last. It was his *ace in the hole* and never failed to deliver. Sometimes the creepy atmosphere of the country pile worked like a charm. At others, he would lay it on thick with tales of previous occupants coming to a grisly end. Ever since the day he and Sable found the chamber with that ancient menhir, he hadn't ventured back into the unlit depths of the tunnel network. No buyer ever asked to go that far, even if some expressed a curiosity about their reach.

What worried him now, was Marina's unflinching enthusiasm for everything he showed and told her about the house - even the horrific bits. If he didn't come up with a plan, she might put in an offer. Unless that worked out way below market value, Kate's folks would accept it. For a property professional, this should have been a source of delight. But two things played on the fifty-year-old's mind. First, he couldn't shake a certain pervasive jealousy at the thought of someone else owning the Grange. This was mad, and the kind of thing his ex-wife used to claim about him. What made it worse, was that David couldn't lock down why he felt an inner longing for the weird house. With every ounce of rational thought, he regularly struggled to downplay or dismiss Sable's assertions of his connection to that home. Second, he couldn't remember the last time someone turned his head in such a spectacular fashion. Marina gave him butterflies in his tummy, right from the outset. Her perfume drugged him like the petals of a fragrant spring flower. Her attractive, unblinking stare turned his legs to jelly. Every time she brushed past him on the viewing, or allowed those slender fingers to rest on his forearm, he burned to sweep her up in a ravenous embrace. And if time between meals is a gauge of hunger, David was a starving man in the world of affective appetites.

"How far do the tunnels go?" Marina peered into the darkness beyond the halo of electric lamp light.

"Quite a way. But you need a torch to explore them. Sadly, I didn't think to bring one, as people rarely ask to be shown around." David was lying through his teeth. The everyday, tiny pocket torch he took on each viewing, pressed against his body. A jacket lining bulge from the object prodded him in the ribs as if in punishment for the falsehood.

"Oh, that's a shame. I'd want to see it all before committing to buy. Wasn't there a torch on the wall near the top of the steps?"

David's mind raced for a suitable excuse. "It's unreliable. Due to health and safety considerations, I must insist on at least one heavy duty torch each. Preferably some recently tested ones. With litigation culture the way it is… Well, I'm sure you understand."

Marina looked deep into his sad eyes. David tried to hold fast, but felt a little like a prisoner under interrogation. Flagrant dishonesty wasn't his forte. He'd never gained Kate Warren's comfort with it.

"Can we come back another time to finish up the tour?"

David thought. He couldn't very well say 'no.' Delay was the only option. Time to work on a better strategy to discourage her. That was now his best hope. "Yes, we can do that."

"And do you have suitable torches somewhere, or should I buy a pair?"

"It's okay. I know where I can lay my hands on a

couple."

Marina stepped past him in the cellar entrance's direction. "Thank you for showing me around today. I enjoy your company." She shot him a quick wink.

"I was wondering if you'd like to go out for a bite to eat with me?" The man tried not to trip over his words. He was out of practise at romance by far too many years. His good looks remained into middle age, better than one might have hoped. But a smooth-talking Lothario, he wasn't. The proposition blurted out with zero finesse.

"I'm not a big one for dining out." The reply was matter-of-fact.

"Sorry." David swallowed hard.

"What for?" She stopped and turned, lips pursed.

"I don't know. For asking. Crossing the line."

Marina stood straight in front of him at a distance David found a little unnerving. But her words soothed some of his discomfort.

"I'd like to spend more time with you. I prefer one on one that's all."

David perked up a little. "Far from the Madding Crowd? How very Thomas Hardy. I know some quiet restaurants."

She shook her head. "Do you like to walk?"

"Yes."

"Could we go somewhere close by? If you bring the torches along, we might combine that with another look around down here."

David attempted to hide his disappointment. Like a dog with a bone, she would not let this go. Did Marina want to go out with him at all, or was the beguiling woman only desperate to get her hooks into the manor? "Okay. How about Saturday? A wander round Shaftesbury; grab a coffee outside on Gold Hill. A picturesque excursion without too much hustle and bustle. Then back here to explore dark, dodgy tunnels of little use to a home buyer. What do you say?"

They reached the cellar steps. Marina studied David for a moment.

"I'd like that. Thank you."

*   *   *

"Do you own the whole building?" Marina examined the attractive timber-framed exterior of David's flat in Cerne Abbas. She had just arrived out front and rung his bell.

"No." David shut the main door and unlocked the car for his guest. "I rent an upstairs flat. Sounds odd for an estate agent, I imagine."

Marina expressed no opinion as she got comfortable in the front passenger seat. "Did you bring the torches?"

"Yes, they're in the boot."

"So, why would your renting a flat sound odd?"

"Because of my job. Partner in a firm, too. The late ex-wife used to make a big deal out of my housing status." David started the engine and pulled away.

Marina watched the hedges drift by. "Aren't you wealthy?"

"What makes you say that? The job? Our business

does well. I'm thinking of *buying* a home soon."

"Any idea where?"

"No."

"I'm surprised you haven't gone for the manor."

"How come?"

"You seem attached to it. You know it well."

"It's been a prominent feature of my life for some time. Funny. I could afford it now if I wanted it."

"But you don't?"

The question hit David like an express train. He'd not given serious consideration to buying Meoria Grange for himself. That seemed like a crazy idea in the plain light of day. The house of horror. The place where his ex-wife and daughter were killed by something science and common sense couldn't explain. Yet the seed of that suggestion landed on the fertile soil of his raw emotions with surprising agency. It was one daft way to keep Marina from meeting an untimely and horrific fate: Gazumping of a humanitarian and ethical nature. That didn't solve the yearning inside to draw her closer to him though. He considered her question about being wealthy. Could she have read about his treasure trove good fortune in the news? Was this attractive and provocative younger woman: Kate Warren - Mark II? A gold digger out for what she could get? David shook the paranoia from his brain and chastised himself with an inner monologue. *You're so frightened of getting burned again, you'll find any way you can to paint a prospective partner in the same light as Kate. Take a chance, David, before you run out of life to take it with.*

Early summer light added an atmospheric haze to the long, sweeping cobbled street of Gold Hill in Shaftesbury. A collection of characterful cottages with both slate and thatched roofs followed the descending, right-hand curve out of sight. David always liked to come here. He remembered the bread commercial featuring a lad pushing his bike up the hill, from back in the seventies.

"It's a beautiful spot isn't it?" He didn't turn his head away from the view as he verbalised the thought for Marina.

Her voice was almost a whisper. "Lovely."

"There's a shop over the way that sells semi-precious stones and crystals. I bet they'd have one to match your eyes." David was still trying too hard to convey interest.

Marina turned away to stare along the ridge. "Is there somewhere we can sit?"

"Yes. There's a bench with a great view of the hills up top."

"David? Hi." The familiar tone of Tracey's voice from the office cut through the dreamy stillness.

David looked up. "Hi Tracey. Are you out shopping with your husband?"

"Not quite. Shopping *for* my husband. Our anniversary's coming up. Thought I'd find an unusual present in one of the independent shops round here."

"Great. Oh, I'm being rude. Allow me to introduce you to Marina."

Tracey followed the direction of his hand.

Marina studied the woman before them. David watched her smile a silent greeting.

Tracey fidgeted. "Pleased to meet you."

David nodded to himself. Perhaps he wasn't the only one that striking emerald gaze unsettled? Somehow the thought helped him relax. "Would you like to join us? There's room on the bench."

"No, that's okay. I promised I'd meet some old friends for a spot of lunch at the coffee shop." She fixed her eyes on David. "Have a good weekend. See you Monday."

"You too. Have fun." David scratched his cheek and knitted his brows together as he watched her stroll off. In the distance she paused and looked back to deliver an almost melancholy wave.

Marina leaned across into his field of vision. "Can we go back to the house now?"

* * *

David pulled up the handbrake and put his car in neutral. Marina peered out at the roofline of Meoria Grange through the passenger window. The man killed the engine and withdrew his key.

"Would you honestly want to be rattling around in this place all by yourself? It could get lonely."

"I'm used to being alone." Her words were flat. She detached the seatbelt and climbed out of the vehicle.

David hurried to join her. She had already reached the top step by the front door before he ambled over, clutching two chunky electric torches and the house key. He fought for new excuses or diversions that would keep them from an exploratory of the tunnel network. Or should he drag her down there, show this stunning woman the ancient stone and have done with it? If the result was anything like his previous excursion, she'd be running for the door in no time. But then he'd lose her. Plus, things didn't work out too well for Sable Masters after she ventured into the depths with him. It was a quandary from which there was no obvious route of escape.

"Would you like to go round the whole house again? You know, to put the cellars and tunnels back in context?" It was the best delaying tactic he could muster on the spot.

Marina pushed open the door and moved in ponderous, thoughtful steps through the downstairs hallway and atrium. She kept her back to him as she spoke. "You don't want me to buy this house, do you?"

"I... Well, I err-"

"Why?" She swivelled on the spot, her smooth alabaster forehead streaked with frown lines.

David's shoulders sank. He placed the torches on a mahogany side table standing against one wall. His eyes closed while he collected his thoughts and took a deep breath. "Honestly?"

"I'd like to know."

"Okay. The truth is, I don't even know myself. Not in so many words. This place pulls me in. The house and I have a history - some of it heart-breaking and horrible. And I never thought I'd feel this way about another woman. Especially one I've only just met. How's that for a list of reasons?"

"Excuse me?"

"Huh?"

"The last bit with the woman. What are you talking about?"

"I'm talking about you." There, he'd said it. His cards were well and truly on the table now.

Marina's eyes scanned his face and posture. "Are you trying to protect me from something?"

"When we get to the end of the tunnels, you'll find out for yourself."

"Don't bother. I'm not going to buy it."

David's face reddened. He had never been so embarrassed in his entire career. What kind of estate agent was he, anyway?

Marina's forehead relaxed. "But I still think *you* should." She drifted closer and slipped a lithe hand around his waist. "You like me then?"

David held her gaze this time. "What's not to like?"

"I was starting to wonder."

"Sorry. I'm a mess inside."

Marina rested her full volume curls against his left shoulder. Soft, warm breath teased David's neck like invisible, enticing fingers. "Please let me in, David. I don't want to hurt you; don't want to take anything from you." Her lips brushed the nape of his neck then moved to whisper in his ear. "How long has it been?"

The man gulped. "Since what?"

Her voice became husky and playful. "You know."

David felt his crotch stir with aching arousal. "Far too long."

If his awkward but successful attempt to discourage this buyer from purchasing the house seemed unprofessional, it paled into comparison with what happened next. A passionate embrace and breathless tongue wrestling conducted in the hall, led to him scooping the slim, attractive brunette into his arms as if she weighed nothing at all. For the briefest moment, it almost felt like the portrait of Jacob Backhouse smiled at David, like *The Laughing Cavalier*. It seemed pleased as he stomped by on his way up to the master bedroom, swinging Marina's shapely legs past the old oil painting. The next few hours were the most joyful, erotic and fulfilling the middle-aged estate agent could remember. The couple's naked bodies writhed and tumbled, soaked with musky sweat. Watching Marina rise and fall above - head thrown back lost in open-mouthed ecstasy - made his Jamaican honeymoon with Kate feel like a detention at school by comparison. While on top himself, David drove deeper than he thought possible. His tingling body may have plunged into a chasm of pure paradise, but it was the overwhelming sense of loving connection that trumped all physical bliss.

When all was said and done, they lay together in a radiant afterglow of passion's embers. Something about this mind-blowing encounter cleared David's head, like a cleaner brushing cobwebs from a long-forgotten room. He had found a much-needed moment of clarity at last. Now it was time to make some important life changes.

16

The Whole Truth

"It's a nice day, Dave. How about we take a stroll round Borough Gardens with our sandwiches?" Charles Pembry leaned against the door frame of his partner's office, clutching a brown paper bag.

"Why not?" David beamed. He secured the desktop computer and retrieved his jacket with a spring in his step.

The pair wandered through the park in sunshine that embraced them with its comforting warmth. They passed the bandstand and watched kids entranced by the ornate fountain. Charles rubbed his chin and squinted. "If I didn't know better, I'd say you've been enjoying the delights of *Lady Labia*."

David stretched. "And *do you* know better?"

"Well, I thought so. Are you seeing someone?"

"Yeah."

"Have I met her?"

"You've seen her. Briefly, anyway."

Charles stopped at a bench and sat down in silence. He let the brown sandwich bag dangle between his legs with limp fingers. "It's not Marina, is it?"

"Did I tell you her name?"

"I believe you mentioned it. Tracey said you introduced her in Shaftesbury over the weekend."

David nodded. "That's right."

"And she's the same one who came in to ask for a viewing at Meoria Grange?"

"Yep. Honestly Charlie, she makes me feel like I'm twenty all over again."

Charles bit his lip and lowered his head.

David's buoyant mood evaporated. "What's wrong? I thought you'd be pleased."

Charles glanced away across the well-maintained grass. "When I said you should start *seeing* someone again, I had no idea you'd take my words at face value."

"What are you talking about?"

"Marina isn't real, David."

David paused. "Charlie, if this is some kind of joke, it's not making me laugh."

"It's not making anyone laugh. You're my friend; I'm worried about you. So is Tracey."

"But you said Tracey told you I introduced her to Marina in Shaftesbury."

"Yeah. She followed your gaze to an empty bench seat. Said you were so deadpan and not given to cracking jokes, that she went along with it and gave a *'Pleased to meet you,'* or something very much like it."

David's mouth went dry. "The day Marina came into the office, you said it looked like we were having a good chat."

"I said it looked like *you* were having a good chat.

319

That's why I came to see if everything was okay. Then you fetched the house keys and left-"

"With Marina."

"On your own. Trust me, Dave. I stood there and watched you walk out the door alone."

David put a hand up to wipe perspiration from his forehead. "But we've made love. She's like an amalgamation of every dream girl I had as a kid, and she loves me. I've never felt so fulfilled."

Charles' eyes watered at the desperation and disappointment written across his friend's face. "Listen to yourself a moment. When does anyone *ever* meet someone like that? I'm not a mental health professional, but it sounds like something inside has wound so tight it's snapped. No shame in it. What with all the stuff you've been through, it's hardly surprising."

"Have I done anything else at work to embarrass the firm?"

"No Mate. Tracey won't even talk about Saturday with anyone else. You know how discreet she is. She only told me because we've all been close for so many years. And because - like me - she's hoping you'll have a rest and get help."

"I could take a little time off while I move house."

Charles' face brightened. "You've found a place? Excellent. There now, that can add to stress. Good news, though. Where are you moving to?"

David shielded his eyes from the sunlight. "I've bought Meoria Grange from Kate's parents."

His business partner's mouth dropped open. "Oh,

my God. David, please tell me you're kidding. You're not, are you?"

David shook his head. "It's something I have to do. Now I've got the money-"

"Have you been going there a lot?"

"I know what you're thinking. It hasn't driven me insane. Marina helped me see it as the right decision."

"Marina helped you see it as the right decision and you're not insane? David, we've established that Marina isn't real."

"So you say." His face became drawn. "But she's real to me."

Charles placed a hand on his colleague's shoulder. "Guess we know why she didn't buy the house herself. The money would never have transferred across, would it?"

"So you think I've lost the plot?"

"I think you're suffering inside and it breaks my heart. All you ever wanted was to settle down and enjoy a family life like the one you knew growing up. Thanks to Kate that was ripped out of your hands. But you need not conjure up a fantasy female to compensate. You're a catch, David, and a bloody good one at that. Don't turn inward and go where your friends who love you can't follow."

David sighed. Where did he go from here? He was able to see, hear, touch, even taste Marina. How could she be a figment of his imagination?

Charles spoke again. "After three decades, do you trust me?"

"More than anyone I know."

"Then trust I'm telling the truth." He pulled out his sandwiches. David joined in and they munched away in silence for a time. A young mother pushed a giggling child past them in a buggy. Charles swallowed a mouthful of lunch and brushed crumbs from his lap. "Oh, with all the other business, I forgot to tell you: Sarah's expecting."

"Seriously? That's brilliant. You and Claire must be thrilled."

"To think the two of us will be grandparents."

"You've come a long way from your 'Top Gun' fixation and Astra GTE days."

Charles threw back his head and laughed. "I'd give anything for five minutes back in the eighties again. But I think five minutes would be enough. The old days were fun, but I like my life now. A good home, a loving wife and a wonderful family."

"Sounds perfect."

Charles looked at his friend with mournful eyes. "You'll find it too, in a way that suits. I know you will."

David folded his hands. "That's the problem. It feels like I already have."

*　*　*

That same afternoon David sat at his desk, mind wandering in realms of which he wasn't consciously aware. In a motion similar to automatic writing, one hand gripped a ballpoint pen and doodled the same name over and over on his notepad: *Marina George*.

Tracey appeared on his office threshold, pulling at her clothes with uncomfortable fingers. David lifted his head as the assistant spoke.

"Hi." She held up the front page from a set of property details depicting a photograph taken outside his new home. "I've removed this from the window now we've sold it. I usually toss them, but know you often keep old shots of that house. So I thought I'd better ask."

David's mouth wrinkled into a weak smile. "Thank you, Tracey. Yes, I'll take it."

Tracey placed the thick paper down on his desk and turned. At the door she hesitated. "I told Charles that I saw you on Saturday."

"He mentioned it."

She looked round. "I said you introduced me to someone."

David pushed his chair back and stood. "It's alright, Tracey. He explained everything."

Tears filled the woman's eyes. "I want you to be well and happy. That's all."

"I know." The phrase floated out in a resigned whisper.

Tracey crossed the small floor and kissed him on the cheek. She pulled out a handkerchief and hurried from the office to the staff toilet.

David looked back down at his desk. On the left sat the details of his impressive new home, bearing the title *'Meoria Grange.'* On the right, his notepad swarmed with the scribbled name *'Marina George.'* His gaze shifted from one to the other and back again. All colour drained from his cheeks and he grabbed his jacket.

"Charlie, I'm going out," he called with force on a purposeful march to the door.

In his office, Charles held the desk phone away from his head to reply. "Take all the time you need."

"What are you trying to do to me?" David's shout resounded across the manor atrium. The front door which he had thrown open, swung shut behind him. "Come on, show yourself." His face went crimson, veins pulsing in his neck. Charlie's revelation he might have lost his mind caused anger to surge through David's torso. There seemed only one thing worthy of blame: this place.

A soft knocking tapped on the front door. He span, grabbed the handle and yanked it open.

A pair of sparkling green eyes met his. Marina's mouth curled in an uncertain twist. "David. Are you okay?"

David looked her up and down.

The woman continued. "I saw you coming down the driveway, so I followed." She hesitated. "Is everything alright?"

The estate agent glanced at his Ford Focus, the only vehicle parked outside. "Where's your car?"

"Oh, I was walking along the ridge when-"

"In those shoes?" His eyes flashed down to a pair of thin-strapped, high-heeled sandals. "Who are you?"

The man didn't wait for a reply. He turned and

stormed back into the hallway, leaving the door open for the curious woman. She followed inside and closed the portal with a gentle click. Cautious fingers stroked the wood, like feet tiptoeing around a sleeping giant.

David threw up his hands and laughed. "Marina George?"

"Yes?" Her subdued voice came in meek reply.

He looked at her across the hallway. "Marina George? It's an anagram of Meoria Grange."

A wry smile - still meek - rippled across her face. "So it is. Gosh, I'd never thoug-"

"Don't give me that." David raised a strong right index finger like someone pointing a gun. "I'll say it again: Who are you? *What* are you? Is this some psychotic episode I'm having, because apparently nobody else can see you?"

Marina stood still and watched him in unblinking silence.

David ran a hand through his hair. "So are you a figment of my imagination?" He lifted his gaze to the rafters and called out to the house. "Are you trying to drive me insane, like you did Mark Chambers? I'm in the frame now, aren't I? You always do it to your new owners."

"Not all. Not you. Never you." Marina spoke with an expressionless face that never left his.

"Well, my colleagues think I've gone round the bend, because I'm carrying on with someone who isn't there."

"I *am* here, David." She walked towards him with slow, calm steps.

David's heart thudded. His voice trembled and tears welled up in his eyes. "Who are you?"

"I am Meoria." The words came out with tender loving-kindness. "We are one."

A vision of Sable Masters' involuntary trance danced behind David's widening eyes. He shook his head in desperate disbelief. "It can't be true."

The beautiful woman stood right in front now. "You are my bonded one, come back at last."

David's eyes narrowed. "You think I'm a Geomantic Energy Well guardian?"

Confusion caused the feminine head to list.

David adjusted his delivery. "Human terms, I guess. I saw a man in a dream many years ago. Someone from an ancient tribe who once lived nearby. He underwent a ritual at the stone in the cellar of this house. Presumably it formed the hilltop back then."

The woman's eyes lit up at the tale. "Turil."

"Turil? Was that his name?"

She nodded. "Turil, your first form at the time we were joined."

"He died fighting another tribe, yes?"

Her head lowered. "Yes."

"Then Jacob Backhouse bought this land before the civil war and built the house."

Her eyes flashed from sorrow back to joy, like a little child who has been scolded and then given a new toy. "We were so happy together in your form as Jacob."

"And he fell supporting the King in battle against the Parliamentarians."

Again her head sank.

"I don't know the name of the guy who put in the plumbing and electrics."

"Henry Dove." She clutched hands to her chest as if hugging an invisible memory. "You had such plans for the house as Henry. Every day felt exciting and new."

"But a riding accident cut those plans and days short?"

A single tear rolled down her left cheek. She reached the slender fingers of one hand towards him. "And now David Holmes."

David's first instinct was to recoil in horror. He caught himself part way through the reaction and stopped. Meoria paused, her hand not quite touching his arm.

David watched her. "At what cost? Do you have any idea of the lives you've taken or ruined?"

She froze and looked crestfallen.

He went on. "You destroyed my own daughter."

Again her head rocked with bewilderment. "I drove those out who stood in the way of our reunion. Their fears were plain, so I confronted the invaders with them."

David shook his head. "You have no concept of humanity, do you?"

Her eyes watered.

David sighed. "No, of course you don't. You don't understand. Sable was right. How can you, you're not human yourself."

"I love you, David. I've been waiting for you to return."

"That's what you meant the other day when you

said you were no stranger to being alone."

She nodded. "Your life cycles are so short. When you ascend, I am left behind to wait; longing for the joy of our union once more."

"And do you always look like this?"

She touched his arm now. "No more than you look like this. When you connected with the stone, I received an impression of the form you would find most appealing as David. I don't observe earthly matter or physical attributes when I see you in my heart."

"Your heart? You're a ruthless killer. Sable Masters didn't take her own life, did she?"

"She wanted you; was hoping to lure you into her arms. You were not hers to hold, and she sought to confuse you. To delay you from my embrace."

David gawped. "And I thought I'd already married the ultimate jealous wife. You take the biscuit." He shuddered at the near joke made at Kate's expense, so close to the spot where this creature slew her. "So why now? Why didn't you appear when I first came to scope the cellar, all those years ago? It would have saved a lot of time, trouble and untold human misery."

"You weren't ready. Whenever you come back from the upper light, it wreathes you in forgetfulness. That is the way of things with your kind. But inside, the soul energy never truly forgets. Over time, your innermost being hears my call." Her face lit up. "Then, we are reunited." She let go of his arm, twirled on the spot with joy and wrapped her hands behind his neck.

David reciprocated at her waist and gazed into the

most adoring, deep green eyes he had ever seen. This thing - whatever it was - loved him with an intensity beyond the comprehension of mortal man. It could kill without pity or remorse and would never stop until they were together again. But it could also love in total purity, holding nothing back. "So what happens now?"

Meoria placed her forehead against his. "Now you own the home that should always have been yours; we are one energy as it was at the first."

David glanced around. "And if I want to change the house in some fashion?"

"We can do whatever you wish. It will be so wonderful to share in the joy of your vision, like before."

"Like before." David repeated the words under his breath. "There I was growing up and thinking I would steer my own course through life."

"So you have. Steered it with your inner compass."

"Back to the harbour where it belongs?"

"Just so."

David snorted. "I know an estate agent is supposed to love property, but Charlie would say I'm taking that to an unhealthy extreme."

Meoria blinked.

David squeezed her. "Never mind. It's a device we call humour."

"I know something of humour. You taught me a little once."

"When? Oh, you mean as Jacob, Henry, or whoever."

"Yes."

"Shame I didn't teach you not to slaughter people."

Meoria rested her head against his shoulder. "Why are your kind so afraid of transitioning to the light? Is it because you forget what awaits?"

"Some people are afraid of what awaits. Others fear that nothing awaits. Most dread pain in the process."

"Your shells become brittle and broken, until they can no longer contain your life energy."

"Death. The end, for some."

Meoria shook her head, and those curls tickled the man's nose. "The end for none. There is no end. Your energy remains in flux for a time. Then it reforms anew in this realm with fresh physical clothing."

"There's no end for you either, is there? You never die."

"No. Nor do I forget. In the times between your cycles, I yearn for our brief moments of togetherness."

"Sable said the bonding ritual used my energy to balance yours. At least, that's what the ancients believed."

"Yes, it's true."

"So the land prospers and you don't kill anyone?"

"Unless they come here to harm you, my love."

"Why can't Charlie or Tracey see you? It would make my life a lot easier."

"My power extends only a short way beyond this place."

"To Dorchester or Shaftesbury?"

"The limit of my range. It causes a huge drain on my reserves to appear in this form to more than one human at a time. The only person I wish to appear for is you."

"We won't be throwing any dinner parties for the Hembrys then, will we?"

When their eyes met, David knew he had his answer. Now he finally had all the answers and a way forward, if he wanted it. The choice wasn't difficult to make. His soul sang at the ecstasy of this reunion with Meoria. He cleared his throat.

"I would say my old life is about to die, but that's not true. I'm about to start living my old life again after a hundred year break, aren't I?"

Meoria kissed him on the mouth for one moment with moist, tender lips. When their mouths parted, her voice hummed with a deep longing. "A hundred long years, bonded one. I love you."

* * *

"Last day on the job. I know it's a cliché, but I've got to say it, Dave: the end of an era." Charles Pembry plonked a book-sized, square, gift-wrapped package on his business partner's desk.

David sat back in his chair and picked up the parcel. He gave it a gentle shake near his ear. "It's not your stapler, is it?"

Charles put his hands on his hips. "Give me some credit, Mate. I know Claire says I'm a useless shopper, but that's below the belt."

"Sorry Charlie. Should I open it now?"

"Yeah. We'll do the proper gift and presentation from the rest of the office later. This is a little something from me to you."

David tugged at the wrapping paper. It came away with a rustle to reveal two items: A boxed model car and a DVD. He laughed. "A die-cast Vauxhall Astra GTE and the film of 'Top Gun.' Only you."

"Not too corny?"

David stood and wiped moisture from one eye. "Means more than I can put into words, old friend."

The two men embraced. Charles stood back with reddening eyes, but remained clasping David's upper arms in his hands. "You don't have to do this, you know."

"Charlie, I-"

"I know. I know once you make your mind up about something that's it. I'm not interfering. All I'm saying is that Arthur and James gave this partnership to both of us. Anytime you want to come back, the position is yours."

"Thanks."

"So, are you still seeing her?"

"It's probably best if I don't get into it."

Charles stepped away, watching his partner with misty eyes. A realisation dawned. "I'll never see you again, will I?"

David stood eyeing his friend and colleague of thirty years. His head shook in a hesitant motion. "I don't think so."

Charles wrung his hands. "I wish you'd get help. If you need anything - I mean anything at all - pick up the phone, day or night. I'll be there."

"I know you will, Charlie. I couldn't ask for a better

friend, and I'll never have another like you. But you were right. I'm going where you can't follow. At least, not in a way that would make any sense."

"You were always the better agent."

"You were always the better man. Claire chose well."

"You might give my wife a call and remind her of that. I left the bloomin' toilet seat up again this morning. You'd think I'd have learnt by now. That's what she told me."

David grinned. The pair hugged and slapped each other on the back once more.

17

A Bride in Mourning

In the decades that followed David Holmes taking up residence at Meoria Grange, the nearby valleys flourished in a way not seen in living memory. That time became known as *'The Golden Years'* by lucky residents of Sydling St. Nicholas, Cerne Abbas, and their environs. Every growing thing thrived, from garden flowers to the local watercress beds. Any hiker enjoying a jaunt along the Wessex Ridgeway, would notice a palpable sense of wellbeing and contentment on that section of the trail. It even earned the location a nickname of *'The Happy Valleys'* among the walking community. On wandering past the impressive old, three storey Portland stone manor house that crested the ridge, the sensation was one of such euphoric bliss it became a favourite walk for many. An almost addictive tonic to the stresses and strains of life in the modern world. Passers-by rarely glimpsed the reclusive gentleman who inhabited that house. There were stories from over forty years ago that once tragedy had befallen several previous occupants. But if there were any spooks or spectres nearby, the aura at the Grange only felt like one of peace and tranquillity. Nobody under the age of sixty seemed to have any idea who the owner was. Those who did, usually plied their tales over a beer or three in the local hostelries. Some said he was an outsider (he'd only moved to Dorset from Wiltshire seventy years previous, after all). Others reckoned him to be an eccentric millionaire who'd made his fortune selling antiquities. A few claimed he was an estate agent who once lived in both Sydling St. Nicholas and Cerne Abbas for a time, before winning the lottery. Younger folk believed this to be nothing more than silly rivalry between neighbouring villages. Whoever he was, he kept himself to himself.

* * *

"Good morning, Sleepy Head. I've made you breakfast in bed." That voice, so ethereal, musical and beautiful never ceased to thrill David's soul. Gentle lips kissed the ninety-year-old man on his forehead as he opened a pair of tired eyes. Meoria looked no different to the day he had first seen her. But then, why would she? Beyond all natural comprehension to David, was the unchanging way she looked at *him*. To Meoria he never altered; never got any older. His energy was alive and fresh, forever joined to her own while his time on earth remained. Ever seeking it again when it was taken away above. She would never stop loving him, never leave nor berate him. A delicious smell of smoky bacon and scrambled eggs wafted into his nostrils. Those nasal passages now ran thick with white hair, like the few skimpy strands that adorned

Devon De'Ath

his pale, wrinkled head. David lifted his aching back from the mattress while Meoria plumped his pillows for support. He reached one trembling hand out to clasp her well-manicured digits.

"I love you, my strange angel." He patted her. "This looks marvellous." He studied the cooked breakfast. Internet grocery deliveries had been one invention David adopted soon after his departure from Strong & Boldwood. Anything that enabled him to stay at the Grange and go out as little as possible. Meoria could only travel so far with him, and he got odd looks from passers-by, nattering away to an invisible person. Being away from her was agony. He never wanted to leave again. But, something inside heralded an event with little respect for his preference and he knew it.

"I love you too, bonded one." She propped herself up on the bed beside him and stroked his head while he ate. "Every day we are together is a joy."

"Meoria?" David's face darkened.

"Yes, Darling?"

"There may not be many days left."

She wrapped her arms around his shoulders and squeezed him tight to her chest. "Please don't say such things. How can I bear another season without you?"

His eyes twinkled. David raised his head to meet her loving stare. "I'll come back to find you again. I promise. I will always come for you."

"I know you will."

They sat in a communion of quiet only the intimate understood.

On his way downstairs after dressing, David regarded the portrait of Jacob Backhouse. He lifted one wizened finger to stroke the canvas, echoing his cleaning efforts that day he first discovered it as a twenty-year-old man. A van crunched to a halt outside. As the pensioner made the bottom stair, a letter landed on the doormat. The postman was already driving away before David reached the correspondence. Its postmark was local. The envelope bore a return address for a Mrs Sarah Thomas.

"Sarah Thomas?" David pondered aloud and scratched his chin. "Ah! Sarah Pembry's married name was Thomas." He ambled over to a large chair by the living room fireplace and sat down to open the letter. Clicking fingers - painful from arthritis - unfolded a typed sheet of paper. He read to himself with downcast features:

'Dear Uncle David,

I don't know if you will receive this letter. If you do, I hope it finds you well and happy.

I haven't contacted you before (in accordance with Dad's wishes we leave you alone) but I thought you should be told that he passed away last month.

We lost Mum two years ago to a stroke. Dad was never the same afterwards. About six months ago he had a bad fall. It broke my heart when he realised he could no longer cope and moved into a nursing home. With no future to hope for and memories of Mum so painful, he appeared to focus on *other things. Whenever we visited, all he talked about were the good old days. Those earlier years with you two as estate agents, blazing a trail through the Dorset property market. For a few brief minutes it was as if the lights came back on inside him, and age slipped away. He died in his sleep and we buried him next to Mum.*

Wherever do the years go? I've retired now. I'm looking forward to spending some peaceful days with my husband, spoiling our grandchildren at every available opportunity.

I miss you. My brother Grant and I often speak about 'Dear Uncle David.' Dad would never hear a harsh word spoken against you. I'm sure the loss of Andrea and Auntie Kate was a horrible blow. I don't pretend to understand what else happened. My father always refused to comment, other than with the same old line: 'He's in a happy state, but needs to be left alone.'

Sorry to be the bringer of sad news. May you find peace and contentment in your own remaining days.

Love and best wishes,

Sarah Thomas (nee Pembry).'

David brushed a hand across the letter. His stare moved to a side table near the fire. There sat the die-cast Astra GTE and 'Top Gun' DVD Charlie had given him forty years before.

"David?" Meoria appeared at the entrance to the living room.

The old man's gaze rose to meet hers. "Charles Pembry passed away. His daughter sent me a letter."

His voice cracked as he waved the piece of paper.

Meoria hurried over and perched on the seat. David couldn't hold back a sob of emotion. The woman cradled his head in her hands with the tender affection she always lavished on him. She kissed the silvery hair then whispered. "It was the end of his cycle, my love. How I wish things could be different for you. How I wish they could be different for *us*. You'll see him again for a time. Then it will be my turn to mourn."

The overwhelming power of her adoration enveloped him. Her presence soothed like an unseen balm. He watched flames crackle and dance in the fireplace. They cast leaping shadows across the rug - a place he and Meoria had made tender, passionate love so many times over the last four decades.

The day wore on. As the sun set, David and Meoria cuddled up on a rattan sofa. It faced westward from the orangery across the rolling Dorset hills. A tightness gripped the old man's chest. He placed one hand beneath the beautiful creature's chin and turned it to face him. "It's time, Dearest."

The woman whispered with a heart-rending gasp. "No."

David squeezed her. "Will you help me upstairs?"

David lay back on the mattress in their large, comfortable bed. For the first time in ages, his body no longer ached. Meoria tucked him in, her pupils large and moist. David could always get lost in those eyes. They had enchanted him from the first moment she walked into his office. He placed a finger across her trembling lips.

"Shh now. We both recognise this as a passing phase. Soon I will come back to you, renewed and strong again."

Meoria locked her mouth onto his in one final, intimate physical exchange. She felt his energy break away from her own, fracturing the balance she had known since his return. That energy lifted towards the ceiling with the feminine creature staring after it. She wept. "Don't leave me, David. Please don't leave me." She clutched onto his lifeless torso. But if anyone could sense the essence of David was no longer there, it was her. His life energy had gone.

From the attic, down the hallways, to the furthest depths of the cellars at the Grange, Meoria's wailing cry split the peaceful stillness. The house foundations shook, and the walls echoed with the desperate howl of her aching bereavement.

Down in the valleys, the waterways gushed with a sudden surge like an inland tidal wave. People walked out of their houses to stare at the sky as if a rumble of unusual thunder had rent it in two. To their surprise, they found many plants in their gardens twisted and dead. The stems contorted and shattered, like necks wrung by some furious assailant. It was a considerable time before even the most skilled of gardeners could get much to grow there again.

* * *

"I always wanted to get a look inside this place." A thin man of slight frame in his early sixties, opened the front door at Meoria Grange. He peered through the gap, scanning up to the ceiling with bright but beady eyes.

"It's in an amazing spot, Mr Carlson." The head of a pretty girl of around twenty with bobbed red hair, joined the other to steal a glimpse. "How long has it been vacant?"

"A few months, Jenny. It's okay, you can call me Andrew. We cultivate an informal atmosphere at Strong & Boldwood. My old mentor, Charles Pembry - God rest his soul - always said that was the wish of our founders." He stepped across the threshold into a hallway and large atrium. The slender girl followed, adjusting a light pair of wire-framed spectacles.

"Has it never been up for sale during your career?" She leaned around the doorway into the living room.

"No. It belonged to a previous partner in our firm, you know. David Holmes. I met him once. I was a new starter when he retired aged fifty."

The girl clipped across the hallway to catch sight of the kitchen beyond the staircase. "He retired at fifty and lived in a home like this? Wow, he must have sold a lot of houses."

Andrew Carlson swayed on the spot and chuckled. "I'm sure he did, but I don't think it was that on its own."

"What then?"

"I don't know the full story, because Charles never

told me. In fact, the only time I ever saw him angry was when he caught some of us newbies gossiping about his old partner. Anyway, there was talk that David's ex-wife and daughter once owned the property and got murdered here. He came into money, bought the place and retired after a mental breakdown or illness. Lived here like a recluse until the day he died, as far as anyone knows."

Jenny shuddered and crossed her arms over her chest to rub the opposite shoulders. "Creepy."

Andrew's eyes narrowed. He was enjoying the role of storyteller. "That's not the weirdest bit."

"Oh God, what else?" Jenny fidgeted and looked around, as if the walls were about to come alive and swallow her up.

"They never found David's body."

"What?"

"When the bills stopped being paid, the council sent someone out. Police broke in but the place was empty. Everything looked immaculate. Someone had even made the bed up with fresh laundered sheets. Upstairs there was a box containing his will, a full history of the house and details of modifications to the property the old boy had undertaken. A new bathroom, updated electrics, and some fresh kitchen cabinets, mostly. Nothing too major. They'll look dated now, no doubt. Given his age, the authorities wrote him off after a short search. He left the place to an estranged niece, along with his money. She doesn't want to see it. Asked us to get a good price."

"Great to be his estranged niece. Crumbs, do we

need to tell prospective buyers all that? I mean, it seems like a fabulous house until you hear those worrying stories."

Andrew looked towards the staircase. "We'll be selective in our disclosure. Shall we look around?"

Jenny went ahead up the stairs. At the bend she paused by the painting of an English cavalier. "Any idea who this is?"

"According to the documentation David Holmes left behind, it's Jacob Backhouse - the man who built Meoria Grange."

"It's a strange name for a home isn't it?" Jenny snorted and wrinkled the upper part of her nose. "If I was buying this place, I'd change it to *Wessex Ridge House*' or something more normal. Friendlier too."

A door slammed on the landing above.

Jenny's face dropped. "What was that? Is someone else here?"

"Shouldn't be. I imagine it's the wind. Draughty old piles are often like this. Don't let my stories unsettle you. Let's focus on the positives; this place has so much potential. Think about the commission."

"Yeah, positives." The girl wasn't convinced.

Andrew brushed past her and climbed the remaining stairs to the landing. "I know the house is a bit long in the tooth, but let's see it for its possibilities. Many people would love to own such an exquisite slice of English history. Others will keep the protected features and rip out everything else to modernise it according to their tastes." He swivelled to face back down to the girl, lifting his spread arms like a magician. "No doubt we'll soon find somebody with better decorative taste than that sad, lonely old boy who lived here."

A pair of unseen hands pushed Andrew Carlson hard in the back. He flew forwards down the upper flight and collided with his young assistant. The pair crashed against a wood panel on the wall. It split with a sharp crack.

"Mr Carlson - Andrew, are you alright?" Jenny staggered up and clutched onto her winded and red-faced employer.

Andrew withdrew a bright red handkerchief and wiped sweat from his brow. Mouth open without verbal response, he looked back up to the empty landing.

Another crack arose from the damaged wood panel. The pair twisted to watch the split cladding re-join and heal like a wound closing in rapid time.

Jenny shrieked. "Oh, my God. Did you see that?"

Andrew nodded. He grabbed hold of the banister for support.

"Andrew, I don't want to stick around here any longer, do you?" The girl shook and whimpered.

On both upper floors, a resounding rhythmic crash broke the silence again. Doors flew open and slammed shut in hasty succession. Their sound rang through the structure like a firecracker reverberating off the walls of a cavern. An eerie blue mist seeped from a bolted panel door in the staircase's side. It glowed and swirled about the intruders, now huddled together beneath the portrait. From out of the curious cloud, an inhuman but feminine voice hissed in anger. "Get out."

Andrew and Jenny were on their feet in a flash. They stumbled and tripped over one another in a frantic scrabble to make the hallway and relative safety of the front door. The vibrant vapour flew around the atrium, then slithered through the air like a giant snake rearing up to strike. The words came again with ever increasing pitch and volume until the terrified estate agents' ears whistled in pain. "Get out. Get out. Get out!"

They dived across the threshold and ran for Andrew's vehicle. The engine gunned and caused them to skid away down the driveway with a shower of gravel and dust.

At the far end of the private road, Andrew pulled up.

"What are you doing?" Jenny clasped her hands together beneath her chin as if in prayer.

"For Sale board." Andrew puffed and gripped his chest. The scare had brought on a sudden stab of pain. "We'll hammer it in and go. Think they'll be drawing straws in the office for who does a viewing up here." He staggered to the rear of the car and retrieved a wooden board and mallet from the boot.

"What happened in there? I'm not coming back. Shit, I'll get another job first." Jenny got out to help him position the notice.

Andrew hammered the *'For Sale'* sign deep into frost-heavy ground. "There, that'll do."

Jenny stared down the long private thoroughfare leading up to what she now considered a creepy, haunted house. "Do you think anyone will be mad enough to buy it? What if the viewing goes okay and they don't realise what's lurking inside?"

Andrew followed her gaze and fought to catch his breath. With a shake of the head he shrugged and closed his eyes. "Caveat Emptor."

ABOUT THE AUTHOR

Devon De'Ath was born in the county of Kent, 'The Garden of England.' Raised a Roman Catholic in a small, ancient country market community famously documented as 'the most haunted TOWN in England,' he grew up in an atmosphere replete with spiritual, psychic, and supernatural energy. Hauntings were commonplace and you couldn't swing a cat without hitting three spectres, to the extent that he never needed question the validity of such manifestations. As to the explanations behind them?

At the age of twenty, his earnest search for spiritual truth led the young man to leave Catholicism and become heavily involved in Charismatic Evangelicalism. After serving as a part-time youth pastor while working in the corporate world, he eventually took voluntary redundancy to study at a Bible College in the USA. Missions in the Caribbean and sub-Saharan Africa followed, but a growing dissatisfaction with aspects of the theology and ministerial abuse by church leadership eventually caused him to break with organised religion and pursue a Post-Evangelical existence. One open to all manner of spiritual and human experiences his 'holy' life would never have allowed.

After church life, De'Ath served fifteen years with the police, lectured at colleges and universities, and acted as a consultant to public safety agencies both foreign and domestic.

A writer since he first learned the alphabet, Devon De'Ath has authored works in many genres under various names, from Children's literature to self-help books, through screenplays for video production and all manner of articles.

Made in the USA
Middletown, DE
15 July 2024